## Head-On Heart

'I thought you wanted to get an early start to LA in the morning,' Amity said weakly. 'We're searching for the holy grail, remember? We should go back to the motel and get some sleep.'

But Amity's will power was threadbare. At this point, she would have followed Daniel to hell if he'd promised to make love to her beside a brimstone lake.

Daniel led her outside, where Amity took the first breath of fresh air that she'd had in hours. The sky was vast. Far from the urban light pollution, countless stars were visible across a background of sheer black, as if they'd been swirled on black velvet with a giant paintbrush. The gravel lot was almost empty. The darkness seemed to sing. The night, left to itself, was carrying on with its own secret life.

'You know, I may have already found it,' Daniel said, squeezing Amity's hands. He bent down to give her a kiss, and it was simple and sweet and almost chaste, like a gesture from an ancient legend.

*By the same author:*

**TAMING JEREMY**

To find out more about Anne Tourney's
books please visit www.annetourney.com

# Head-On Heart

Anne Tourney

*To Prosser,*
*July '07*

In real life, always practise safe sex.

First published in 2007 by
Cheek
Thames Wharf Studios
Rainville Road
London W6 9HA

Copyright © Anne Tourney 2007

The right of Anne Tourney to be identified as the Author of
the Work has been asserted by her in accordance with the Copyright,
Designs and Patents Act 1988.

Typeset by SetSystems Ltd, Saffron Walden, Essex

Printed and bound by Mackays of Chatham PLC

ISBN 978 0 352 34090 0

All characters in this publication are fictitious and any resemblance
to real persons, living or dead, is purely coincidental.

This book is sold subject to the condition that it shall not, by way
of trade or otherwise, be lent, resold, hired out or otherwise
circulated without the publisher's prior written consent in any form
of binding or cover other than that in which it is published and
without a similar condition including this condition being imposed
on the subsequent purchaser.

# Late Saturday Night, Eight Years Ago

## (Somewhere in a Condemned Warehouse in Lower Downtown)

Sweat, beer, smoke, testosterone – the male reek of the mosh pit went straight to Amity's head, leaving her dizzy and strangely turned-on. She didn't know how she'd ended up in this sweltering maze of flesh, but she knew she wasn't going to be able to shove her way out anytime soon. Frantically she scanned the crowd for the girl who'd brought her, but finding Manda's raven-dyed head in the thicket of black T-shirts, black tribal ink, and black dreadlocks was hopeless.

Twelve twenty-one a.m. The opening band had wrapped up its set almost half an hour ago, and the beasts were getting restless in the vacuum it had left behind. An excess of energy rattled the storage vault turned underground club. As one of the few girls in the box – and a girl under twenty-one, at that – Amity was getting jumpy. Guys kept bouncing off her like electrons, grabbing her waist or hips by accident or design before they zoomed away to crash into each other. She was glad she'd worn her big black CBGB shirt, instead of the purple tube top that Manda had wanted to lend her. That slinky tube would have been a swimming pool by now, filled with the draught beer that had been spilled on her by crowd surfers.

'Three-Way!' a voice shouted, a hoarse bellow soaring above the din. Someone else took up the cry, and soon the two words had turned into a raucous chorus, accompanied by the tribal banging of boots against the concrete floor.

The band was late – way late. So was Amity. She'd told her stepmother that she'd be home by midnight, but here she was, with no prayer of escaping this club even if she'd wanted to. She was here for the long haul, at the mercy of a band she'd never heard of. Manda, who was the closest thing that Logan High School had to an indie rock journalist, had sworn up and down that 3-Way Dream was going to blow the roof off the alternative scene. So far they'd only produced an EP with a local label called EarWaxx, but it was only a matter of, like, *minutes* till they broke big and, if Amity didn't catch them at this venue, she'd regret it for the rest of her life.

As a swap for the free write-up that Manda had given the band on her webzine, some promoter had opened the club's fire exit to let two high-school grads inside that night. The thrill of sneaking into one of the city's temporary underground venues had worn off long ago. Amity hadn't been impressed with the first band, Scoresby, but then she hadn't expected miracles from a band named after the cheap Scotch that her dad's poker buddies drank. Now she was tired, bruised and wildly desperate to see the inside of her bedroom again.

Then she saw Daniel. Lean, solo figure, standing in the middle of the stage with a black guitar slung over his shoulder, shading his eyes with his hand and smiling sheepishly, as if he'd just stepped out of bed to find a rowdy audience in his room.

'Sorry kids,' he said into the mic. 'Daddy overslept.'

His apology was a wry, smoky purr – the sound struck Amity in the gut before she'd even heard him sing. She froze where she stood, as the rest of the crowd vanished in a roaring blur. Seconds later, a bassist and a drummer materialised on stage, but Amity would hardly see them that night. She would wake up the next morning with a fractured rib and a garden of bruises blooming across her body, but she never felt the brutes who crashed against her in the pit.

All she saw, heard and felt was Daniel. His voice, coarse and sweet at the same time, like honey poured over fine gravel. His hands on the black Gibson, hips moving hypnotically as his fingers worked the hell out of the strings, producing sounds that leapt from harmony to ear-splitting dissonance with the speed of a manic's mood swings, threaded with blues riffs straight from the Delta. Her own fingers began to dance against her belly as they tried to capture that river of notes for themselves. Her memory absorbed every detail of his face and hands and body – the focused intensity in his dark eyes, the muscles working in his jaw, the scar on the back of his right hand, the lines of his long-legged body. Halfway through the set he pulled off his shirt and threw it on the floor and, when she saw the glistening planes of his chest and abdomen, Amity's pulse went into a helpless overdrive.

She'd only had sex once in her life, and now she was convinced that she never wanted to have one of those fumbling, half-naked collisions again. This cacophony of sound and sensation was infinitely better. Bass hashing out a rude, off-kilter backbeat, drums firing out a fierce counterpoint, and Daniel's voice and guitar on top of it all, shaping the songs as he shaped the raw vibrations that were thundering through Amity's blood.

*I've never felt this way before.* That was the phrase girls said over and over again, sometimes when they talked about sex, more often when they talked about some mystical, sky-high ideal of romantic love that they'd imposed on whatever thoroughly average male they were dating. Three weeks later, the girl would have forgotten the dweeb's name, as she soared skyward with someone else.

What Amity was feeling at this moment was hard and real. Nothing like it – she'd heard nothing like the sounds these three musicians were making, and she'd sure as hell never dreamt of playing anything like that on her old Johnson six-string.

She could see the muscles in Daniel's jaws clenching as he alternately attacked and seduced the strings – playing nice, playing nasty. The tendons in his forearm quivered as his right hand tore up and down the Gibson's sleek neck, and his passion made her want to rip herself open. She was wet all over – wet with sweat, spilled booze and something slick and secret that was turning the crotch of her panties into a pool of syrup. The rhythm of the song was as insistent as a train, driving her inevitably towards something so new it hadn't been named yet; she didn't know when she'd reach that destination, but she was getting there pretty damn quick.

The pounding in her ears and chest matched the pounding of Daniel's chords, matching the throb deep in the pit of her belly. She felt an urgency as keen as the shrieks of feedback set off by Daniel's guitar. Some faceless stranger brushed against her chest, and her hardened nipples tingled with the contact. Then an undertow of hands and arms were lifting her towards the ceiling, and she was on her back, staring up at a constellation of white lights, spinning and rolling over a hundred heads and shoulders. She felt a lurch of panic, thinking she would have to fall, but she didn't. Borne by the crowd, borne by the music, Amity kept riding. Up, up, up ... until someone's merciful hand grabbed her smack between the legs, and the runaway train inside her exploded, leaving streams of shuddering pleasure in its wake.

One of Amity's friends had come for the very first time on prom night, on a hotel bed that her boyfriend had covered with rose petals. A girl in Amity's English Comp class had written a near-pornographic essay about hitting her first peak in a mountaintop jacuzzi, with her stepmother's boyfriend. Manda had had her first climax in the back seat of a limousine, with a B-list rocker she refused to name.

Amity had her first full-blown orgasm crowd-surfing in a mosh pit, listening to a dark-eyed, utterly intense guitarist named Daniel pound out music like she'd never heard.

So it began.

## Chapter One

# A Four-Letter Word for 'Friendship'

As soon as the blonde with the heavy frontal artillery strolled up to the stage and wrapped her fingers around the microphone, Amity knew she might as well pack up her six-string and go home. It didn't matter that the blonde sang like an alley cat trying to howl through a hairball; she'd won the audition before she opened her black-glossed lips. Probably had something to do with the phoenix tattooed across her cleavage – the bird of resurrection rising across the awesome hills of her breasts.

Watching the guys in the band respond to the blonde's performance, Amity figured there was a lot of resurrection going on in this garage.

GIRL SINGER NEEDED TO FRONT LOCAL BAND, the ad in the city's weekly free rag had read. Any band that could afford to advertise in an actual print publication, as opposed to tacking up Xeroxed flyers on the bulletin boards of coffee shops and second-hand guitar stores, was worth a shot. Too bad they couldn't have been honest about the kind of 'singer' they were looking for.

HAWT CHICK WITH MASSIVE HOOTERS NEEDED TO DRAW DECENT CROWDS. Now that would be a refreshing example of honesty in advertising.

'Knock, knock, knocking on heaven's doooor,' the blonde wailed. Great, Amity thought. Flashing your assets to win an audition was one thing, but did the girl have to sacrifice classic Dylan on the altar of her knockers? Actually, she sounded more like the Guns n' Roses cover of that song, complete with Axl Rose's signature wail – the blonde had probably never heard Dylan's original.

Amity sighed and fished a can of beer out of the cooler that had been set out for the girls who were trying out that night. She usually didn't drink before she sang, but when you already knew you'd lost, there wasn't much point in abstaining. The only reason she wasn't on her way out of here was that she had some promising eye contact going on with the drummer.

A lot of girls wouldn't settle for a drummer, but Amity thought drummers were cool. Drummers were the infantrymen of the rock world, carrying the rest of the band on the sturdy shoulders of their rhythm. Easy enough to overlook them, until they weren't there, and your set caved in like a cardboard box in the rain. This guy wasn't the cutest one in the band, but he had sexy lynx eyes, rock-climber's shoulders and a pierced tongue, which he'd flashed at her a couple of times.

Amity knew what it was like to be overlooked. In a subculture whose feminine ideal was a blonde blown up to comic-book proportions, skinny brunettes got overlooked a lot. She glanced down at the small valley of cleavage that she'd created with her leather corset – bought at a thrift store for $7.50, just for this night. She'd pulled the laces of the corset so tight that her eyes crossed, but she still couldn't produce more than a gentle outcropping.

Along with the corset she'd worn a camouflage-print miniskirt with a heavy studded leather belt, fishnet stockings and combat boots. If Amity had ruled the rock world, she would have had the standard audition attire be a baggy T-shirt and old jeans or yoga pants, no make-up allowed. Women would sing a lot better if they didn't have to worry about whether their bustiers were holding up, their black lipstick was smeared across their teeth or their mousse was going south on them.

Reality wasn't half as kind as Amity's fantasies. If you didn't pay homage to the god of Superficial Appearances, you wouldn't get very far in this business. At least her get-up had caught the drummer's attention. Every time his green eyes met hers, and held her gaze steadily as he worked his sticks, Amity felt a throb in the pit of her belly that spread warmly through the rest of her body.

As soon as the blonde's solo ground to a merciful halt, the five other girls who were left got up to leave. Hostility wafted off their nubile bodies like a trendy drugstore perfume, leaving an acrid after-scent. Amity watched them sympathetically. She used to feel like that after she lost an audition, until she learned the three key truths about life as a girl in the rock'n'roll universe: 1) it wasn't fair, 2) it never had been fair, and 3) it never would be fair. Ever.

If you had a few good songs, and you really wanted your chance to sing them, you just had to be very Zen about the whole thing. Sit back. Inhale. Crack open a beer, snag yourself a nice young drummer and settle down ... for at least an hour or two.

'Hey. Weren't you going to sing tonight?'

Lost in thought about the cruel reality of garage-band life, Amity hadn't heard the drummer walk up to her. He pulled a Diet Coke out of the cooler, shook the ice off his hand, and rolled the can up and down the back of his neck. Then he lifted his soaked white tank top to apply the can to his belly, giving Amity a good look at the tightly knit muscles of his abdomen.

Nice. Very nice. Smooth, toasty skin, dewed with just enough sweat to salt an egg. A tribal tattoo covered the rippled hardness between his pectorals and his navel. Amity shrugged, pretending that she hadn't noticed his little preening session.

'The audition's over. She won it with her, uh, lungs.' Amity nodded at the blonde, who was now encircled by the remaining three members of the band.

'Yeah, the rest of the boys are into lungs.'

The drummer grinned. He had a small scar on his right cheek that deepened when he smiled. Nothing like a scar in dimple's clothing to start Amity's engine.

'What about you?' Amity asked.

'I'm more into legs. Long and lean. Like yours. They're perfect.'

His gaze roved down the length of Amity's thighs, caressed her knees, and lingered on the shapely contours of her calves and ankles. This guy was on point. He'd immediately picked out her best feature, complimented her on it, and woven the compliment into a pass within thirty seconds of introducing himself.

'Thanks,' Amity yawned and kicked her feet in the monster boots. 'I wouldn't say they're perfect, but they do their job. Walking. Holding me off the ground. That kind of stuff.'

He clasped his fingers and stretched out his arms, flexing his biceps. On the slope of his right shoulder was another tattoo, a stick figure with a big head and a crudely drawn face.

'What's the tat on your arm?' Amity asked, her curiosity piqued.

'What does it look like?'

Amity squinted at the tattoo, with its ludicrous leer. 'Like the universal men's room icon. With dirty intentions.'

The drummer laughed, flashing his tongue stud. Amity's heart did a double-thump. She'd heard about the miracles that a man could work with a pierced tongue, but she had yet to experience any of them.

'That's my icon,' he said. 'Stick Man. 'Cause I'm a drummer. Get it?'

'Got it.' Amity couldn't help laughing back.

'My name's Gregg,' he said. 'With three Gs. What's yours?'

'Amity.'

'Listen, Amity. How'd you like to audition for me after everyone else clears out?'

Ah, yes. The private audition. What he'd gained in sheer sex appeal, the drummer had just lost in overdone pick-up tactics. God, Amity thought, I'm too young to be this cynical.

'Thanks, but I've got to get home. I'm getting up early tomorrow.'

'Work?'

'Nah,' Amity scoffed. 'Church. What do you think?'

Amity began to scoot off the elevated work table where she'd been sitting. Gregg blocked her, planting his hands on either side of her hips. He smelled good. Very good, for a musician, as if he'd taken a shower and done his laundry sometime within the past twenty-four hours. The sweat on his skin was fresh and sweet. No booze seeping out of his pores, no scrim of cigarette smoke. His sculpted shoulders looked burnished in the dim overhead light of the garage. Amity wanted to lick them.

'I'm serious,' he said. 'I want to hear you sing. We don't have to do it here, if you're not comfortable. I know a place we can go where there'll be a crowd.'

'I came to sing for *this* crowd,' Amity reminded him. But she was melting.

'What can I say? These guys suck.'

Amity glanced at the rest of the band, who were paying heavy court to their new lead singer. 'And you don't?'

'I can appreciate eye candy as much as the next male. But you're serious about your music.'

He took a couple of steps back, giving Amity just enough room to escape if she wanted to, removing that fresh, intoxicating smell that was making her want to tear off his thin excuse for a shirt and cover his torso with love bites.

'How can you tell?'

'You're the only girl who brought your own guitar. And the case looks like it's been around the world three or four times.'

Amity tried not to smile, and failed. 'Not around the world. But it's been around the city a lot.'

Gregg smiled back, flashing the scar/dimple again. His eyes were the same shade of green as Amity's tabby cat, Diabolicus. But Diabolicus had been neutered, and Gregg ... well, Amity's guess was that his masculine parts were very much intact.

'You're probably thinking I just want to get laid,' he said.

'Something like that.'

'I'd be lying if I said I *didn't* want to get laid.'

'At least you're honest.'

'But I want to hear you sing first.'

Amity edged off the table, landing on her feet about two inches from Gregg. In her boots, she was exactly his height, and her mouth was so close to his that she could have kissed him without taking a single step forwards. She could swear she felt his heart beating; maybe drummers had stronger pulses than ordinary mortals. Being close to him was so sweet. She'd really rather stay here and breathe in his scent and give him a full-body tongue bath. But singing for another musician, who was genuinely interested, was a chance she couldn't pass up.

'Let's go,' she said. 'Take me where the lights are shining.'

There weren't many lights shining at the dive where Gregg took Amity. The place was slightly bigger than a shoebox, and a good half of that box was taken up by the stage. An old man wearing a hat and suspenders sat on a stool in front of the microphone, lovingly strumming a guitar and singing a Robert Johnson song, 'Come On In My Kitchen'.

'He's good,' Amity said.

'He's real,' Gregg agreed. 'There's no fake shit here. That's why I brought you.'

'I'm flattered.' Amity looked around at the crowded dingy bar. 'I guess.'

Gregg put his hand on the small of her back and steered her towards the bar. There weren't any empty barstools left, so he found Amity and her guitar an empty space against the wall, where they waited while he went in search of beer.

A musician who bought drinks for his dates, Amity noted. She was impressed. Then she saw that the bartender, a curvy redhead in her late thirties, was giving Gregg the beers with no subsequent exchange of money. From the long steamy look that the two of them shared, Amity could see how they'd struck on that arrangement. Oh, well. At least this was one beer that Amity didn't have to buy.

The elderly bluesman had finished his song to the sound of raucous applause.

'Maybelline's going to sing next,' Gregg said, handing her the cold bottle of beer. 'Then you're up.'

'Maybelline? Isn't that a brand of lipstick?'

'Not this time. Check her out.'

Maybelline was a knockout of a woman dressed in a white sleeveless gown. She reminded Amity of a tall glass of iced coffee – double cream, no sugar. Her posture was so elegant that Amity found herself unconsciously straightening her own spine. It wasn't until she clasped the microphone in her slender, manicured hand and leant into the spotlight that Amity realised she had to be pushing seventy.

A stunning seventy. If Amity could look like that, or sing like that, when she was that age, she'd be damned glad to have a name like Maybelline. Maybelline's voice reminded her of Nina Simone – smoky, searching. She could go low and sultry, then soar up to a range where she was crooning in the sweet, high tones of a child. She sang about love and lost dreams. She sang about men who make you crazy, and men who make you want to kill them, and men you want so much that you're willing to drop everything to follow them wherever they go. And all these men, Maybelline seemed to imply with her sad, siren's smile, would dump you in the end.

Hypnotised by the singer's crooning vocals, Amity felt the narrow walls of the dive fall away. What are my dreams? she wondered. What do I want so much that I'd drop everything to chase it? When will I find anyone I love enough to leave my lame boring life?

She didn't notice that Gregg had been pulling her gradually closer, making a muscular cradle for her with his torso. Moving subtly against her, his hips and arms felt like a physical expression of the music, which blossomed into a slow hot make-out session when he pushed back her hair and nuzzled the soft slope between her earlobe and her collarbone. Before she knew it, Amity was turning in his arms to meet his mouth. His lips were tentative at first, and dry, but soon the kiss deepened into a warm wet tongue-tangle that made Amity so limp she wanted to slide to the floor, taking Gregg right down with her.

But Gregg did the opposite – instead of letting Amity fall, he wrapped his hands around her bottom and lifted her off her feet, holding her just high enough above the ground that she felt like she was floating. There weren't many advantages to being too thin, Amity thought, but this had to be one of them. From an elevated angle, she could do some serious kissing. She held Gregg's face in her hands and let her lips run wild. Whenever she felt the smooth ball of his tongue stud, a flash of sparks exploded in her belly.

Amity didn't care if her boots ever hit the ground

again, but the kiss had to end sometime. When Maybelline finished her last song, the little place erupted into a roar of appreciation. The singer bowed like a lily bending in a breeze.

'Your turn,' Gregg said into Amity's ear.

Amity shook her head. 'I can't.'

'What do you mean? That's why I brought you here.'

'I can't follow her. She's too good. She knows everything. I don't know anything yet. I'd feel like a dweeb.'

'But listen –'

'No.' Amity picked up her guitar case, which was still propped faithfully against the wall. 'I want to go home.'

She pushed through the crowd. After taking a few steps, she turned.

'Aren't you coming?' she asked Gregg.

He grinned, giving her a tantalizing flash of lynx-green eyes and silver tongue stud.

Under normal circumstances – if the word 'normal' could be applied to Amity's life in any way – she didn't do one-night stands. When she first saw Gregg watching her as he pounded his skins, Amity never thought she'd be following him back to his one-room basement apartment for a night of blistering passion. She just thought she'd like to kiss a drummer with a tongue stud.

But when he offered to carry her guitar back to his place (he didn't have his own car; the band shared a beat-up Chevy van from 1986), Amity changed her mind. The gesture touched her for some reason; it seemed sweet and old-fashioned, like something her mom's dates would have done, if her mom had carried around a Johnson acoustic.

'You must be a folkie,' Gregg remarked, after he'd lifted the case out of her hand. Without the instrument, Amity always felt off-balance.

'Not really. I just like to play acoustic. And I've had Blue Molly forever, so I carry her around for luck.'

It was too dark to see his expression, but Amity could tell that Gregg was giving her an odd look. 'You named your guitar?'

'Yeah. Blue Molly. Molly because I liked the name, and Blue because ... well, she's blue. She's closer to me than most of my family members, and I don't have that many friends.'

'What about boyfriends? Anyone in the picture right now?'

Gregg put his free arm around Amity's waist. Her body fitted perfectly against his, her slight curves knitting into the smooth grooves of his torso. He was warm, and he still had that heady tang of fresh sweat. As they walked together, their hips and outer thighs brushed together with each step. The friction of his jeans against her fishnet-clad skin made Amity shudder.

And he had asked her if she had a boyfriend. Which meant that maybe whatever they were going to do tonight would amount to something more than a quick roll on his mattress.

'Nobody serious,' Amity said. Nobody at all was more like it, but Gregg didn't have to know that.

'Great,' Gregg said, holding her tighter. 'So there's no one to object if I take you home and do terrible things to you?'

'I might object,' Amity said. 'It depends on how terrible you are.'

Gregg put her guitar down, wrapped her in his arms, and kissed her. The kiss was pure liquid heaven, his tongue slipping past her lips and weaving through the soft interior of her mouth. His hands slipped under her bustier – a tight slide, but he managed it – and kneaded her skin. Though he couldn't reach her breasts, her nipples tingled in response to his touch, and she wished she could strip off the damn leather contraption right there on the street so he could caress her all over. She felt a raw moan forming deep in her throat and she didn't bother to hold it back.

'How's that?' Gregg asked, when he finally broke the kiss.

'Terrible,' Amity whispered.

Fortunately they didn't have much farther to walk; after that liplock, Amity's legs were so wobbly that they couldn't have carried her more than a couple of blocks. As soon as they got into his apartment, Gregg lived up to his self-declared reputation as a leg man. He lowered Amity onto his mattress, removed her boots, and pulled off her fishnets. She lay back and let his mouth work its way from the soles of her feet all the way up to her inner thighs, his lips grazing on her skin. Whenever his teeth nipped her flesh, Amity would let out a little gasp of surprise and pleasure. She got a lot of praise for her legs – usually rah-rah compliments that she gave herself when she looked in the mirror, because there wasn't much else that she liked to look at. But no one had ever worshipped her this way.

Once he had her thighs draped across his shoulders, Gregg wore them like a skin stole for the rest of the night. Her knees stayed locked around the back of his neck while he pulled down her panties and showed her what a pierced tongue could really do.

Tongue stud, meet my clit, Amity thought, her mind coasting into a hallucinatory mist of sensations. The tiny silver ball was able to coax feelings out of her that she'd never experienced before – shimmers and sparks that alternately made her moan and growl and sigh, until she was soaring so high that she couldn't hear herself anymore. Unlike most of her lovers, Gregg didn't treat her orgasm like a finish line. He let her come into his mouth, and after the molten tide ebbed into a ripple and faded away, he started all over again.

By the time he was ready to get inside her, Amity was

too limp to respond. She lay back and languished in her afterglow as he unlaced her bustier, his fingers fumbling with the ties as if he were a kid unwrapping a Christmas present. Off came the bustier and her tight miniskirt. Naked, she lay underneath him as he unwrapped a condom and entered her quickly, moving inside her with all the speed and urgency of a man who's been putting off his climax for an hour. Somehow she found the strength to wrap her legs around his waist and tilt her hips, to draw him in deeper. The muscles in his arms trembled with the effort of holding himself back.

'Go ahead,' she said. 'It's your turn.'

When he came, she squeezed him with her thighs as tightly as she could and milked him with her inner muscles. The orgasm left him speechless; he rocked back and forth inside her, saying absolutely nothing for what seemed like a very long time, and when he took a breath it sounded like he'd just been born.

'Incredible,' he gasped. 'You're absolutely incredible.' Gingerly he lowered himself onto the mattress and lay on his back. 'I never thought an acoustic chick could do that to me.'

'You'd be surprised,' Amity replied, her lips curving into a *Mona Lisa* smile.

Somehow through the post-sex haze, Amity remembered that she had to go to work in the morning. She managed to untangle herself from Gregg's limbs and make her way home before dawn, her blood still pumping from the naked workout. Before she'd left Gregg's apartment, he'd woken up long enough to scribble his phone number on her palm with a green felt-tip pen before collapsing back onto his mattress.

'That's my cell,' he mumbled into his pillow. 'Call me.'

'I'll think about it,' Amity said, as casually as she could. Then, just to cover her bases, she pried the green pen out of Gregg's hand and scrawled her own number down on a fast-food napkin that she found on the floor. *Amity (Acoustic Chick)*, she wrote below her digits. She made a tent out of the napkin and propped it on the pillow opposite his snoring head.

Getting ready for work, she couldn't stop thinking about Gregg's supple body, his agile hands, the smoked-almond flavour of his skin. She couldn't shake the sensation of his sleek, studded tongue ... lunging through her lower lips like a dolphin playing in saltwater breakers. Now all she had to do, she thought, as she splashed cold water on her face, was keep her sanity until sometime after dark.

*Remove all body jewellery, cover all tattoos.* It was company policy at the Multinational Federation of Mortgage Offices, which the staff fondly referred to as MOFO. For Amity, MOFO was just another gig in hell. The only saving grace of temp jobs was that, like car wrecks, someone eventually cleared them off the road, and you got to move on.

Humming a few bars of Dylan ('I Shall Be Released' seemed to fit the mood of a Monday) Amity tugged the studs and rings out of her eyebrow, nose, and lower lip and dropped them in an empty Tiger Balm jar on her bookshelf. Then she wriggled around in front of her mirror to make sure that no ink was showing under her white rayon blouse. No need to tame her brown hair; it hung long and straight enough to satisfy any mortgage applicant. All she had to do was whirl a lint brush over her skirt to catch stray cat hairs, and she looked no more threatening than the 21st century's answer to Alice in Wonderland.

Which could have been sexy, in a kinky sort of way, if the sub-zero climate in MOFO's file room didn't strip her of any desire for sex.

Before she headed out, Amity poured kibble into her tabby's food dish, a ceramic bowl painted with the words 'Tuna Breath'. Then she stopped to salute the gods, who hung on posters around her room. Hendrix, Dylan and Johnny Cash, then Iron Maiden and Alice Cooper, Bonnie Raitt and Sheryl Crow, and finally, her idol of all idols, Daniel. Daniel, Zak and Randy, the members of 3-Way Dream, had hung beside her bed since Amity was eighteen. Three existential desperados, shot in black-and-white, gazed down on her, their eyelids heavy with ennui, as she kissed her fingertips, then laid them on Daniel's mouth. All three of them were hot, but Daniel was her man. His diabolical black eyes had been watching her get dressed and undressed for longer than a lot of couples had been married.

With her usual reverence, Amity placed Blue Molly's case in its stand. Blue Molly didn't get enough action anymore. Her main function these days was to snag Amity's panties as they went sailing across the room in the general direction of her laundry hamper. Last night had been her first outing in months. Too many mortgage applications, not enough music – that had been the story of Amity's life lately. But after last night, everything was going to change. Amity could feel it.

'So what's *your* story, baby?' asked the guy who manned the coffee cart in the lobby of MOFO, when Amity stopped to get her morning chai. He seemed to think that if he asked her that question every day, with the same leer on his lips, she would eventually strip off her clothes and fall naked at his feet, panting her confessions.

'I don't have one yet.'

Didn't he get tired of hearing the same answer? The coffee guy wasn't Amity's type. His face wasn't bad – he had a heavy-lidded look of boredom that she found mildly intriguing – but his hands looked squishy and his fingers were stubby. Hands were key.

'Everyone has a story.'

'Well, I guess mine's flash fiction. The end.'

Amity grabbed her chai and walked away, swinging

the black attaché case that she'd got as a college graduation gift from some relative who thought she'd get a real job. Amity loved the case. It made her feel that a cooler life was in her grasp, as if she could be called away at any moment for a sexy adventure with John Travolta and Samuel L. Jackson. So far, she didn't have anything to put inside it but a peanut butter sandwich, a tube of lip gloss, a yellow legal pad and a couple of pencils. You never knew when you might need to scribble down a few song lyrics. One of these days, she might even write her story.

Once upon a time, there was a girl with pipecleaner arms and legs who carried a guitar named Blue Molly everywhere she went. When she wasn't plucking the strings, she wore the guitar slung behind her back, like a country singer. But most of the time, Blue Molly rested against her waist, bouncing along to the rhythm of her slim hips when she walked, and whenever a popular song came into her head, she didn't have to wait till she got home to work it out on the frets.

In junior high, the guitar girl started to write her own songs. She wrote songs while she was waiting for the bus. She wrote songs in the school cafeteria. Most of her lyrics were about hot, passionate love: kisses that lasted for days, fingers strumming her skin, bodies melting into each other. She wrote songs with dirty lyrics, songs with titles like 'When You Make Me' and 'My Lips Down There Are On Fire', and sang them to boys behind the bleachers for a quarter a song. She herself had never been kissed by a boy, not even a chicken-peck, but she had faith that it would happen one day. All she had to do was wait for her breasts to fill out and her freckles to fade.

Ten years later, Amity was still waiting.

Oh, she'd been kissed. Just not in any way that resembled the mind-blowing, earth-shifting, lip-and-tongue extravaganzas that she'd dreamt about. She had a bit of cleavage to call her own, when she wore the right bra and leant over at a 45-degree angle, pushed her upper arms against her rib cage and took a deep breath. But she still had her freckles; if anything, she had more than ever, even on parts of her body that never saw the sun.

Somewhere out there was a gorgeous, intense, musical man who liked his girls long, lean and speckled. All Amity had to do was locate him in the hordes of totally average tone-deaf guys who wanted women who looked like ageing cheerleaders.

If Amity ever found this guy, she'd have to prove to him that she was much sexier, in her own way, than any staggeringly beautiful Maxim cover girl. And get him to feel thunderbolts whenever her lips met his. And make him realise that he loved her so much that without her, he didn't even want to breathe ... minor things like that.

'You're late,' said Barbara Bellicosi. Husky as a linebacker in her aqua suit with matching heels, the department manager caught Amity by the arm.

'I'm not!'

Barbara pointed to the clock that hung over the cubicles, where MOFO's more diligent employees were already obediently installed. The clock said that it was ten after eight. Amity's digital wristwatch – waterproof, in case she ever decided to escape the landlocked world for a year-long scuba-diving expedition – said that it was still 7.58.

'We need to talk,' Barbara said, her fingers forming a vice around Amity's elbow. Amity could already feel a bruise taking shape. She thought Barbara would take her to her office, a cubicle-and-a-half near the westward window. Amity had been hauled off to that corner a few times, most recently because she'd told one of the other temps that in spite of the fact that she'd been working for MOFO for thirteen weeks, she privately believed that mortgages were a capitalist scam.

But Barbara wasn't heading for the corner today. She was dragging Amity down the path she'd just taken, past the water cooler and the rows of potted bromeliads, along the fudge-ripple marble floor that led to the reception desk, where a Eurasian girl yawned as she flipped through a copy of *Vanity Fair*. Though her exquisite beauty made her look like a permanent installation, Amity recognised the girl for what she was, another temp. The girl smiled, not very pleasantly. Amity saw a message in her exotic eyes.

*You're outta here.*

'Amity, today is your last day at MOFO,' Barbara announced. 'I already spoke to the agency. They'll have something else for you by next month, I'm sure.'

'Next month?' Amity squeaked. 'My rent's due next week. I need my cheque on Friday, or I won't be able to cover it.'

'Well, if you communicate your situation to the agency, I'm sure your representative can expedite the process of finding you a new position,' Barbara said.

Amity narrowed her eyes. 'Do you have to practise to talk like that?' she asked. 'Or do those chunky words just flow after a while?'

Barbara's jowls quivered. Her waxy rose lips pursed, and for a second, Amity felt sorry for her. She pictured Barb getting ready for work that morning, carefully choosing a shade of lipstick that would compliment the colour of her suit and her frosted pouf of hair. Maybe she had a meeting with the corporate office that morning. Or maybe she was in love.

'Good luck,' Barbara said stiffly, steering Amity to the tall glass double doors.

'You know, Barb,' Amity said, before she left MOFO forever, 'you look pretty in chlorine blue.'

Amity always had a send-off for her temporary bosses, but she never hung around long enough for the reaction. Instead of waiting for Barb's response, she slipped through the double doors, swinging her attaché case and walking briskly – mustn't keep Travolta waiting.

'It must suck, being, like, thirty years old and having no job,' sighed the dreadlocked teen who made Amity's double chai latte. Her pretty face puckered in commiseration, as if she actually had an insight into Amity's experience.

'I'm not, like, thirty,' Amity said, regretting that she'd told the barista why she was lounging around at a coffee shop in the middle of the morning in front-office attire. 'I'm twenty-seven. By the way, you have a bug in your dreads.'

The girl wandered off, looking bewildered as she combed her matted locks with her fingers. Amity picked up her paper cup and stalked out of the coffee shop. She had planned to sit there for an hour or two, postponing the time when she'd have to go back and face her empty apartment, but she wasn't in the mood to be pitied by a gainfully employed adolescent.

Her studio looked lonely. Diabolicus was nowhere in sight; for such a fat feline, he had an uncanny ability to make himself invisible. Dust motes spun through the sunlight, drifting down onto the tangle of sheets on her futon and the skirt and bustier she'd shed that morning. Amity felt an unfamiliar pang of loss. Usually she faced the end of a temp job with a joy that bordered on dementia. Today she just felt like a loser.

The light on her answering machine was blinking. Amity's heart skipped a beat. She had no reason to suspect that Gregg would call her so soon. Rule number one of sleeping with musicians was that you never expected them to call (this was even more critical than the no-cash-loans rule, or the no-more-than-one-night-on-the-couch rule).

Sure enough, Gregg hadn't called, but when Amity

played the message, she was more shocked than if he had.

'Hey, Sis! Guess who?' cooed the female voice, sweet as synthetic maple syrup. 'It's been ages. Lots of catching up to do. Listen, sweetie, the reason I'm calling is that I need a gi-normous favour from you. I need a ride. The catch is, I'm in Vegas. And I was thinking, wouldn't it be cool if you drove that sexy convertible out here and we took a road trip together?'

Amity stood staring at the machine. 'No way! Try the bus!' she shouted.

'It's not just me,' the recorded voice continued through Amity's explosion. 'I've got a few friends who need a ride too. We're stranded in a hotel that's costing us a hundred bucks a night. We seriously need help. Listen, Sissy, call me back as soon as you can. We can't afford this room much longer. 'Kay?' The voice burbled a phone number, then the message ended.

'Airhead,' Amity muttered. 'Like I'd really waste a road trip on you and your sleazy stripper buddies. Why don't you text-message your pimp?'

She threw herself down on her futon and lay on her back, staring up at the ceiling. She couldn't remember the last time her stepsister Heather had bothered to call her. Because of Amity's sporadic employment, she was of little use to Heather as a source of cash, but now she had something that Heather needed.

The T-Bird. Amity's gorgeous metallic-blue convertible, the 1966 model that her father had lovingly restored and left to Amity when he walked out on his mismatched family.

Now Heather wanted to be chauffeured through the desert in that classic beauty, with her entourage in tow. Whether she was flaunting her perfect figure in a sequined G-string in front of total strangers, or using her mother's credit card to buy Dom Perignon for her best friend's bachelorette party, Heather loved to impress. Taking a Greyhound back home would be way too pedestrian for her tastes, if not for her wallet.

But Amity found herself replaying the message and writing down the number anyway, probably for the same reason that she was always breaking her rules about being co-dependent with musicians. As hard as she worked to be hard, Amity couldn't get rid of her gooey centre. She was a sucker for a lost cause.

Speaking of lost causes, why not call Gregg? She'd scribbled down his cell number before taking her shower that morning. He was probably still in bed. Maybe he'd invite her to come over, help him wake up. Amity's pulse quickened as she thought about how he would smell and feel, wrapped in sheets that were still warm from the night before. He'd reach up and pull her down onto his mattress, take her into his arms and kiss her deep and slow, and her stress would dissolve in the heat of his mouth like sugarcubes in the rain...

'Hello?'

Amity was startled when Gregg picked up on the first ring.

'Um, hey. It's me.'

Silence. 'Who?'

Amity felt a coldness in her stomach, which gathered into a ball of ice. Six hours after giving her the greatest serial orgasm of her life, Gregg didn't remember the sound of her voice.

'Me,' she repeated, all fake cheer. 'Amity. From last night. Remember? The girl you were wearing around your neck for three hours.'

'Oh, yeah. How's it going?'

He couldn't have sounded less thrilled if she'd been an agent from the IRS, calling to remind him that he was being audited the next day. She'd called too early. Or maybe too late.

'Not so good,' Amity said. 'I lost my job this morning.

I was hoping I could come over and you could cheer me up.'

Might as well ask for exactly what I want, she thought. Gregg didn't seem to be in any frame of mind to pick up on subtle suggestions.

'Oh, shit,' he said under his breath, probably thinking that Amity couldn't hear. 'Listen, Amy –'

'Amity. You dropped a syllable.'

'Amity. Whatever. Listen, you're a sweetheart, and I'd like us to be friends –'

'Kind of late for "just friends", isn't it? After everything we did last night?'

Gregg gave an exasperated snort. Amity didn't have to work very hard to picture the matching expression on his face, the boredom in his green eyes. He probably went through this little speech five or six times a week.

'What we did last night was fuck,' he said.

'Fuck,' she repeated. 'Fuck.' The word didn't have a very pleasant reverb. It sounded like a body bag rolling down a flight of stairs.

'Right. You got it.'

'But you want to be friends.'

'Yeah. Sure. I mean, we'll see each other at parties and shows and stuff.'

'So you consider "fuck" to be a four-letter word for "friendship"?'

Gregg gave a jerky, uncertain laugh, a man-giggle. 'If you want to put it that way.'

'I'll tell you exactly how and where I want to put it,' Amity said, but Gregg broke the connection before she could go into any anatomical detail.

She also knew a five-letter word for 'friendship': Amity. And that's all she'd been offered from the men she'd dated, slept with or loved. Maybe she'd have better luck if she changed her name to Aphrodite.

Or she could start calling herself Heather; that was a heck of a lot sexier than being named after a Quaker virtue. Amity's stepsister never had any shortage of men falling in love with her. They dropped at her feet like victims of chemical terrorism, unable to resist her bodacious figure, her big blonde hair or her puffy angelfood lips. Heather didn't swear, she didn't pierce odd parts of her flesh, she didn't swill beer out of cans or try to play the guitar in public. On the whole, she was pathetic. Amity almost felt sorry for her.

But pity wasn't on Amity's mind as she picked up her phone and dialled the number of the hotel where Heather was staying. All she could think about was getting as far from Denver as possible before her rent was due. When you needed to escape reality, you couldn't do much better than Vegas.

## Chapter Two

# You Gotta Pet Your Muse

In the years before he disappeared, Amity's father had done two things that had had a huge impact on Amity's life. He had married Heather's mother, Candi, and he had left Amity his 1966 metallic blue Thunderbird convertible.

That car had been the object of his undying devotion – baby, lover and deity all rolled into one piece of utterly cool machinery. Like all great gifts, he had come by the car through an accident of fate, or karma, winning it in a poker game when he was thirty years old. The T-Bird had helped him win his second wife, Candi, a former showgirl who was drawn to bright, shiny objects.

Candi had strutted into Amity's world when Amity was fourteen, bringing with her a truckload of pink luggage, a vicious Pomeranian who had given Amity an abiding fear of dogs, and a daughter named Heather. Living with her new stepsister, Amity felt like a Third World village that's been occupied by a global superpower. Heather was sixteen years old, going on twenty-five. She trailed a string of boyfriends, whose desperate phone calls suddenly tied up the telephone line in Amity's house. Her morning bathroom ritual lasted so long that Amity had to learn to wash off with the garden hose so she wouldn't miss the school bus. Heather and Candi were on perpetual mother–daughter diets to tame their abundant curves, and the refrigerator teemed with cans of Slim-Fast and bottles of Evian.

Synthetic disco-pop blared on the stereo in Heather's new bedroom, where Amity's father had once played Skynyrd albums during poker games with his buddies.

'Heather and Candi are nothing but Spandex and synth,' Amity had complained to her father. He had nodded, looking shell-shocked.

Amity's father was a simple guy, a mechanic who liked a good game of Texas Hold 'Em and made a wicked creamed-cheese-and-grape-jelly sandwich. He had an intimate understanding of high-maintenance automobiles, but he couldn't cope with a high-maintenance woman.

When he walked out on his marriage, Amity's father left the house to his second wife. He left Amity the T-Bird, granting it to her in a note tucked in the corner of her bedroom mirror: *Take good care of my sweetheart. She's yours now. I'm taking the old Honda and heading somewhere West.* Amity knew that the word 'sweetheart' didn't refer to Candi.

As stepmothers went, Candi wasn't too bad. Her heart was in the right place – somewhere under her left mound of silicone – so she didn't fight Amity for the T-Bird and she let Amity live in the house until she left for college. This gave Heather plenty of time to turn Amity's life into a prototype of hell. Heather was just bright enough to invent a nickname for her stepsister, and she was popular enough to make it stick. For the last two years of high school, the skinny girl with stringy brown hair and a blue guitar was known by the entire student body as The Amityville Horror. Or Amityville. Or, simply, The Horror.

The name sucked. But then, Amity expected high school to suck, so she wasn't disappointed when the last years of her adolescence never blossomed into a teen dream of love notes, chocolates and unprotected sex. And though she and Heather never became friends, a weird bond developed between them, like a twisted cactus growing in the fallout of a nuclear explosion, as they lived through the aftermath of being abandoned by the only father figure that either of them had known.

'Men always leave,' Heather told Amity, with all the matter-of-fact worldliness of a forty-year-old streetwalker. 'That's why you have to leave them first.'

'I'd never leave anyone. I believe in love,' Amity declared.

Heather, sipping a can of Slim-Fast, laughed so hard that chocolate liquid sprayed out of her nose. 'Dream on, Amityville! Fantasising about dead rock stars doesn't count as love. You're eighteen years old, and you've had about three dates.'

Amity shrugged her bony shoulders. 'I've got time.'

Besides, the guys in 3-Way Dream weren't dead, and though Amity would never give her stepsister the opportunity to shoot down her most cherished fantasy, she believed that she and Daniel were destined to get together, if only for half an hour in the back of a tour bus (Amity was a heavy daydreamer, but at least she was realistic). Every time she watched him on MTV, on the grainy black-and-white video of 'Save My Soul', and saw the close-up of his hand strumming the strings of his guitar as his gravelly voice scraped out the lyrics, Amity knew that hand was going to lay a claim on her skin one day. She'd taped that video and watched it over and over, until she knew Daniel's hands better than her own. There was a deep white nick on his fourth knuckle, and his pinky was slightly crooked. His nails were uneven, as if he chewed them, and Amity knew that when he ran his hands down her naked torso, those jagged nails would leave tiny red lines on her skin, and she'd look at those lines later and wish they'd never fade.

And when he huddled over his guitar and stared into the camera, one eye half hidden under a thick wave of dark hair, Amity got chills imagining the time when he would be holding her body instead of that instrument, and gazing down into her eyes with all the intensity he was pouring into the camera's lens.

Amity's fixation on Daniel was more than a teenage crush. Sure, she did all the usual girly things – memorising every issue of 3-Way Dream's fanzine, writing down their lyrics in her diary, giving herself a temporary tattoo of Daniel's face with a ballpoint pen. But when she wasn't crushing, she was working out Daniel's songs on Blue Molly, trying to capture the eerie pentatonic blues-flavoured chords that were his speciality. Sometimes those chords triggered tangents of her own, hypnotic states where she left 3-Way Dream far behind, to jam to the sounds in her own head.

Years after that conversation with Heather, Amity's faith was starting to fray, but the heart of the fabric was still strong. Even in her darkest days of loneliness, despair and sexual frustration, a girl with a blue guitar and a blue car had to feel like there was someone special waiting for her, behind the next curve in the road, or at the next open mike night at a half-empty bar.

What kind of troubadour would she be if she didn't believe in love?

The hardest part of leaving town was abandoning Diabolicus. Amity's neighbour across the hall, a single computer programmer in his forties who worked from home, had offered to take Amity's pet. As soon as the cat saw his new digs, with the big fat sofa wedged under a sunny windowsill, he trotted away from Amity without a backwards glance.

'It's only temporary,' Amity reminded her neighbour. Tears prickled her eyelids as she handed over the Tuna Breath dish and a half-empty bag of kibble. 'I'll be back sooner than you think.'

Her neighbour gave her a long look. 'Really? A troubadour like you? I imagine once you hit the road, you won't stop rolling.'

Amity had never thought of herself that way: a shiftless traveller, roving from one place to another with her guitar strapped to her back. In fact, she'd been feeling more like a stick planted firmly in mud.

'I always swore I'd never leave anyone,' she said. 'And here I am, dumping the only male who's ever stuck with me.'

'You aren't dumping him,' her neighbour said. 'I'm sure the cat understands. Listen, Diabolicus and I will get along famously. We're a couple of lifelong bachelors. Look at him – does he seem to be suffering?'

He nodded at the cat, whose sausage-like body was already lodged deep in the sofa cushions, directly under a sunbeam. His almond-shaped eyes were closing as he lapsed into a contemplative slumber. Amity had had the cat since she was fifteen. He wasn't a kitten anymore. At his age, Diabolicus needed a sunbeam, a sofa and a caretaker who could afford to buy him canned food every now and then.

Leaving her apartment was much easier, at least from an emotional standpoint. In the four years she'd lived in this building, Amity hadn't put down any roots. She'd made a few sweet memories in the bed with a cute painter who'd been hired to freshen up the halls; she still felt small aftershocks of arousal when she remembered the way he'd had her take off all her clothes and lie face-down on her mattress, while he applied a brand new paint-roller to her back, her bottom and the backs of her thighs.

His white overalls were easy to slip out of; in fact, she didn't even know that he'd undressed until he gently parted her legs with his knee, slipped into the nook between, and coaxed his way inside her. By that point, Amity hadn't needed much coaxing, her lower lips were as warm and unctuous as the creamy paint that sat untouched in his paint tray. She and her painter screwed the afternoon away, breaking occasionally to share a beer – a long lazy exchange of love and liquids. There was still a lightning streak of eggshell white on the hardwood floor beside her bed, left by the sole of his sneaker when he dug into the floor for added traction as he came.

But the rest of her stuff held no allure for her anymore. The mirror, where she'd studied her reflection with more dismay than pleasure, would be left by the dumpster behind the building, where some other lonely single girl would find it. So would the bookshelf, with its collection of leftover college texts, and her crusty old microwave, and mismatched assortments of pots and pans. Obviously it wasn't true that every pot had a lid, Amity thought, as she threw her kitchen utensils into a box for disposal. Her love life – or lack thereof – proved it.

She didn't take anything with her from her closet but her jeans and boots, a few T-shirts and tank tops, her leather jacket, miniskirt, fishnet stockings. Her business suit, heels and panty hose were dumpster-bound. She did take an open box of strawberry-flavoured condoms that she found in the back of her drawer – always best to think of a condom box as 'half-full' – and her rock posters. And of course, her blue guitar. The thought of hocking Blue Molly for some extra gas money flitted across her mind, but she knew she'd never do it. Pawning your instrument was a cheesy cliché, an easy way out for a wannabe who secretly knew she'd never make it.

Amity left an envelope taped to her landlady's door with a cheque for 73 dollars inside and a note promising to send the rest later. The cheque would clean out her bank account; except for the last paycheque she had coming to her, and her credit card, Amity would be driving off to Vegas dead broke.

'Viva la Visa,' she said to herself as she climbed into the T-Bird, fired up the engine and headed for the nearest gas station.

Loaded up with road maps, sunscreen, bags of beef jerky and red liquorice, and a twelve-pack of bottled water, Amity headed out of Denver. Driving the big bird made her feel small, but safe and free as she settled into mental cruise mode. Guys in pickup trucks, sports cars and work vans gawked and honked at the sight of a lone brunette driving a classic convertible, but in her mind, they were already falling away, along with the city itself. She was alone with the highway and the sky, Sheryl Crow playing on the stereo that her dad had installed. Her passenger, the only friend who mattered to her at the moment, reclined beside her, her long neck tipped up to the sun.

'What would I do without you?' Amity said to Blue Molly. Muse, confidante, mascot, struggling sister of ambition – the guitar was everything she had left, but she was more than enough.

Amity felt a songwriting attack coming on. She pulled off the interstate at a truck stop, found a shady spot under a tree and parked the T-Bird. Then she dug around in her duffel bag until her fingers made contact with the smooth surface of a hardbound notebook.

The notebook was almost as critical to Amity's mental well-being as Blue Molly. The book was filled with staff paper, so that she could scribble down arrangements of her own songs, but she also recorded her thoughts on those lines, and her fantasies, and her lyrics. Leaning back in the seat and propping her heels on the dashboard, Amity began to write. She hummed a melody to herself, making up the lyrics as she went along. She always had a burst of creativity whenever she left another temp job. Those gigs seemed to suck the juice right out of her, but as soon as they were over, she'd feel the urge to write again.

> *In the blue of the evening*
> *Sweet shadows surround you,*
> *The lady comes in, and settles beside you.*
> *Don't push her away, or she might leave forever –*
> *You gotta pet your muse, baby,*
> *Gotta pet your muse.*

Amity chewed the end of her ballpoint and studied the verses she'd written. Not bad. The song was mellow, laid-back; she'd need a strong bridge to inject some passion into it. When it came to songwriting, Amity was big on passion. If she'd been born ten years earlier, she could have written power ballads for heavy-metal bands.

With the lyrics out of her system, she went on to update her diary.

> *Destination*: Las Vegas, Nevada
> *Mission*: Rescue Heather from her own stupidity
> *$$$ spent on gas*: Lots – all on my Visa. I'm going to blow my credit limit before we hit Nevada
>
> Here I am, sitting in the parking lot of a Flying J in the middle of a weekday afternoon. Lost another job. Shocker. Now I find myself on a mission of mercy, riding off to Vegas on my fiery blue steed to save Heather from her own vile impulses. Who knows what she's been doing in Sin City? Or *who* she's been doing? I can tell you one thing, I won't be letting any skankster wannabes ride in my T-Bird. That would be dangerous. No hitchhikers, either; Heather has a thing for sexy hitchers ever since those old Bugle Boy commercials came out, with that stud standing at the side

of the road in his tight jeans. No more men for me. I'm a priestess of my muse now. Triple-G Gregg cured me of my lust for males. I'm going to be celibate forever. Celibate and unemployed – that's me.

Amity sighed. She closed the notebook and shoved it back into her duffel bag. It was getting harder to pretend that losing all those jobs didn't matter. Drifting from one sterile office setting to another had worked for Amity so far, but she was starting to get this nagging feeling that she ought to be coming down to earth pretty soon, settling in for a landing. With no job, no man, no apartment – and now, probably no cat, since Diabolicus was so comfortably installed with her former neighbour – Amity was rootless.

Two years ago, that freedom would have thrilled her. Today, with thoughts of an empty bank account hovering over her like a bird of prey, freedom felt scary. Leaving one hand on the wheel, Amity yanked open a bag of cherry liquorice with her teeth.

'This is going to be my last escape ever,' Amity promised Blue Molly, as she gnawed a mouthful of rubbery red candy. 'One last road trip, then we'll find a permanent address. How does that sound?'

Blue Molly had nothing to say.

'I know it's been hard these past few years. I promised you that I'd be famous by the time I turned 25. Well, I'm not famous yet, but I've written a few songs. I've had steady gigs ... pretty steady. People say I'm good – or I *could* be good, if I'd work at it. Listen, after this road trip, I'm going to settle down. Maybe we need to move to LA. Maybe that's why I haven't made it yet; I haven't been around the right people. If I took you to some of those clubs in LA, we could make it. We'll play in bars, coffee houses, wherever we have to go to get heard. I admit I haven't tried hard enough, but that's going to change. Everything's going to change, as soon as this trip is over. I promise.'

Amity heard a thump. She turned her head to see her battered guitar case, plastered with peeling concert stickers, sliding down the seat onto the floorboards.

'Fine,' Amity sighed. 'You don't have to tell me. You've heard all these promises before. Jeez, Lady, you're even more cynical than I am. If you can just hold on for a few more days, I'll find a way to get you all the glamour and glory you've always wanted.'

Amity ran a quick calculation in her head. Thirteen hours. That's how long the drive from Denver to Vegas was supposed to take. But there were so many distractions along Interstate 70: velvet green mountains and twisty red canyons, diners and dinosaur museums, morning mists and evening storms. She could easily stretch the trip out to two days, if she wanted to. Then she'd meet up with Heather and her friends in Vegas, and of course there would have to be a certain amount of gambling and debauchery to make the trip worthwhile. Three days' worth, at least – and then she'd have to drive the whole crew back to Denver before she could even think about moving to Los Angeles.

The available balance on Amity's Visa had been about $7,000, last time she actually looked at her monthly statement. That should be enough to buy a little fun and freedom before she got back to reality again. She'd have a couple of thousand left over to get herself into a new apartment. This time, she'd be a responsible tenant. She would pay her rent on time, with the proceeds from her *real* job. She would even stick to her No-Musicians-Overnight rule, so there would be no mysterious banging or thumping, moaning or jamming coming from her apartment late at night.

'Give me one week,' Amity begged Blue Molly. 'No, make it two weeks. Two weeks, and I'll land somewhere, get a job, and start writing songs for real. We'll both be famous by the time I'm thirty.'

A truck rumbled through the parking lot, making the convertible vibrate. Blue Molly slid all the way to the floor with a final, sceptical thud.

When she was sleeping, Heather looked like a Botticelli angel. Daniel always stopped breathing for a few seconds when he came across her like that, sprawled out on her back, her long corkscrew curls spread across the pillows like spirals of precious metal peeled from a solid brick of gold. Her perfectly pointed chin was tilted upwards, her puffy lips were partly open, and her tawny eyelashes fell across her cheeks with such sweet symmetry that Daniel's fingers itched to pluck out a song about them.

A whole damn song about eyelashes. That's the kind of thing that Heather did to him. Even the smallest details of her beauty gave him a hard-on to write lyrics. Too bad he couldn't seem to get any of those words past the huge wall of lust that slammed down when he looked at her.

He set down the plastic cup of nickels that he'd earned playing the slot machines downstairs that night, and pulled off his shirt as he walked across the room. He unbuttoned his jeans as he stood over his sleeping bride and pushed them down his lean hips. He still couldn't believe she was his now. On the fourth finger of her left hand was a gold-painted ring, studded with a pink chunk of plastic encircled by rhinestones. He'd bought the ring at the Casbah's gift shop, choosing it right off the Super Deals rack. Heather wore the ring with pride ... at least he liked to think that the look on her face when she held out her left hand and squinted at the plastic trinket was pride.

One day, he'd write a song about that ring, too, and

play it for Heather. She'd be wearing a real rock by then, a whopper of a diamond, and they'd laugh about the bubblegum toy that he'd slipped on her finger the night they got married at the Casbah Hotel's private wedding chapel, the Temple of Love.

Remembering that ceremony made Daniel vaguely queasy, possibly because his stomach didn't want him to forget the three bottles of cheap champagne he'd shared with Zak and Randy in an alley behind a liquor store before the wedding got under way. The boys had tried to convince Daniel that he was making a mistake. Daniel didn't know how to tell them that the moment he saw Heather, the reckless stars in his personal constellation had finally seemed to fall into place. He wasn't sure how he would explain this to his parents, either. He thought he heard a plaintive echo of his mother's voice when he slipped the ring on Heather's finger: *Your father and I don't mind that your new wife isn't Jewish, sweetheart. But are you sure she really loves you?*

Daniel was sure ... as sure as a man could be, when he'd met his bride. He'd seen the sparkle of sheer delight in Heather's eyes when he promised to stick with her till death did them part. And though that sparkle had been snuffed out for a moment when she saw the tacky pink ring, Daniel knew her joy was genuine. As soon as he found a steady source of income, he would buy her a ring that would prove without a doubt that she was the woman he loved.

For now, the closest thing to a rock that he could give her was right between his thighs. Daniel tugged the warm sheet out of Heather's fingers, and pulled it down slowly, exposing her creamy skin inch by inch. Her full breasts, with their rosebud nipples, her taut belly, her hips – Heather's hourglass figure reminded him of the first guitar he'd ever owned, the black Epiphone that he used to cradle against his body like a lover.

'Wake up, sweet thing,' he whispered, as he climbed onto the bed and parted her thighs. 'It's me.'

Heather's angelic face puckered. 'Me who?' she muttered. 'Damn it, who turned that light on?'

Her hand flopped around on the night stand as she tried to find the lamp without opening her eyes.

'That's the sun coming through the curtains,' Daniel said. 'It's after ten o'clock, baby.'

He persisted in his mission to get between Heather's legs, in spite of the fact that she had clamped her thighs shut. Coaxing them apart was like trying to open an oyster with a plastic knife, but Daniel was determined to get to the silky pink folds in between. Heather was always in a foul temper when she woke up, he reminded himself. Her bitchiness had nothing to do with her new husband, the love of her life.

'I've got something for you,' he murmured. Daniel ran his thumb up and down the strip of fur that pointed like an arrow to the paradise between Heather's thighs. Her shaved bush was only a shade or two darker than the long curls that trailed across her pillow. She had to keep herself trimmed so that she could wear her string bikinis and sequined G-strings. As hot as she looked in that stuff, Daniel often wished that she would let herself grow wild down there, so he could sink his fingers (among other things) into a jungle of gold hair.

'What?' Heather opened one blue eye.

'It's hard, and it's huge – well, kinda huge – and it's all yours, if you want it. Think you could open up for me a little, darlin'?'

A smile turned Heather's mouth into a valentine. She threw off the rest of the sheet and raised her knees, wrapping them around Daniel's hips and pulling him down on top of her, into her. Daniel's heart sang. His baby was always ready for him, even in the sourest of moods. She was already rocking her hips, but he didn't give her what she wanted right away. Instead, he kept his cock pressed against her mound so she could feel what she was missing, think about how much she wanted him, maybe even go a little crazy.

'Tell me what you want,' he whispered into her ear, as his lips left feathery trails of kisses down the length of her throat.

'You know what I want.' Her voice was still husky from the night before, when she'd worked her shift at the casino, walking in and out of the rafts of cigarette smoke.

'Yeah. But I want to hear you say it.'

'Oh, come *on*, Daniel. Don't play games.'

'Does this feel like a game?' He kissed the very tip of her nipple, then circled the flesh with his tongue until it peaked. Then he ground the firm nub oh-so-gently between his teeth.

Heather moaned and picked up the pace of her rocking, trying to force him to slide into that warm, wet nook between her legs. He was more than ready to do just that, so ready, in fact, that he had to bite his lip and play a few bars of Bach in his head to keep himself reined in. When Bach's counterpoint didn't work, he started to think about the things that had been stressing him out lately. He thought about money, and he thought about his band, and what a mistake it had been to try to bring 3-Way Dream back together.

The other guys hadn't changed at all; they'd just become more extreme versions of the jerks they used to be. Randy was in desperate need of rehab, and Zak's greatest ambition in life was to screw enough showgirls to cast his own musical.

'Hey.' Heather's hands clasped his face. 'What happened? You felt like a battering ram three seconds ago.'

'Just a momentary lapse. Trust me, it won't last.'

And it didn't. Being back in the moment with Heather sent Daniel's blood rushing back where it belonged, and before long, he was gliding into her, engulfed by her warm, fragrant softness. He could hear the liquid sounds he made as he slid back and forth inside her, the sounds of the honeyed friction that he loved so much. Faster and faster, the strokes generating an electricity that was too much to bear, and with his gorgeous new wife moaning and writhing under him, it wasn't long until he felt that familiar heat deep in his groin. His muscles went taut, and Heather reached up and grabbed his head, pulling him down for a deep French kiss that lasted along the whole, gut-wrenching ride of his orgasm.

Before he could catch his breath, Heather was pushing Daniel down to the edge of the bed, spreading her thighs at a butterfly angle. He knew what to do, and he did it with gusto. He loved eating Heather just after he'd made love to her; she was overflowing with juice, and wild to come. When he felt her back arch, he reached up to grab her nipples, tweaking them as her back curved into a beautiful bridge.

No matter how she moaned during foreplay, Heather never made noises when she came. She always clenched her teeth, and though there was no question that she was feeling pleasure, she wouldn't vocalize it at the critical moment. Her silence always left Daniel feeling slightly uneasy, and just a bit let down. He liked feedback.

Feedback or not, making love to his new bride was still the closest he'd ever get to heaven.

'I still can't believe this,' he said, sinking back onto the hotel's scrawny pillows. They didn't make hotel pillows like they used to; the ones he remembered from his early days on the road had been as deep and soft and reassuring as a long afternoon nap with a voluptuous woman. On the other hand, it could be that his band just couldn't afford to stay in the kinds of hotels that treated their guests to luxury bedding.

'Can't believe what?' Heather mumbled.

'This. You. That we're married. I feel like some loser who stopped by a slot machine on his way out of a casino, bet his last quarter and hit a million-dollar jackpot.'

He could feel Heather cringing beside him. 'Don't call yourself a loser. It's bad for my self-esteem.'

'Just a figure of speech. All I meant was that I can't believe how lucky I am to have snagged a woman like you.'

'That's better.'

Heather snuggled up beside him. Then she caught sight of the ring on her left hand, and her pretty face sagged into a pout.

'I'm not going to feel like a new bride until I get a real diamond,' she said.

'I thought you liked pink.'

'A pink diamond, maybe. Not a pink piece of... glass.'

'And you thought the gift shop ring was romantic.'

'It was, at first. Now it's getting old. I'm starting to feel like trailer trash.'

A whiney note sharpened the edges of Heather's newborn kitten voice.

'Listen, sweetheart, it won't be long till we start making big bucks again. As soon as we get paid from this tour, I'll buy you a real diamond. It might be small, but it'll be real.'

*As soon as we get paid.* Dread snagged Daniel deep inside his chest and held him like a meat hook; he could actually feel the vertigo as his feet swung back and forth over the abyss. He hadn't told Heather that the band's new manager had disappeared. Last time they'd seen Ernie, the manager had been waving to them from the open door of a rented Cadillac, a cocktail waitress draped on either arm. *See you guys first thing in the morning,* Ernie had said, with a leering wink. *Although my morning probably won't start before three in the afternoon.* The Caddy had disappeared down the Strip. Ernie hadn't showed up at the meeting the next day. Zak and Randy had been so hungover that they didn't realise their manager wasn't there.

But Daniel had been stone cold sober. He wasn't too worried when Ernie didn't show. When he didn't answer his cellphone, Daniel started to worry. And when the clerk at the front desk told Daniel that Ernie had checked out, leaving all his own bills paid, but none of the band's, Daniel's worry exploded into panic.

'The guy must have had a family emergency,' Daniel had muttered to himself, pacing the hotel lobby, raking his hair with his fingers. Good thing he was wearing his hair on the long side again – it gave him something to hang onto in times of turmoil.

*Family emergency?* sneered a sceptical voice in the back of Daniel's consciousness. *Dream on. Sewer rats like Ernie don't have families.*

Daniel still hadn't told Heather that Ernie had bailed. It had been hard enough telling Zak and Randy. The looks on the guys' faces had hit him like fists in the gut. No rage in those eyes, no true disappointment, only resignation at hearing the old, familiar fucked-over-again refrain.

'Hey. At least we got to get out and play,' Zak had said with a shrug. 'Got my ABC's taken care of – arse, booze and coke.'

'Better than flipping burgers,' Randy agreed. 'And we did get some cash up front.'

Cash up front. Right. That would barely cover the hotel bill. Meanwhile, Daniel had a new bride to take care of, and the honeymoon was already headed for a crash-landing.

There had to be a legal way to get money fast. Heather was already making plans for the condo they were going to rent when this gig ended, the cute sports car she wanted to buy. She was complaining about her wardrobe – she'd need something besides G-strings and go-go boots to wear when she got back home – and dropping ominous hints about her wedding ring several times a day. Daniel had fallen in love with a high-maintenance woman. And though he knew he was doomed, Daniel wanted nothing more than to make his golden-haired Botticelli girl happy.

He'd been up all night searching for answers, wandering from one casino to the next, up and down the Strip, looking for a kindred soul who could tell him where Ernie was, tell him how to pull cash out of thin air, tell him the meaning of his wayward meandering life. He was on a vision quest in Vegas, seeking any kind of illumination of the path he should take, even if the illumination came from a flashing neon sign that said: FAST CASH.

Fast cash. The key to paradise lay at the front door of a pawn shop. At two in the morning, the place was closed, but the storefront was lit up like Christmas morning to display the glories of its merchandise. Was there any city on earth that could offer anything like the treasure-packed pawn shops of Vegas? Hardcore gamblers would sell their family heirlooms, their grandmothers' wedding bands, their kidneys, their first-born children, their very souls to get the cash to pay off monster debts, or keep the roulette wheel spinning. Some poor bastard had even committed the sacrilege of pawning a classic guitar. Nestled in a mound of glittering cellophane, the axe gleamed like a black shark caught temporarily in a mermaid's net. Who had been graced by fate to hold that beauty? Who had stood up on a stage with that axe and felt its thunderous purr like a sweet musical electrocution?

Keep drooling, baby, the instrument seemed to mock Daniel. You'll never be able to afford me. Not even from a pawn shop.

Drooling in front of the pawn shop window brought

back a memory that he'd held down for many years, a memory that brought a harder pang than the break-up with the first girl he'd loved.

Twenty-two years old, and he'd felt like he was fifty – wrecked and wrung out from two years on the road with 3-Way Dream that had brought nothing but gigs that rarely paid and a long string of disappointments. The grinding winding tour had taken them from one bar or club to another, where they'd pounded their hearts out for audiences who sometimes loved them, and sometimes wanted to turn them into road-kill. With nothing but one EP under their belts, printed by an indie label, some sporadic airplay on college radio stations, and no distribution to speak of, the band had drawn more blanks than anything else. Daniel had taken odd jobs at gas stations and motels to keep gas in the van, fuelling his body with peanut butter and cheap beer, and writing. Writing song after song, in a flood of inspiration and desperation, struggling for that one hit that would break them all through. That journey brought him to a pawnshop that was the twin of this one – for all he knew, it *was* this one – holding the one thing he owned that had any value at all, his first Gibson Epiphone.

He hocked his Gibson Girl for twenty bucks. A single crumpled bill, dirtied by who knew how many hands. The guy behind the counter at the pawnshop told Daniel he was getting a great deal. The only reason he was getting so much for the old instrument was that the man felt sorry for him.

'I'll be back for her,' Daniel had promised. Watching his black beauty disappear across the counter into the old man's grimy, tobacco-yellowed palms, Daniel had felt like he was selling the love of his life to a pimp. He'd had that guitar since his fifteenth birthday. She'd been with him through high school parties, college garage bands, through a few small triumphs and a thousand kicks in the teeth. Every song he'd written that was worth its three or four minutes of life had been worked out on her frets.

'Sure you will,' the pawnshop dealer said.

'No, really. I will,' Daniel insisted.

And in all fairness to his Gibson Girl, Daniel had come back. He was back in that same pawnshop, ticket in hand, five weeks later. Those five weeks were a bridge that led from his old life to a shining new one. The band caught the attention of a small-time manager, who was owed a favour by a big-time record producer, and within a matter of days, the guys who'd been sharing a single jar of peanut butter were reviewing contracts. Cash seemed to end up in Daniel's hands whenever he opened them; he had no idea where the money was coming from, but it felt damn sweet to have something in his pocket besides cocktail napkins with girls' phone numbers scribbled on them.

But it wasn't enough money to get his Gibson Girl back. When Daniel went back to the shop, she was gone.

'You were supposed to hold on to my guitar for three months!' Daniel said. He wanted to reach across the counter and grab the greasy polyester collar of the pawnshop dealer's shirt, but he held back.

The pawnshop dealer rolled his thick shoulders and shifted his eyes. 'Shit happens. It's gone. What can I say?'

'Who bought her? Give me the guy's number.'

'Can't do that. We don't give out our customers' names.'

Daniel raked his fingers through his hair. He felt as if the floor under his feet was rolling, wavelike.

'Look. I'll pay you. Hundred bucks, cash, if you tell me the guy's name.' Hands shaking, Daniel pulled out his wallet. Same old billfold he'd been carrying for years, cracked and hardened from a lot of trips through the washing machine in the pocket of his jeans, but for once it was filled with bills. Daniel peeled five twenties off the stack and held them out to the pawnshop dealer. The bills vanished into the dealer's meaty paw before Daniel could blink.

'It wasn't a guy. It was a girl. Hot little number – a redhead, if I remember right. Tight jeans. Halter top. Said she was starting her own band.'

'Who isn't?' Daniel said impatiently. 'What was her name?'

The dealer screwed up his face and stared into the distance, as if he were crying. 'Sadie. No, that's not it. Carrie.'

'Don't you keep records?'

The dealer laughed. 'What do you think this is? City hall?'

The man's face disappeared behind the red mist that covered Daniel's eyes. He'd never had the impulse to kill a fellow human being before, but this guy was looking less like a human and more like a sewer rat by the second. The dealer must have seen something dangerous in Daniel's face, because his phlegmy laughter dried up quick.

'Her name was Sadie O? Grady,' he said. 'She had one of those squiggly things after the O ... a question mark.'

'Nice. Where does she live?'

'No idea. She mentioned that she was staying with friends in a trailer park off the Strip. Name of the band was Bush Babies. Couldn't forget that one if I tried.'

Daniel let go of the breath he'd been holding. 'Thanks.'

'Now get the hell out of here and don't come back,' the sewer rat said. He began to lower his beefy body towards a place below the counter. It didn't take a psychic to know that he was reaching for a weapon.

Daniel didn't need a second invitation to exit stage left.

He never did find Sadie O? Grady, or the Bush Babies. That didn't surprise him. The name of the band had probably changed five or six times by the time Daniel got wind of it, and he never really believed that the chick had called herself Sadie. The only thing he knew for sure, the one truth that would haunt him for the next five years, was that someone else was holding his black beauty. Some other musician was receiving that magic that used to flow through her strings with almost no effort on the player's part. That axe had a power and a voice all her own; the guitarist was little more than the middleman. Or middlewoman, as the case may be.

Life turned into a tornado soon after they broke their first deal with a big name label. Recording sessions in real studios, touring by bus instead of by van, real food, new clothes, and girls by the dozens, if not the hundreds. Zak and Randy were ecstatic. They drank up 3-Way Dream's success like a couple of desert dogs slurping water from a garden hose.

Daniel always knew it couldn't last. Through one city, one country after another, the ghost of his first guitar followed him. He knew he was crazy for being so superstitious. But he also knew he was doomed without his Epiphone. She'd guided his career like the needle on a compass; he hadn't always understood where she was leading him, and the paths she'd pointed out had sometimes come close to killing him. But in the end, she'd always brought him back to true north.

'I know you're somewhere in this city, Girl,' Daniel sighed as he peeled himself away from the pawnshop window.

Or somewhere out in the yawning desert that surrounded the dazzling oasis of Las Vegas. Or somewhere in the suburbs of Orange County, or the backstreet studios of LA, or the bars of Austin, Texas. The Epiphone could be anywhere. Only a fool would think he could track down one old electric guitar – probably dinged up beyond belief by now – and beg, buy or steal it back from the poseur who thought he owned it.

King Arthur didn't consider himself a fool when he sent his three knights off in search of the Holy Grail. Some quests were impossible. You knew that from the first step that you took, but you took that step anyway, and the next one, and all the steps that it took to reach your goal, because the gleaming, shining object of your quest was the source of your salvation.

*Chapter Three*

# Licking the Jar

Las Vegas by daylight was a whole different animal than it was after sunset. On a blistering hot midmorning, the city was a tired, ragged beast, its coat brown and dusty, knots of bone poking out from under its hide. Half of Las Vegas Boulevard seemed to be under construction, and Amity got a few whistles from guys in hardhats as she cruised by in her convertible at the speed of a geriatric snail. She checked them out from behind her oversized five-dollar sunglasses and gave the cute ones a flash of tongue. Looking at all that sunburnt male flesh, slick with sweat in the Nevada sun, was already getting her juices flowing.

Traffic on the Strip was agonisingly slow, but Amity wasn't in any hurry to get to Heather's hotel. If she'd had more than a few bucks in her pocket, she would have stopped at a casino to play a few hands of blackjack and snag a free cocktail, or hang out by the hotel pool. She had a sudden urge to pretend that she'd never heard of Heather; who said Amity couldn't just get lost in Vegas? She couldn't remember the last time she'd had a vacation. But then, you couldn't really claim that you needed a vacation if you didn't have a job.

Vegas wasn't the place to mull over your career failures, at least not when you were flat-out sober and drenched in sunlight. Amity leant back in her car, flexed her fingers on the wheel and settled back to enjoy her escape. It was easy to forget reality when you were driving past monstrous replicas of the Sphinx, a medieval castle, the New York skyline and the Eiffel Tower. There were the brand new themed super casinos, the glamour palaces, and in the shadow of all that wealth were the older seedier places, like the Casbah, where Heather and her friends were staying.

Along the way, Amity passed a boarded-up wedding chapel, an abandoned replica of a quaint country church sitting in the middle of a weedy vacant lot like an anachronism dropped off a spaceship from the nineteenth century onto the surface of Planet Vegas. The little white building had been tagged with graffiti, and the remnants of a lattice trellis lay in smithereens on the dirt yard. A billboard standing several yards from the deserted Chapel of Endless Love boasted a giant advertisement for a web site called VASECTOMY.COM.

'OK, it's official,' Amity announced over her shoulder to Blue Molly. 'Love is dead. What are we supposed to sing about now?'

Heather's hotel wasn't going to supply any creative inspiration. The Casbah had been built to resemble a sheikh's palace in the middle of a desert oasis, but the palace was looking bankrupt and the palm trees drooped at a dispirited angle. The three life-size plaster camels standing in an island in the middle of the parking lot didn't do much to boost Amity's confidence in the hotel valet's driving skills. And she didn't like the way the valet was ogling her T-Bird as he held out his hand for her car keys. Amity didn't trust her automobile with other drivers under the best of circumstances, but now that the convertible was the closest thing she had to a permanent address, she was even less willing to hand over her keys and let a stranger slide behind the wheel.

'No, thanks. I'll park her myself,' she told the pimply kid in the tacky white uniform. Her words came out sounding more snappish than she'd intended, and she felt bad when the guy's face sank with disappointment. It was bad enough that he had to wear a polyester Sergeant Pepper jacket with gold epaulettes; the kid didn't need some nearly homeless chick treating him as if he weren't good enough to touch her vehicle.

'It's nothing personal,' Amity reassured the valet. 'She's just all I've got right now. Me and my car and my guitar – we're all alone in the world.'

Now it was the valet's turn to look at Amity as if she were a refugee from Loserville. As he eyeballed her Iron Maiden T-shirt and road-grimed jeans, he was probably sizing her up as a trailer park hooker who'd cruised in from the boondocks to plump up her wallet in Vegas over the weekend.

'Whatever,' he said, and left Amity to navigate the hotel parking lot alone. He also didn't offer to carry her luggage. She had to drag her suitcase and guitar all the way across the lot and through the hotel lobby. The slot machines were in full swing, being plugged with quarters and nickels by zombified men and women who stared at the spinning displays with glazed eyes. The relentless ding-ding-brrrr-ding of the machines filled the air. The Casbah was one of the cheesier hotels in Vegas, too far off the Strip – and off the radar of good taste – to attract any high-rollers or glitz goddesses. Its fake Moroccan interior was a tribute to a cinematic glamour that it could never hope to possess. The plastic palm trees needed a good dusting, and the faux-stucco walls were stained with cigarette smoke. One of the floor managers was strolling around with a fez on his head and a stuffed monkey perched on his shoulder. It was all too much for Amity to handle in broad daylight.

'I always knew Heather would end up in a place like this,' Amity muttered to herself. Checking out the cocktail waitresses, with their huge hair and bejewelled bras,

Amity realised that this was where girls ended up after they frittered away too many brain cells on hairspray and peach schnapps in high school.

Amity took the elevator to the third floor, where Heather had told her she was staying. She glanced at her reflection in the elevator's mirrored walls, then promptly averted her eyes. She looked like exactly what she was: a straggly wannabe rocker chick with a banged-up six-string. Heather wouldn't expect anything less from the Amityville Horror.

A stack of dishes and an empty champagne bottle sat on a tray on the floor outside Heather's hotel room. Amity stopped and stared, not at the leftover food, or the plastic glasses half-filled with flat champagne, but at the blonde waif who was squatting on the carpet beside the tray, stuffing sandwich crusts and crumpled napkins into her open backpack. The girl started when she realised that Amity was standing over her, staring.

'What are you doing? Are you hungry?'

Amity thought about offering the girl some spare change, then remembered that she didn't have any. Meanwhile, she tucked away the idea of stealing leftover food from room-service trays for possible use in the future.

With a haughty sniff, the girl brushed her lank platinum hair out of her eyes, which were rimmed with smudgy black kohl. She wore a black T-shirt embroidered with shiny beads, tight black jeans that made her skinny legs look like pipecleaners, and brutally heavy Doc Martens. Definitely an alternative flavour.

'I'm not going to eat this stuff,' she said, her babydoll voice oozing contempt. 'I'm keeping some of it, and I'm selling the rest on eBay. I got here first, so back off.'

Amity wasn't about to infringe on this crazy chick's territory. 'You're selling my sister's trash?'

Wow, Amity thought. Where have I been all these years? Working lousy temp jobs, when I could have been selling Heather's dirty napkins and pizza crusts on the internet. If I could snag one of her dirty thongs, I might never need to work the temp agencies again.

The blonde got to her feet. Petite but mighty, she stared Amity down. 'I don't know who your sister is. The stuff I'm stealing belongs to Him.'

She pronounced the word 'him' with a distinctly capital H.

'Him who?' Amity asked.

The girl blew air through her black-painted lips in an exasperated poof. 'You ought to know. You're going into His room.' She shot Amity a look of envy. 'So what do you do?'

'I'm unemployed. I play the guitar.'

And in her limitless spare time, Amity apparently had surreal conversations with spooky tweakers in rundown Vegas hotels.

The girl planted her fists on her hips and tapped the toe of her Frankenstein boot on the orange carpet. 'No, I mean what's your speciality? Head? Hand jobs? Anal? How are you going to get in there?'

'Well, I'm going to knock on the door. And when someone answers, I'll walk inside. I'm not a hooker or anything, if that's what you think.'

The girl looked incredulous. 'You really believe it's that easy? Gawd, you must be, like, a total newbie.'

'I'm here to visit my stepsister,' Amity said, edging towards the door. The girl's eyes had taken on a maniacal gleam. 'I'm pretty sure she'll let me in without doing anything gross or illegal to whoever she's in there with.'

'Listen, let me go in with you,' the blonde suggested, her craftiness tinged with desperation. 'We'll work something out. I'll give you half of what I get from selling this stuff.' She pointed to the trash in her backpack. 'Just give me an intro. I have to meet Dan. I have to. I mean, he's everything...'

'No thanks. You can keep whatever you get.' Amity pounded on the door with both fists.

The door opened. Amity stepped inside, and quickly secured the deadbolt behind her.

Then she turned around, and saw who was standing in the room. All of a sudden the scene in the hallway became brilliantly, shockingly clear.

'You want to travel around the country looking for *what*?'

Heather's Christmas-bow lips tightened into an incredulous knot. She was standing in front of the vanity table at the hotel, her blonde curls still crackling from the brushing she'd been giving them. Daniel had just told her about the journey he wanted them to take, his quest for creative and spiritual salvation.

'I need to find my first guitar,' Daniel said. His hands flopped at his sides, helpless to assist him in pleading his case. 'It shouldn't be all that hard. I know the name of the woman who bought it from the pawn shop. All I have to do is find her. And then maybe find the next person who owned it after her. And the next person after that, and so on, until she's in my arms again.'

'You. Are. Smoking. Crack.' Heather's curly mane whipped around her face as she punctuated each word with a shake of her head. 'No wonder we can't afford this room anymore. You're back on drugs.'

'Hey! I've never taken any drug stronger than aspirin,' Daniel protested. 'Randy's the one who had the drug problem, and he's clean now. Or trying.' Daniel came up behind Heather, took her by the shoulders and turned her around to face him. It was hard to get his new bride to turn away from a mirror. It was even harder to melt that cast-iron scowl on her face into the sweet, sexy pout that he'd fallen in love with.

'Look, baby, I know this sounds insane, but I have to

find that guitar. *Have* to. Nothing's gone right since I hocked her. None of my successes have turned into anything but a flash of glitter and a few bucks that are long gone.'

Heather must have seen the fractured light of longing in Daniel's eyes, because her shoulders relaxed under his hands. Her face softened – she was his love kitten again.

'OK. What do you want me to do?' she asked.

'Nothing. You don't have to do anything. Just come with me. Be there for me. I'll find the Gibson; all you have to do is be my guardian angel on the road. Can you do that?'

Heather chewed her lower lip. Her blue eyes swerved towards her vanity table, to a heap of sequined bras and thongs, and the stack of bills that she'd carefully straightened and counted the night before.

'You know, I've got my own career, too,' Heather said. 'I couldn't get established as a dancer anywhere if we were on the road. And it's not like you'd be making enough money to support us if you were spending all your time looking for that old guitar.'

Daniel winced. 'My Gibson Girl isn't just some "old guitar", sweetheart. She's a classic. The first electric guitar I ever owned. She was the legend of my life, and I handed her over to some sleazeball so I could buy peanut butter and beer for the guys in the band. Can't you see how guilty that's made me feel all these years?'

'Jeez, honey, you're so dramatic. It's not like you killed somebody...'

'But it *is*. That's exactly what I did. I killed part of myself, Heather, the part that was faithful to the kind of music I wanted to play when I was fifteen years old. I killed the part of myself that wasn't a sellout –'

A two-fisted banging interrupted his impassioned speech.

Heather stiffened. 'Who's pounding the door down?'

'Don't open it. It might be one of those strung-out groupies. The only fans I have left are absolute freaks.'

'Let me at her. I'll kick her arse,' Heather threatened, looking about as capable of kicking arse as a Persian kitten in high heels.

Daniel let go of Heather's arms. His wife scampered away and flung open the door. The door immediately slammed shut behind the visitor, who bolted it behind her.

'Amityville! Oh-my-gawd, sis, you really came!'

Behind the masses of Heather's curls, Daniel couldn't see much of the person who was filling her arms. He caught a glimpse of a tall, skinny girl with long brown hair snagged in Heather's embrace. The belly of a black guitar case protruded from behind the girl's back.

'Who is that?' Daniel asked.

Heather stood back and let him see the brunette in all her glory. Her face was streaked with a drab paint mixed from sweat and desert dust. Her hair, if it had been styled in any particular way when she left her house that morning, had lost any semblance of order to the wind. She wore an old Iron Maiden T-shirt with the sleeves cut out, over a grimy white wifebeater and hip-hugging jeans. No boobs or hips to speak of, but she had a tight figure, if you liked the lean, hungry look.

Daniel didn't care much for that look himself. It reminded him too much of the way he'd been a few years ago, and the way he was about to be again.

'This is our ride back to Denver,' Heather bubbled.

'I'm also her stepsister,' the brunette added. 'There was a relationship between us before I showed up to give you guys a ride home. My name's Amity, by the way. Not Amityville.'

Daniel must have been standing in a patch of shadow, because when he took a few steps forwards to inspect the girl more closely, her jaw dropped as if she were seeing him for the first time. She suddenly wore the same slack, stupefied, pre-hysterical stare that Daniel had seen on hundreds of girls during his brief bout with fame. He didn't get that stare much anymore. Amity's reaction flattered him, but it also left a bittersweet taste in his mouth.

'You're D-D-Duh...' she stammered.

'Daniel Goldstein,' he finished for her. 'Nice to meet you. Heather never told me she had a sister.'

'Goldstein?' Heather gave him a confused look. 'I thought your last name was "Gold".'

'It is. Was. Used to be.'

Daniel had shortened his last name years ago, when 3-Way Dream signed their first contract. He'd always meant to have his name legally changed, but he'd never got around to it. Something kept holding him back, maybe leftover guilt from his loving Jewish family, who had always been supportive of his music, even when they were mildly bewildered by it.

'When we bought you that fancy electric guitar, we thought you'd want to play it in your father's band,' Daniel's mother had lamented. 'That music you write, sweetheart... well, it sounds like your guitar is defective. Like your parents didn't care enough to buy you a really *nice* instrument.'

Daniel's mother was a perpetually befuddled beauty, the kind of woman who would need help crossing the street if she weren't stopping traffic with her looks. Daniel had inherited her thick, ink-black hair and deep brown eyes, along with his father's gift for music. Dan Goldstein, Senior, sang lead in a popular local band called the Swizzlestix. The 'Stix', as they informally called themselves, were booked for months in advance, playing at weddings, sweet sixteen parties and other events commemorating life's milestones. The boys in the Stix could play everything from torch songs to beebop, classic rock to Top 40 hits, and even heavy metal if the crowd was right. They played a kick-arse cover of Megadeth's 'Train of Consequences' that was requested at every bar mitzvah they ever played.

'You got your mom's looks and my singing voice,' Daniel's father used to say, with a sigh of gratitude. 'Thank god it wasn't the other way around.'

Though Daniel's parents had showered him with genetic gifts, he hadn't used his full family name for years, and he had no clue why he'd suddenly done it this afternoon. Something about the dusty brunette with the banged-up acoustic guitar made him want to tell the truth.

'Well, anyway. Amity's here to take us all back home.' Heather clasped her hands together and did a little happy-dance. 'I can't wait to get back to Denver. I've got soooo many plans.'

'So do I,' Daniel said, hoping the tone of his voice would remind Heather of the talk they'd been having before her sister showed up. But Heather refused to make eye contact with him as she scurried around the hotel room, snatching up scraps of satin lingerie and stray shoes. She dragged a suitcase out from under the bed and began tossing her belongings inside at random. Amity stood frozen, gawking at Daniel with eyes the size of dinner plates.

Daniel rubbed the back of his neck and stared at a stain in the carpet. He'd never really felt comfortable with female adoration. Part of Heather's appeal had been the fact that she wasn't impressed with his reputation. She'd never heard of 3-Way Dream; she'd been into techno and hip-hop back in those days. She had no appreciation for the traditions they'd tried to carry on, the chords and vocals of Daniel's delta blues driven by Randy's relentless, primitive percussion, all of it undercut by the hyperactive crunch of Zak's surfer punk bass. For Heather, Daniel's main selling points had been the fact that he worshipped her and that he 'rocked in bed' (her words, not his).

'You OK, Amity?' Daniel asked. 'Can I get you a glass of water? Instant coffee? How about a whiskey straight up?'

'You got my name right. No one ever gets my name right the first time,' the skinny girl said.

'That's because it's *weird*,' Heather piped in. 'Nobody calls their kid Amity, unless they want the whole world to give them a hard time.'

From the way Amity held herself – arms tense, fingers curled into fists, shoulders curved in under the weight of her guitar – Daniel guessed that the world probably *had* been giving her a hard time. And for whatever reason, that thought gave him a pang of regret.

'Take a load off,' he said. 'Let me take that guitar for you.'

He held out his hands, and slowly, Amity lifted the strap over her shoulder, never taking her eyes off his face. She wasn't what he'd call a hottie, but there was something about the way Amity looked at Daniel with her clear cinnamon-brown eyes that snagged him deep down. It was more than the ego boost of being adored by a groupie; this girl really seemed to recognise him, the way you recognise someone you knew long ago, before they were anybody.

He had to admit that her attention, weird as it was, was turning him on. When he got close to her to take her guitar, he smelt a hint of gasoline that she'd probably splattered on her jeans when she was filling up her car. He smelt the desert wind, and hair that hadn't been washed in a couple of days. And layered over all of that was the coconut-scented sunscreen she'd slathered over her bare arms for a long ride in the sun.

'Let me guess,' he said, brushing a dead bug out of the hollow of her collar bone. 'You drive a convertible.'

Her thin body reacted with a long, sustained quiver when Daniel touched her. A new guitar always responded the same way. The look in her eyes changed from awe to suspicion.

'Yeah,' she said. 'It's a '66 T-Bird.'

'It's the coolest car. I wanted us to drive home in style,' Heather said. Oblivious to the moment that had passed between Amity and Daniel, she had stopped throwing her own things into the suitcase and had started in on her husband's. 'Hey, Amityville, let's decorate it before we hit the road.'

'What do you mean?' Amity asked warily.

'Oh, you know. Get some pink Silly String, write "Just Married" all over it, cover it with toilet-paper roses and hang some empty cans out of the trunk. That way people will know you're escorting a couple of newlyweds back home.'

Daniel saw the change in Amity's face, the subtle shift into an all-too-familiar disappointment. He saw her throat twitch as she swallowed that bitterness down.

'You two are married?'

'Yep.' Heather flashed the pink ring. 'I'm wearing this for now, but Daniel's going to buy me some fantabulous bling as soon as he hits it big again. Isn't that right, baby?'

Heather draped herself across her new husband and gazed up into his eyes.

'Absolutely,' Daniel said. He gave his wife a big kiss. He knew it would hurt Amity, but better to give her a little pain than to drag it out. Truth was, he was married now. Committed. And as if the promises he'd made to Heather in the Temple of Love weren't enough, Amity wasn't his type.

Not even close.

For Amity, the most awkward part of this scenario wasn't seeing Daniel in the flesh. It wasn't the sense of having a cannonball of longing fired at her solar plexus, or juggling the thousand-and-one impulses that her nerves were shooting to the most sensitive part of her body. The worst thing about this whole meeting was that Heather seemed oblivious to the fact that she was now married to the man Amity had spent half her life wanting.

For Heather, Daniel Gold was any another guy, one of the many who'd fallen at her feet without any effort on her part. He just happened to be the first one who'd managed to hang onto her long enough to slip a ring on her finger. Not just any ring, but the only one that Amity could ever have imagined herself wearing. Any guy could walk into a jewellery store and ask a sales clerk to help him choose the same diamond solitaire that every other white-bread American bride was wearing that month. What could more perfectly express the impulsive heat of true love than a chunk of pink glass?

Now Heather was wearing that pink glass ring. And all she could think about was the diamond solitaire. If she noticed that Amity's heart was fishtailing back and forth in her chest as she stared at Daniel, Heather didn't let it show.

Did Heather have no memory of the poster that had hung on Amity's wall? Had the image of Amity crawling through her bedroom window after sneaking out to a 3-Way Dream concert faded so quickly from her mind? What about that bitterly painful conversation Heather had had with her stepsister, when she told Amity that she was crazy to spend her time dreaming about a rock star, when she could be chasing 'real' guys?

He looked 'real' enough right now, standing so close that Amity could see swirls of chocolate brown in his pitch black eyes. His fingers, when he reached out to brush that bit of bug debris off her shoulder, felt as solid and warm and vibrant with life as anything that had ever touched her skin. More so, because Amity had memorised the shape and texture of those fingers years ago, and she'd been waiting for them to make contact with her body ever since.

That contact lasted only a millisecond, but it jolted through Amity's skin, muscles and bones with all the force of a lightning bolt. That current brought her eighteen-year-old self back to life, with all its confusion and wild desires; her knees turned to strawberry jam, her mouth filled with invisible cotton, and her mind went into a tailspin of waking wet dreams. Amity and Daniel, rocking together in a sweaty tangle of legs, arms and sheets. Daniel's mouth pressed against the ankh tattoo below Amity's belly button, as his fingers kneaded her small breasts. Amity pinned to the wall under the weight of Daniel's body while he found his way inside her, into the moist, secret darkness where she knew he'd always belonged.

'You OK, Sis? Earth to Amityville!'

Heather's crimson-tipped fingers snapped in front of Amity's eyes. The crisp noise jerked Amity out of her fantasies.

'Don't call me that,' Amity said.

Heather's eyebrows wrinkled. 'Call you what?'

'Amityville. That's not my name. I'm not a town. And I'm not a horror.'

'Coulda fooled me,' Heather muttered, but she backed off. 'Standing there like a dead hitchhiker in a zombie movie. Listen, sweetie, we want to hit the road as soon as possible. I can't afford this place for one more night –'

'Amity just got here. Chill, Heather. No need to rush.'

Amity didn't hear a word Daniel said after he spoke her name. He pronounced the word with all three of its syllables. No one ever got Amity's name right – not the first time, usually not the second or third.

'Well, we have to get going soon,' Heather huffed.

'Tomorrow,' Daniel said. 'Let's all have some fun

tonight. We're in Vegas. God knows, reality will still be there next week.'

'But my job won't,' Heather whined.

'I'm sure there's more than one dancing gig in Denver,' Daniel reassured her. 'You're so beautiful, baby. You could dance anywhere on earth.'

He rubbed Heather's shoulders, and the tension seeped visibly out of her body. Amity felt a stab of envy, thinking how it must feel to be stroked, soothed by Daniel's hands. Heather had always been lucky, but now she'd hit the jackpot. Daniel looked just as good as he had in the early days of 3-Way Dream, possibly even better. Time had left him leaner, given him a harder edge. He still had that brooding, introspective air about him that Amity loved; she'd always thought he looked haunted, but it had never occurred to her that his ghosts might be anything more than part of the identity he presented on stage.

In her head, Amity was already composing lyrics about Daniel, and about how she'd lost him before they even met. Love was always such a disappointment.

Sex, on the other hand, could heal a lot of heartaches. And right now, some potential healing was presenting itself at the door of Heather's hotel room.

'I feel like hammered shit,' announced the half-naked guy with the dishwater-blond hair who had just walked in. He looked like a surfer who had just woken up on the beach after an all-night bonfire bash.

'You're Zak,' Amity said.

The surfer, who was actually 3-Way Dream's bass guitarist, squinted at her. 'Last time I checked,' he said. He rubbed his eyes and gave her an elevator look, from boots to eyebrows, spending most of his time checking out the expanse of space between her crotch and her collarbone. His grin was two parts lust, one part mockery.

'Who are you? *What* are you?' Zak asked. 'If you're here to give blowjobs, you're wearing the wrong outfit.'

'She's here to give us a ride, arsehole,' Daniel said. 'Unless you want to hang out in Vegas by yourself.'

'Wouldn't kill me,' Zak yawned. 'I'm getting lots of play here.'

'Too bad it's all on your back,' Daniel replied.

'So? That's why we're in this business. Booze, drugs and babes.'

'That's why *you're* in this business. Some of us are serious about music.'

'Oh, yeah. I forgot. You're Mister Big Artist Man,' Zak sneered. 'Well, if you're so great, why were we all cooling our arses for the past three years? And then all we can get is a lousy gig at a shithole in Vegas?'

'Hey, you don't like it? Feel free to go solo at any time, dude!'

'Who says I can't? Who says I don't have any talent?'

'Uh ... everyone? You play that bass like a one-armed spastic lumberjack, dude.'

For the next ten minutes, Zak and Daniel bickered back and forth like a married couple, snarling accusations that had clearly become as familiar to them as the songs they'd been performing together for years. Zak was a lazy drunken pussy-hound. Daniel was an uptight self-righteous dickhead. Amity sighed and sat down on one of the hotel armchairs to wait it out, while Heather continued her packing. Amazing how women got such a bad rap for bitching and nagging; when it came to catfights, no one got down and dirty like a couple of male musicians.

Heather caught Amity's eye and mouthed the words, *They do this all the time*. Amity smiled back, enjoying a rare moment of sisterly empathy.

'Are you two done yet? We're hungry!' Heather shouted.

'Screw you, bitch,' Daniel muttered to Zak. 'Let's go get something to eat.'

'Screw you double, bro,' Zak said cheerfully. The storm

clouds in the room blew over as quickly as they had gathered. 'You and Heather go ahead. I've got my lunch right here.'

Zak sauntered over to Amity's chair, took hold of her hands and pulled her to her feet. Then he wrapped his arms around her in a hug that was surprisingly sweet, a little boy's hug, only Zak wasn't all that little. Especially below the waist. As he purred into Amity's ear, Zak pressed his pelvis against her, letting her feel him harden. For a perpetual partier, he had a very firm fit body. His bare chest and arms felt so warm and hard that Amity felt herself melting. What he lacked in subtlety, Zak made up for in blunt up-front sex appeal. Amity had always thought he was the cutest member of the band, after Daniel.

'You've got a tight booty, little girl,' he whispered. 'Wanna stay here and take a nap with me?'

'Hey! Hands off my sister.' Heather slapped Zak's arm. He moved away, pouting.

'Just getting to know her. What's your name, sweet thing?'

She gulped. 'Amity.'

'Amnesty? Don't tell me – hippie parents.'

Heather snorted. 'Right. It's *Amity*, dork.'

'You probably should have asked her name before you did that full-body press,' Daniel added. 'Sorry, Amity. Zak needs to be sent to obedience school with the other puppies.'

'We'll talk,' Zak promised. He wrapped a strand of Amity's hair around his finger and tugged gently.

Heather pointed to the door. 'Go to your room. Put on some clothes. You can't go down to the buffet in your boxer shorts.'

'Catch you later,' Zak said, giving Amity one last wink.

Zak's eyes really were as blue as they appeared in his videos, pure Pacific Ocean. His crooked smile sent

Amity's pulse into a hopscotch beat. Zak wasn't Daniel, but he was the next best thing for now: one-hundred proof fun. After her lousy experience with Gregg-with-Three-Gs, and the crushing blow of discovering that Heather was married to the man of Amity's dreams, a little fun didn't sound half bad.

Amity assumed that Zak would ditch her as soon as some cocktail waitress caught his eye down in the casino, but for the rest of the afternoon, he never left her side. He brushed his arm against hers as they filled their plates at the buffet, then sat beside her at the table, feeding her chicken fingers and miniature meatballs from his plate. Whenever Amity looked up, she found his blue eyes focused steadily on her; she wasn't used to that kind of attention, and it turned her into a red-cheeked mumbling idiot.

When she wasn't staring down at her plate, or sneaking glances at Zak, Amity was watching Heather and Daniel. Daniel was so wrapped up in Heather that he barely touched his food; he was too busy devouring his sexy bride instead. He murmured in her ear, making her blush. He held her hand and nibbled her fingers. He played with her curls, then cupped her chin in his hand and turned her face so that he could kiss her lush lips. By the time the meal – or the pretence of a meal – was over, Amity knew she had a stomach ulcer. That's what happened when the twin monsters of jealousy and despair gnawed at your gut for an hour.

'We're going upstairs for a while,' Heather cooed, waving at Amity and Zak as Daniel dragged her away from the table. 'You kids play nice.'

'Thank god!' Zak erupted after they'd gone. 'That lovey-dovey stuff was making me want to puke.'

Amity decided that she liked Zak very much.

Zak kept his promise; he and Amity talked. Or Zak talked, and Amity tried.

'So tell me your story,' he asked. 'Where did you come from? What makes you roll out of bed in the morning?'

Amity pondered these questions and twisted her swizzle stick through the golden-brown liquid of her drink. Her life was a lot like a Long Island. To the casual observer, the glass seemed to be filled with nothing more potent than the typical iced tea – served at picnics, sweetened with saccharine, maybe zested up with a slice of lemon. But from Amity's perspective, her life had the potential to knock that observer on his or her complacent arse. She knew she had a destiny. She just didn't know how to make it anything but a dream.

'I came from a little yellow ranch house in the 'burbs,' she said. 'Growing up, my family life was pretty boring. There was me, my dad, my stepmom and Heather, all living in that house, trying to figure out how we'd all ended up together. I went to school. Played the guitar. Didn't date much, just lusted after a lot of musicians. I don't know what I wanted more – to sleep with them, or to *be* them.'

'Well, being the typical guy that I am, I'm curious about who you wanted to sleep with,' Zak said.

'Daniel,' Amity said, without hesitating. Daniel, Daniel, Daniel. Had there really ever been anyone else?

'Of course. All the girls drool over Daniel. He's got that lone wolf, touchy-feely sex appeal. Back when we first hit it big, they used to call Dan "The Sprinkler."'

'Why?'

'Because he made all the chicks wet.' His voice rose to a falsetto as he mimicked one of the groupies. '"Daniel's, like, soooo intense. Do yah think you could hook me up with him?" Revolting. Talk about a way to wilt my hard-on.'

'It was more than that,' Amity said defensively. 'Daniel's got something special.'

Although her rational brain knew that Daniel was nothing more than a teenage crush, something in her soul had wakened to his music. No cotton-candy crush could have given her the drive to transcribe his guitar arrangements note for note, flipping her old tape recorder on and off as she struggled to capture each phrase, so she could work out the songs on Blue Molly and work them into her own head. Amity had a connection with Daniel, even if its current only ran one way.

'Sure he does,' Zak laughed. 'But I'll let you in on a secret – every guy is born with the same tools between his legs. Throw a lead guitar into the deal, and the women go nuts.'

'No, really,' Amity insisted. 'The first time I heard him sing "Save My Soul", I felt like someone had reached into my chest, pulled my heart out, and turned it upside-down.'

'"Moving inside you/Touching the fire that burns you",' Zak sang. 'Yeah, it's a decent song. We never really got past it. I'll be playing that one for the rest of my career.'

'What's wrong with that? It's a classic.'

'I don't believe in worshipping the classics. I believe in doing something new, every day of your life,' Zak said. 'Once you've had your hit, you should let it disappear into cover-land. Let other struggling bastards sing it. Dan just wants to keep playing the same songs over and over again.'

Amity heard a rumble of that same storm that had been brewing up in the hotel room, when Zak and Daniel had their fight. Zak drained the rest of his Long Island in one gulp, then gave the ice cubes in his glass a vicious rattle. His suntanned face turned long and sullen as he stared at the cards on the video poker screen.

'Can I get you another drink, honey?' the blonde bartender chirped, swooping in with her towel to wipe the bar. 'You paid for the first round; I'll comp you this one.'

She was a statuesque blonde who carried herself with

the self-conscious grace of an ex-dancer who'd never cut the mustard. She was probably in her forties, but looked older and younger at the same time. Her skin was a reptilian tanning-booth bronze, but her eyes had the sweet guileless clarity that you rarely see outside of junior high pep rallies. Her round breasts, packed into a pink Lycra top, were peppered with brown freckles and had a deep crease between them. She hadn't so much as glanced at Amity since she sat down. Amity, apparently, didn't rate in the world of former showgirls. Zak, on the other hand, was getting his own private show as the bartender bent over to display her wares.

'Sure. I'll take another one.'

Amity had to give Zak a couple of mental brownie points for giving the bartender's boobs no more than a cursory glance. Amity would have bet her left arm that the contents of that hot-pink top were surgically augmented.

Amity sighed. During a period of adolescent body-hatred, she'd thought about saving up enough money for a boob job. Trouble was, she didn't really want larger breasts. She wanted a larger life: more talent, more adventures, more sex, more love. Watching the bartender's perky buns wrestle each other inside her hot-pants as she hurried off to make Zak's drink, Amity wondered if the blonde had wanted those same things when she slapped down her money for that overdone boob job. Those breasts apparently hadn't led her much further than this hotel casino, but maybe life wasn't so bad here. Big tips, plenty of second-hand excitement, and you probably got hit on by a lot of married men with fat wallets.

So what if the bartender hadn't made it as a dancer? Sometimes the life you settled for turned out better than the life you'd dreamt of having.

'Tell me, Zak,' Amity asked, 'what do you want out of life?'

Zak's smile came back, lewd as ever. 'What does any guy want when he joins a rock band?'

'Um, I don't know. Musical immortality?' Amity's voice dripped with sarcasm.

'Right,' Zak snorted. 'Guess again.'

'Women?'

'You got it. I won't lie to you. I'm a pussy-hound. I've had more of that than I could count,' Zak said.

'I figured as much,' Amity said.

'But you know what? I remember every girl I've ever been with. I could tell you all their names, right now.'

'Go for it.'

Zak closed his eyes and pressed his fingertips against his temples, as if he were trying to squeeze the list of names out of his skull. 'The first girl I ever slept with was Hilary Hassenpfeffer. Then there was Sally Pine. Then Tracy Kimbrell. Monica Mitchell. Vickie Gilbranson. That's before I got into a band. I can't remember any last names after I started performing. Becky, Stacy, another Stacy, Laura, Heidi, Marla and Darla ... those last two were twins –'

'OK. Enough, enough,' Amity laughed. 'I get the point.'

Zak fixed her with his azure eyes. 'But you're special.'

'Yeah. Right.' Amity almost spit out her mouthful of booze.

'No, really. You're different. Believe it or not, I've never been with a girl who played rock'n'roll. I think the twins played the piano. Or one of them played the piano, and the other sang. But those two played classical stuff, with maybe some Whitney Houston thrown in. I've never slept with a rocker chick.'

'Why not?'

'Dunno. Can't take the competition, I guess. I'm a very insecure guy.'

'I can tell.'

Zak flashed her his grin again. Each time he did that,

Amity felt herself dissolve a little more; she was going to be a puddle of sweet stickiness by the time the afternoon was over. Zak's thigh was pressed against Amity's; she could feel the heat of his flesh through his jeans *and* her own. She had had just enough liquor to let her ask the question that had been hounding her since she walked into that hotel room.

'How did Daniel and Heather hook up?'

'Not to change the subject or anything, right?'

Amity twisted the pink paper umbrella that had come with her cocktail. 'I was just curious.'

'No such thing as "just" curious. Curiosity's a killer. What's eating you up about Heather and Danny Boy?'

'Nothing's eating me up. Heather's my stepsister. I wanted to know how she met the guy she married. That's all.'

Zak gave Amity a long look. 'If that's all, why are you turning that paper umbrella into a pile of confetti?'

'Let's change the subject.'

'No way. You can't change subjects on me that fast when I'm drinking; I'll get the spins. Let's talk about Heather and Dan. What do you want to know?'

Amity took a long sip of her drink. The mixture of rums didn't taste like alcohol at all; if she didn't slow down, she'd be under the video monitor before they could finish another round of poker.

'How did they meet?' she asked.

'Strip club. Heather was dancing. Danny was watching.'

'God,' Amity shuddered. 'How tacky.'

'Not really. Look, Dan and I fight a lot, but we're closer than most brothers. One thing the dude's not, it's tacky. He swears it was love at first sight.'

'Yeah. While she was straddling a pole wearing nothing but a G-string.'

Zak shrugged. 'Love is a mystery. Especially to me. If I see a hot blonde at a strip club, I might buy a lap dance.

Dan bought a ring. Sure, it only cost a few bucks, but that's not the point. He was serious about her. Next thing you know, those two are hitting city hall, then they're getting married at the hotel wedding chapel, with me and Randy as the witnesses. Dan's a romantic, in the worst possible way.'

'What's that supposed to mean?'

'He'll ruin his life for a lame-arse dream.'

When he saw the look on Amity's face, Zak backpedalled. 'Aw, shit. I didn't mean that marrying your sister was a lame thing to do. But Dan's got this weird way of being impulsive and mule-headed at the same time. He'll act on the spur of the moment, then he'll spend months, maybe years, trying to follow whatever crazy vision made him act in the first place. He doesn't know when to give up. Does that make any sense?'

Amity shook her head.

Zak smiled. 'Hang out with us long enough and it will. Odds are, he'll drag you into something, too. He does that to everyone. Hell, Dan's the one who kept the band going long enough for us to hit it big. Me and Randy were ready to quit long before we got famous. And Dan's the one who got us all back together for another tour...'

'So do you think he really loves Heather?' Amity interrupted.

Zak was quiet for a few moments as he pushed buttons, selecting the cards for his poker hand. 'He says he does.'

'What do *you* think?'

'If Dan says he loves Heather, he honestly believes he loves her.'

'Believes it? Or knows it?'

Zak spread his hands in a gesture of surrender. 'Hey, I'm in over my head now. Look, sweetheart, if you want to know about Dan's love life, ask the man himself.'

'I can't,' Amity sulked. 'He's upstairs bonking my sister.'

Zak chuckled. 'OK, I get it now. You're not asking if Dan loves his wife. You want to know if you have a chance with him. Am I right?'

Now it was Amity's turn to make herself look busy pushing buttons. She chose her hand carefully, as if her life depended on it. Just when it looked like she was about to score a royal flush, she came up with a two of spades.

'Loser,' she muttered to herself.

'Hey.' Zak wrapped his arm around Amity's shoulder and pulled her into a half-hug. 'Don't be so hard on yourself. It's just a game. Everything in Vegas is a game. Even the marriages. Easy come, easy go.'

Amity looked up from her glass. 'Are you saying I have a chance?'

'With Daniel, who knows? Me, I'm a sure thing.'

Zak sealed Amity's fate for the afternoon with a kiss that packed a stronger punch than the rum blend she was drinking. Zak's lips were dry and slightly rough, like warm sandstone. He sensed that Amity was shy at first and didn't push her; he let her get used to the rum-drenched sweetness of his mouth, let her start to kiss him back before his tongue entered the game. That tongue was forceful and playful at the same time, skirting the edges of Amity's lips, dancing along her own tongue, flicking the roof of her mouth. When Zak finally broke away, Amity had to take a few seconds to catch her breath and reassemble the scattered jigsaw of her brain.

'We've got an audience,' Zak said.

A couple of college girls were clinging to the bar, staring at Zak and Amity, hissing and pointing. The bigger bolder one leant across the bar, pressing her boobs against the varnished surface and making Amity wonder if she was the only woman in this city who didn't have a rack worth flaunting.

'Aren't you Zak from 3-Way Dream?' the college girl asked.

Zak winked at Amity, then turned to face his fans. 'Nah. I'm Ed. I'm with the organic fertiliser convention.' He lowered his voice and leered. 'Hey, did you say you're interested in a three-way?'

The big-breasted girl wrinkled her nose. 'Fertiliser? Eew.'

'We thought you were someone else,' her friend explained, more politely.

'Yeah. People tell me I look like that Zak guy all the time. My buddies say I sing like him, too. Wanna hear me sing something?'

The girls hurried away. Amity laughed.

'You're not very kind to your fans.'

'Sure I am. If you hadn't been here, I would have taken them both upstairs and shown them the time of their lives,' Zak said. 'But since I've already got a luscious babe on my arm, I don't have to make that sacrifice for my art.'

'You must be ecstatic,' Amity said, savouring the word 'luscious'. No one had ever called her that. Men did not use sensually suggestive, multi-syllabic, euphonic words to describe Amity.

Zak gave her a sly smile. 'Not yet,' he said, taking her by the hand and leading her away from the bar. 'I figure we'll both be ecstatic soon enough.'

Zak's hotel room was identical to Heather and Daniel's in every way, except for the fact that it looked like a small bomb had exploded inside. Clothes were strewn across the furniture and all over the floor. Every flat surface was adorned with an assortment of bottles, mostly beer and Jack Daniel's, many still half-filled with amber liquid. Ashtrays brimming with crumpled cigarette butts sat on the night tables, the vanity and even the mattress, which had been stripped of all its blankets and sheets. A bass guitar took pride of place on one of the gold-striped armchairs beside the window, the only square foot of the room that had been left relatively pristine.

At least the guy had some respect for his instrument, Amity thought. Most men she knew would have apologised for the mess, or at least made a sheepish reference to it. Zak didn't bother. He did, however, remove the ashtrays off the mattress before inviting Amity to sit down.

Plopping herself on the bed, she wondered why she didn't feel more awestruck. Here she was, in a rock star's room – albeit a rocker who was playing casinos in Vegas instead of at the Coliseum – and she felt no more impressed than she had at the age of sixteen, sitting down on the swaybacked sofa in Tony Frazier's rec room. Tony had handed her a can of Pabst Blue Ribbon stolen from his parents' fridge, and as soon as she'd taken one sip, he proceeded to jam his wet tongue into her mouth. Though the scene had lacked any semblance of romance, the weight of Tony's body and the blend of cold beer with hot tongue had driven Amity wild.

'Drink?' Zak asked, locating one of the half-full JD bottles and a couple of cloudy hotel glasses.

'No thanks,' Amity said, remembering Tony and the beer. 'I'm still plenty buzzed.'

'Suits me.' Zak put down the bottle and glasses. 'Booze isn't my favourite means of intoxication, anyway.'

'So what is?'

Amity, who'd been perched on the edge of the stripped mattress, scooted towards the centre and settled back on her elbows. The mattress smelt like Zak's body: musky, male. The scent triggered a raw hot sensation between her legs, and she knew that when she took her clothes off, she'd be more than ready for Zak to do anything he wanted to her.

'Well,' Zak drawled, making his way slowly across the room like a panther stalking its small furry prey, 'I prefer to get drunk on my senses. I like the smell of a woman's skin, her hair, her pussy. I like soft textures. And sounds. Moans, cries, whimpers. There's no high in this world like playing a woman as your instrument. Orchestrating every move she makes, coaxing all those sweet, sweet sounds out of her lips.'

'How do you feel about the texture of latex?'

Zak smiled. 'Don't worry. I'm stocked up.' He opened a drawer in the night stand and produced a box of condoms, already opened.

Then he knelt in front of Amity, parting her legs so that he could wedge his body in between them. He placed his hands on her knees, and worked his fingers up her thighs. She stopped breathing for a moment when he unbuttoned her Levis, never taking his eyes off hers. She lifted her bottom so that he could pull down her jeans and panties. His lips followed in the wake of her clothes, kissing her lower belly, her mound, her inner thighs as he peeled her like a piece of fruit. While he tugged off her boots and socks, Amity wriggled out of her T-shirt and tank top. She wasn't wearing a bra – didn't like them, didn't need them.

'I looove your body,' Zak drawled. His voice had deepened, thickened. 'You're built like a cat. And I dig your fur. Most girls shave it all off.'

'I don't see the point,' Amity said.

'Me neither.'

He hovered over her, stroking the silky brown hair between her legs. Going along with the cat theme, she purred with pleasure. She had a sudden sense of how much bigger he was, before he suddenly took her by the waist and turned her over on her belly. One motion, smooth and effortless, and she was reoriented on the bed, her arse in the air.

'Look at that tight butt.' Zak's voice was thick, hoarse. 'Hard as an apple. That rear end is just crying out to be spanked. Need a spanking, little girl?'

Before Amity could give this question much thought, Zak's palm had landed on her bum, leaving a hot, stinging glow on her flesh.

'Ow-weee!' Amity would have flown off the bed, if Zak's weight hadn't been holding her down.

'Oh, yes. Such a rock-solid little arse, and it looks so pretty with my handprint on it,' Zak murmured. He massaged Amity's burning cheeks, then gave her another few swats, inflicting a pain that blossomed into a sweet, radiant tingle. After every three or four smacks, he caressed her sore flesh with a tenderness that surprised her.

No wonder Zak hadn't been impressed by the bartender's knockers, Amity thought. He was a diehard arse man. Amazing, the profound truths you could discover about rock stars in seedy hotel rooms.

'Now I've got to kiss your bottom and make it all better,' Zak crooned.

As he moved down to kiss the sore places that his hand had left, Amity buried her face in the mattress to stifle a maniacal giggle. She'd never dreamed that she'd have her arse kissed by anyone famous. This was truly a moment to remember.

Her laughter soon died away as Zak began to lick the cleft between her cheeks. When he lifted her hips with both hands and spread her legs apart so that he could tongue the damp space where her bottom met her thighs, Amity gave an involuntary moan. She'd never been licked from behind before, never imagined it was something any of her lovers would want to do. But from the sounds Zak was making as he devoured her, he seemed to be in paradise. She hadn't realised that the tight bud between her cheeks was such a flower of nerve endings, but the sensations he was creating as he probed that hidden spot were driving her wild. She pushed her mound into the mattress, finding a rhythm that matched his tongue work.

It didn't take long for Zak to catch on to what Amity was doing. He burrowed under her body with his right hand until his fingers struck pay dirt. He buried his thumb in the slick channel between her thighs, and when he began to tweak her clit in syncopation with the thrusting and licking and tickling and tonguing he was doing, Amity found herself on the stairway to heaven – or to orgasm, whichever came first.

The last thing she remembered, before she fell apart in a slow-motion liquid explosion of pleasure, was the sound of a female voice wailing like an actress in a cheap porn video. Someone in the neighbouring rooms was being way too dramatic about getting fucked, Amity thought. She herself would never yowl that way, her voice rising to unnatural octaves, lips spilling pleas and obscenities, no matter what was being done to her.

Except that Amity was the girl shrieking like a bubble-headed banshee. She only realised it later, after the last of the rippling spasms had flowed back to the river they came from, leaving her wet and spent and panting on the mattress.

'You sounded just like an actress in a porno flick,' Zak informed her. 'I've gotta tell you, no chick has ever screamed that way for me. And here I thought I was losing my touch.'

'That ... was ... not ... me!' Amity gasped.

'Oh, yes it was,' Zak insisted gleefully. 'Best part is, now it's my turn.'

Zak let Amity have some time to recover. Her mind felt like one of those merry-go-rounds on the playground, the kind you and your friends could spin yourselves. She pictured herself lying in the centre of that big metal wheel, her eyes closed, feeling the world rotate slowly underneath her as her mind floated far above, in the clouds. One by one, her senses floated back, as she heard Zak pulling a condom out of his stash and unwrapping it. She opened her eyes to find him doing something that surprised her even more than feeling his tongue buried in the one part of her body that she'd thought no one would ever want to touch. He made a nest for her out of pillows, lifted her up, and gently set her down in the middle of it.

'You had a hard ride,' he said. 'Now just lie back and relax. I'm going to give you something so long and hard and sweet, you'll never want another man again.'

'Are you sure about that?' Amity laughed. She'd caught her breath, and she was ready for whatever Zak had to give her. She figured his description of his manhood was typical male hyperbole, but as it turned out, he wasn't too far off. When Amity saw his cock, her hand drifted up of its own will to touch it – she just couldn't help reaching for that dusky pink, perfectly arched shaft.

'Don't cover it up yet,' she said, when Zak unwrapped the condom. 'Let me touch it first.'

With Zak kneeling over her, she wrapped her hands around his erection and clung to it for a few seconds, just enjoying its softly pulsing warmth, before she began to explore him with her fingers. She loved the way his foreskin slipped up and down under her palms, like a velvet sleeve, making his cock even more rigid at the core. She loved the way he groaned while she stroked him, not out loud, but deep in his chest, like thunder rumbling far away. And she loved the way his shaft twitched under her fingertips, and the way his abdominal muscles rippled when she reached down below to massage his balls.

'Good hands.'

Two guttural words were all he could manage, before

a muscular spasm tightened his body from head to toe, and he came into the hollow of Amity's belly.

'Sorry. I didn't mean to be that good,' Amity said. 'I guess we didn't need that rubber, after all.'

'Not yet.' Zak flopped down on the mattress beside her. 'Give me a minute or two, and we'll go another round. I swear.'

Before he could make good on his promise, Zak fell asleep. When she heard his snores, Amity realised how tired she was. So much had happened to her today, more than any other day in her personal history. She'd met the love of her life, only to discover that he was married to her stepsister. She'd made up for it by hooking up with another guy, who happened to be one of the best bass guitarists she'd ever heard, in spite of Daniel's remark about Zak playing like a 'one-armed spastic lumberjack'.

And as if all that weren't enough, she'd been given one of the best orgasms of her life.

Amity's father had had a favourite saying, which he used to repeat whenever he found himself in yet another situation where he ended up accepting second-best after losing out on a dream: 'If you can't cut the mustard, you can always lick the jar.' Amity considered that cliché as she lay on the mattress, watching Zak's tanned, taut abdomen rise and fall with each deep breath.

Somewhere in the Casbah Hotel, Daniel was lying on a mattress like this one, with Heather beside him, her golden curls spilling across his chest as they recuperated from whatever games they'd been playing while Amity was busy with Zak. But as she watched Zak sleeping, Amity realised that she hadn't done so badly herself. Zak's cock, thick and pink and coiled up like a snail without its armour, was nestled in his sweat-beaded pubic curls. Amity brushed its head with her fingertips. The shaft began to stir again, and Zak turned to her, sea-blue eyes blinking lazily as he woke.

He saw Amity, rubbed his eyes with the back of his hand, and smiled like a little kid.

Amity smiled back.

Licking the jar wasn't half bad, she thought.

## Chapter Four

# The Flip Side of Fear

The first time she saw Zak in Heather's hotel room, when he walked in looking like death on a stick, Amity had assumed he'd overindulged in some kind of intoxicant the night before. But in the morning, when she woke up in Zak's bed, she learnt the truth – he always staggered around like a hungover half-blind bear after getting out of bed. It didn't matter if he'd been pounding Jack Daniel's all night in a dive bar or sleeping virtuously under a homemade quilt; Zak cheerfully admitted that he was a shitheel before noon.

Zak looked as fresh as a daisy compared to Randy. Amity hadn't even met 3-Way Dream's mysterious elusive drummer. Public sightings of him, outside of the band's performances, were as rare as a solar eclipse. Amity knew she ought to feel privileged to be sitting across from him at a booth at Denny's on the Strip, but she didn't. He was dressed in black, from his dyed shock of hair to his scuffed leather shoes. He wore black sunglasses like Roy Orbison's, that didn't reveal even a hint of the eyes behind them. His skinny, elongated hands trembled as he peeled off the wrapper on a pack of Marlboro Reds.

Once he got the pack opened, Randy proceeded to smoke one cigarette after another, blowing smoke in diagonal streams that barely missed hitting Amity in the face. He tapped away the ashes in a constant, nervous beat, as if he were working out some new arrangement in his head. Grey flecks kept drifting into his cup of black coffee, but the sepulchral Randy didn't seem to mind.

'This is a non-smoking booth,' the waitress reminded them when she came over to take their breakfast orders.

Without moving anything but his chalky, chapped lips, Randy blew a jet-trail of sidestream smoke into her face. Amity felt sorry for the woman, who tried to maintain her plastic smile as she coughed through the cloud. Amity had had plenty of jobs where she'd been forced to smile while being kicked like an empty can. The waitress didn't deserve that.

'Here,' Daniel said quietly, handing the waitress a folded green bill. 'Can we make it a smoking booth, just for this morning?'

Amity had no idea what the bill's denomination was, but it turned the waitress's smile into something radiant and real. Amity longed to be sitting next to Daniel, so she could get a surge of his positive vibes to heal her from the damage being done by Randy's toxic presence. Heather had claimed the space beside her husband, of course, and was hanging over Daniel's shoulders like a blonde vine.

Zak's hand provided a reassuring weight on Amity's leg, but as much as she liked the bassist, he couldn't hold a candle to 3-Way Dream's frontman when the two guys were together. All Amity could think about was finding excuses to reach over and touch Daniel's left hand, which was toying with his spoon. She could pretend she was reaching for the maple syrup. Or grabbing Daniel's napkin by mistake. Or she could just reach out and punch Heather in the jaw, knocking her out cold, and then give Daniel a big French kiss over her stepsister's unconscious body.

Randy would probably enjoy watching something like that. He looked like the kind of guy who appreciated violence, in a dissociated artsy way.

'So Randy. How's life among the undead?' Zak asked, echoing Amity's thoughts.

Randy stiffened. 'If you're trying to give me shit about rehab, don't bother.'

'I wasn't talking about rehab. I was referring to your wardrobe.'

'I like to wear black on sunny mornings,' Randy said. 'Especially when I'm going to be forced to broil in the desert sun in a freakin' convertible for the rest of the day. Whatever happened to that tour bus we rode into Vegas?'

'You know what happened,' Daniel said darkly. 'We got screwed.'

'Some of us got screwed in a more pleasurable fashion than others,' Zak remarked cheerfully.

'No one says you have to ride in the T-Bird, Randy,' Heather piped up. 'You can always hop a Greyhound.'

Yeah, please consider the bus, Amity thought. The idea of driving down the interstate with Randy's radioactive eyes boring into the back of her head was giving her gooseflesh, and not the erotic kind. To think that she'd once considered Randy the sexiest one in the band, after Daniel. Though he looked too anaemic in day-to-day life to man the drums, Randy was possessed by a fierce, demonic energy when he held a pair of sticks in his hand. Drugs had apparently reamed out his soul, turning him into a bloodless husk.

'Too bad you couldn't have seen the guys perform before we left,' Heather said to her stepsister. 'They're better than ever.'

Good old Heather. In spite of all her flaws, she had one overriding virtue – she was an expert at breaking up arguments, breaking up tension and tossing its fragments to the four winds.

'Better than ever? Hardly.' Randy made a contemptuous noise as he blew a smoke ring. The ring wobbled in midair over the table, threatening to come to a landing on Amity's pancakes. 'A three-month gig in the Sultan's Lounge at the Casbah isn't exactly my idea of the big time.'

'So what do you expect? You want us to be playing arenas after we've been off the face of the earth for three years?' Zak asked.

'We were never an arena band to begin with,' Daniel reminded him.

'Maybe not, but we weren't propped up like three stiffs in a casino lounge, playing our same old sets for a handful of zombies in hair-pieces,' Randy shot back. 'We had passion. The fans had passion. Our crowds might have been drunk and stupid, but they didn't need life support. And we wrote new music. What a concept.'

'We'll write new music again,' Daniel said quietly. 'Give me some time.'

'How much time do you need, Dan? I had to rent all my gear, I don't even own a decent drum kit anymore, the skank-artist who was supposed to be our manager is buried in the desert somewhere, and we don't have a tour bus to take us back to wherever the hell we're going next. Where are we going, anyway?'

'Denver,' Heather said brightly.

'Denver,' Randy echoed, sounding like a glum Greek chorus. 'Shoot me now. Why can't we go back to LA?'

'I second the motion,' said Zak. 'We'd be better off heading to Cali. This gig sucked, Danny Boy.'

'Well, I say you all kicked butt,' Heather said. Even Amity heard more loyalty than enthusiasm in her voice.

'We've lost it,' Randy said. 'Whatever "it" was.'

'Speak for yourself,' Zak bristled. 'I'm still hot.'

'Guys, let's not start this again. Not over breakfast,' Heather sighed. 'Let's try to be positive, at least till we get to Denver.'

Daniel laughed. There wasn't even a grace-note of humour in that gravelly sound. 'What happens when we get back to Denver? Will my talent be magically restored?'

'Maybe. Or maybe you'll find something else to do. Like that job I was telling you about,' Heather said under her breath.

'What job? I thought we were all going to keep playing music full-time,' Zak said, suddenly more alert than he'd been all morning. 'If you get some joe-job, Dan, you're never going to be around. You'll be busting your hump to keep your wife in cheap jewellery and G-strings.'

'Hey. Shut up, or I'll come over there an kick your skull in,' Daniel said, but his threat sounded weary, perfunctory.

'Whatever,' Zak said. 'Don't say I didn't tell you so. You'll be flipping burgers before you know it. Then we'll all be fucked. I'll be getting hammered every night. Randy here will slither into a sewer and never be seen again.'

Unbelievably, Randy smiled. 'Not a bad idea, Zak. Your suggestions usually aren't so creative, or so witty. Did you have an enlightening experience last night?'

Zak put his arm around Amity's shoulders and squeezed her tight. 'Several, as a matter of fact. When's the last time you got *laid*, Randy? Or are you still living up to your name?'

Randy snarled, shoved his cigarettes into the pocket of his black Western shirt, and pushed away from the table. He walked out of the restaurant, his stride bow-legged and self-protective. Amity saw him pause in Denny's parking lot to light another Marlboro before he wandered off into the crowd on the Strip, a solitary black-clad cowboy in a river of tourists who all seemed to be wearing the same white T-shirts and beige Capri pants.

'All those stories about vampires being horny all the

time are a load of crap,' Zak said to Amity. 'Once you join the Undead, like Randy, you lose all interest in sex.'

Zak picked up his fork and shovelled a mouthful of waffle and sausage into his mouth, humming to himself as he chewed. Heather cleared her throat and sat up straight, like a little girl at school. Daniel drummed his fingers on the table and sighed.

'Zak, you have an uncanny ability to say exactly the wrong thing at the worst possible time,' Daniel said. 'Now I'm going to have to spend the rest of the day begging Randy to come back with us.'

'Why not just let him take the bus, if he wants to be alone for a while?' Heather suggested.

Amity heartily agreed. Whatever dark memory had been stirred in Randy's brain, she didn't want to have to live with its presence in her beloved T-Bird.

'Because he's a member of this band,' Daniel said. 'And he's still one of my best friends. If I have to tie him up and throw him in the trunk, he'll come with us.'

'Randy lives in the past. He's entirely focused on the negative. That's what turned him into a vampire,' Zak explained. 'He can't let go of the negative shit.'

'It's important to remember the negative shit,' Daniel said. 'Helps us keep the rest of our lives in perspective. It's way too easy to let dreams get swallowed up by the demons in our heads. Or just let them fall by the wayside, out of apathy.'

Icy fingers took a walk up Amity's spine. Daniel might as well have been talking about her; he had even turned his body to face her, leaning over the table with his elbows propped beside his plate, looking at her intently across the cloud of Heather's hair.

'What do you dream about doing?' Amity asked.

Daniel didn't seem surprised by the question. Not at all. He had an answer ready, and he whipped it out like a loaded gun, holding Amity's gaze with steady, dark eyes.

'I want to find my first guitar,' he said. 'My old Gibson Epiphone that I got for my fifteenth birthday. That's the instrument I wrote my first songs on. Every decent song I wrote came out of that guitar. I need to find her, so I can get my gift back. Otherwise, I might as well give up now.'

Heather mewed like an exasperated kitten. 'You're not bringing that up again, are you? I thought we settled all that yesterday.'

'You settled it for yourself, sweetheart,' Daniel said. His voice was quiet, but the gravity of his intention rang out loud and clear. 'Not for me. I still want to do this.'

Heather's dainty hand came down on the table with a chopping motion. 'No. Our plans are set, Daniel. We're going back to Denver, so I can get my gig at the club, and at the end of the month we're moving back to LA We're not going to drive all over the whole country looking for some dumb guitar. You could replace that guitar in about ten minutes on eBay. In fact, you could probably find that *same* guitar on eBay.'

Daniel shook his head slowly. 'This isn't just about putting my hands on that axe again. It's about the journey itself. I need to find my way back to where I was, before I got lost. Do you get that, Heather?'

To Amity, Daniel's words sounded almost like a quotation you'd find on a Buddhist calendar, but she got the gist. Maybe she only got it because finding your first guitar made sublime sense to her. Losing Blue Molly would be worse than losing a limb. Her guitar wasn't anything special – just an old Johnson acoustic – but its body held the echoes of her first original songs, and its strings had been christened with the blood of her fingertips.

Besides, she'd seen Daniel's Gibson in action. The Epiphone's sleek black silhouette had been submerged in her memory for years, but suddenly it was edging its way to the surface, until it became so clear that she couldn't believe she'd ever forgotten the instrument, or the look of focused adoration that Daniel had had on his face when he played her. He'd been holding that guitar the first time Amity saw him, when he stepped onstage, over an hour late, and greeted the crowd like an apologetic lover.

'I get it,' Amity said. 'Believe it or not.'

Heather glared at her and pinched her arm. 'You do not get it, Amityville. What Dan's saying makes no sense whatsoever. He doesn't even know where to start looking for the guitar. He could be driving around the desert for the rest of his life trying to find it. What could be dumber than that? The guitar could have been burned up in a fire, or fallen off the back of a truck. He could be wandering around like some kind of crazy drifter for years.'

'Like a vision quest?' Amity asked.

She'd never known that eyes so dark could turn so radiant, but when she asked that question, Daniel's face glowed as if it were lit by internal candles.

'Exactly,' he said. 'Like a vision quest. A journey that could change the way we look at everything that's happened to us – past, present or future.'

When Daniel said 'we', he wasn't looking at Heather. At that moment, he didn't seem aware that Heather was still sitting at the table. He was looking straight at Amity, and the current of excitement that ran between them was so powerful that it made Amity quiver.

'I want to do it,' Amity heard herself saying. She hardly felt Heather pinching her again, though this time her stepsister's fingernails were going to leave black half-moons in the pale flesh of Amity's inner arm.

'I told you Dan would get you caught up in one of his crazy schemes,' Zak said. 'Though I have to admit, this is the dumb-fuckingest thing I've ever heard. I'm with Heather on this one. What's the term they use for ideas like this? "Wild duck hunt"?'

'Wild goose chase,' Heather said. 'I couldn't have said it better, myself. It's one thing to go looking around for your car when you can't remember where you parked it, or to look for an old friend from high school. But there's just no way to find a guitar. It could be anywhere.'

'If I'm meant to find my Gibson, I'll find her,' Daniel said.

'Dude, that is just so inspiring, it makes me want to shave my head and go up to the mountains and eat rocks,' Zak said.

'I'll help you, Daniel,' Amity heard herself saying. 'I'll drive.'

Heather's jaw dropped. 'You will not! You're driving all of us to Denver. That was the plan.'

A grin was creeping slowly across Daniel's face. 'Plans change, Heather.'

'What about my dancing job?' she cried.

'Those gigs are a dime a dozen for a beauty like you,' Daniel said. 'Take a break. Have an adventure with us.'

Us – he was already saying *us*, Amity thought. Her brain snagged that two-letter pronoun and clung to it with all its might.

'What about the apartment?' Heather went on. 'And the car I want to buy? And all my friends?'

'Finding my Gibson isn't going to take forever, Heather, no matter what you think. I'll give it a few weeks; if it looks hopeless, we'll go home. All that stuff will still be there when we get back.'

'Correction,' Heather said, pushing past Daniel out of the booth. 'It will all still be there when you get back. Maybe. But I might not.'

She stood beside the table, ex-cheerleader-turned-stripper-turned-angel-of-wrath, hands planted on hips swathed in a tight denim miniskirt. Every eye in the restaurant was fixed on Heather; she glowed in her anger, more sexy and stunning than ever. A lump formed in Amity's throat as she thought about how beautiful her stepsister was. Heather was going to get her way again. Amity knew it.

'If you do this, Daniel, you're going to do it alone,' Heather warned. She was shaking with the force of her ultimatum. 'I'll take the bus home with Zak and Randy.'

Daniel sat stirring his coffee. He didn't say a word, and he didn't look at his wife. He just stirred, stared into the coffee as if he were scrying his future, while Amity watched the seconds tick by on the old-fashioned clock over the cash register.

'You do what you need to do, sweetheart,' he finally said. 'I'm going to look for my guitar. Anyone who wants to go with me is welcome to come, but if I have to, I'll go alone.'

Amity exhaled. She'd been holding her breath for so long that when she let go, her chest felt like it was going to explode. Air rushed into her lungs, leaving her high on oxygen, excitement and relief.

'I'm going,' she declared, just in case Daniel hadn't heard her the first time she offered.

'You're a traitor. If you do this, we're not sisters anymore.' Heather said. Her lower lip was quivering. Tears turned her blue eyes into sparkling sapphires. She stamped her foot, in its pretty white cowboy boot, then wheeled around and stalked out of the restaurant.

'I always said, you were the real ladies' man in the band,' Zak remarked. 'You really have a way with women. What's this, your third busted relationship in, like, a year?'

'Shut up, Zak,' Daniel said. 'Heather's pissed off now, but she'll get it eventually. And if she wants to come with us, she can come. I'm not stopping her.'

Now Zak turned to Amity. 'Dan's never going to let you go,' Zak said. 'Wait and see. You do this vision quest thing with him and you may never get back home.'

'I don't have a home,' Amity said. 'My home's with my car. And my guitar.'

And now with Daniel, she thought, but she couldn't

dare say that out loud. Speaking your heart's deepest desires out loud was bad, bad juju.

Amity's life, stagnant for so long, was suddenly happening in bright bursts, like the startling freeze-frames created by the flash bulb of a camera. She saw herself driving down I-70 in her blue T-Bird, screaming the chorus of Tom Petty's 'Free-Falling' at the top of her lungs. She saw herself crashing in the back seat of the car at a rest stop to sleep under the stars. Then she was pulling into the Casbah's parking lot, walking into Heather's hotel room, catching her first live glimpse of Daniel in the flesh, and feeling her heart get squeezed like an orange in a juicer when she found out he was married to her stepsister.

Now she was sitting at a Denny's in Vegas, watching her stepsister hail a taxi on Las Vegas Boulevard. It didn't take more than three minutes for a cab to screech to a halt in front of a blonde wearing a skirt that barely concealed her butt cheeks. With a flash of thigh and a toss of her hair, Heather disappeared into the cab, then she was gone.

Zak had already swaggered off to catch his own ride back to wherever he decided to go. And Amity was here, sitting in a state of grace that felt as fragile as it was temporary.

Easy come, easy go, Zak had said. The phrase hovered shimmering in the air, as glittery and elusive as the promise of winning that brought people in herds to Nevada. Amity didn't have any illusions that Daniel wanted anything from her other than a set of wheels to take him on his journey. But in the recesses of her soul, where she stored all her forgotten crushes and her dusty, discarded fantasies, something stronger than an illusion was waking up and taking hold.

'So how are we going to do this?' she asked. 'Where do we go from here? Where do we start?'

Amity would have bet her left arm that Daniel's hand brushed her arm on purpose when he reached across the table to grab the paper napkin that Zak hadn't touched. Just the slightest whisk of a contact, but it packed a voltage that left Amity shaking.

'Got a pen? I'll show you.'

Hands trembling, Amity dug through her backpack and found a ballpoint that she'd swiped from the front desk at the Casbah. Daniel took the pen and began to sketch out a map on the napkin.

'It all started right here in Vegas,' he said. 'Me, Zak and Randy. We'd come here with a sum total of about seventy-five bucks, taking a break at what we thought was the end of the road. We'd been sliding into the abyss for so long, we didn't even dream of breaking big anymore. We'd literally come here to play out our last hand. I pawned my guitar to buy us something to eat and enough beer to keep us drunk for one more day.'

He'd drawn a star on the map to represent Las Vegas, and now he was drawing circles around it with the pen.

'What do the circles mean?' Amity asked.

Daniel thought for a second. His smile was bitter. 'Circling the drain. I guess that's what we were doing. Kind of sad, how many times you can fail in a lifetime, isn't it? Here we are, back in that same city, making that same, slow circle...'

'No, we're not.' Amity grabbed Daniel's wrist. She'd only intended to make the dismal circling stop, but the moment she realised she was touching him, a hot flush spread over her entire body. She kept her fingers wrapped around his wrist for a second too long before she yanked her hand way.

Daniel gave her a long look. 'You didn't have to do that.'

'I'm sorry. I didn't – that wasn't – I didn't mean to touch you. You probably hate it when random girls touch you out of nowhere, for no reason –'

'You're hardly a random girl,' Daniel interrupted. 'And what I meant was that you didn't have to take your hand away.'

'Really?' she squeaked.

'Your hand feels nice. Your skin is cool. And you have calluses. I like a chick with calluses on her fingertips. It means she uses her hands for something besides taking her credit card in and out of her purse.'

Amity gulped. She stared down at her syrup-smeared plate. Her head was awhirl with stars, and her heart was pounding like something out of a cartoon, a visible valentine trying to hammer its way out of her chest. Daniel couldn't have said what she thought he said. She was having an auditory hallucination, brought on by ten hours driving in the sun, followed by hot sex with a has-been rock star, a cheap pancake breakfast and an unbelievable collision with destiny.

Then Daniel took her hand, found one of those calluses that he liked so much and stroked it with his own fingers.

'You know why this is important to me. You've got the extra skin to prove it. You've done your time on the strings. But I'm still not convinced that you don't think I'm crazy. Here. Check this out.'

He pulled a cracked, dog-eared square out of his pocket and handed it solemnly to Amity. She took it. It was a discoloured Polaroid snapshot, circa 1985, of a scrawny kid with rumpled dark hair. The boy was all but swallowed by the electric guitar he was holding, whose strap looked like it was about to sever his scrawny shoulder.

Amity stared at the snapshot. Then she looked at Daniel. Then back at the picture.

'The kid is you,' she said.

'That's right. The shot was taken on my fifteenth birthday. But don't look at me. Look at the guitar. That's her. My holy of holies. My Gibson Girl. That's who I'm looking for. If I can get her back, I'll be real again. I'll be a musician.'

Still looking at the Polaroid, Amity nodded. She knew that kid. She knew what it was like to hold your first real axe, to feel its weight and power, to know that when you plugged it into an amp, its energy would surge through every nerve, igniting them with sheer electric ecstasy.

'I don't think you're crazy,' Amity said.

'But you think this idea is crazy. Don't you?'

'Yeah,' Amity admitted. 'I mean, what are the chances that you'll find her again?'

Daniel drew a series of lines radiating from the circle on the napkin, like spokes on a wheel.

'I probably have a better chance of winning a million bucks here in Vegas. But those are the same odds that I had when I was trying to make it as a musician. I beat the odds then. I figure I can beat them now. Each one of these lines could be the direction that my Epiphone went. She could be anywhere, with anyone. Some people would look at all those lines and say, hell no, I'm going home. Me, I trust my luck. I believe I can find her. I have faith. Do you?'

'Yes.'

'But you're still sceptical. I can see it in your eyes.'

Her eyes? The last time a man had said anything about Amity's eyes, it was only to inform her that they were bloodshot after a night of slamming tequila shooters in an exceptionally smoky bar.

'That's OK. A little scepticism keeps you grounded.' Daniel grinned at her. 'It's also kind of sexy.'

*Stop coming on to me*, half of Amity was pleading inwardly. *Keep on coming*, begged the other half. Maybe Daniel was truly attracted to her. Maybe he liked to take a stroll on the not-so-pretty side of the female gender every once in a while. Or maybe he was just flirting to keep her interested, so she wouldn't walk away and leave him there with a paper napkin, a table loaded with dirty plates, and a ballpoint pen with the Casbah Hotel's camel mascot printed on it.

'I'm sceptical,' Amity said. 'I'd be lying if I said I wasn't.'

Daniel tapped the pen on the table. 'OK. Tell me something. What's your number-one fear?'

'My what?'

'Your biggest fear. What are you more afraid of than anything else in the world?'

Amity didn't know what to say. She could have trodden water in that question for the next three days. Out of the hundreds of things she was afraid of – from flesh-eating fish to skin cancer to never having a relationship with a man that lasted longer than one night – she couldn't choose the top ten, much less a number one.

'Take your time,' Daniel said. 'There's a point to this question, believe it or not.'

Amity closed her eyes. Gradually a single fear separated itself from the swarm of minor anxieties and phobias that pursued her on a regular basis, until the answer to Daniel's question emerged with such clarity that she wondered why she hadn't seen it right away.

'Well?'

'I'm afraid of not being heard,' Amity said. She twisted her fingers, trying not to give in to her habit of cracking her knuckles when she was nervous.

'Go on,' Daniel prompted.

'I'm afraid that no one's ever going to hear me sing, besides my cat, who's not even with me anymore. I'm afraid that I'm going to fill up a thousand notebooks with song lyrics that are never going to be set to music, or played by anyone but me. And I'm afraid that if anyone ever does hear my songs, they're not really going to listen.'

Daniel didn't say anything for a long time. Neither did Amity. They just sat there, with her biggest fear sitting on the table between them, until Daniel cleared his throat.

'I've always believed that your greatest fear is just the flip side of your greatest dream,' Daniel said.

'Why did you want to know mine?' Amity asked. The question had left her feeling the same way that she did at those rare times when she played her songs for other people: naked, skinned, exhilarated, but wondering if she'd exposed too much.

'Because I thought yours and mine might be the same,' Daniel said.

'And . . . are they?'

That grin was moving across Daniel's face again, and Amity remembered watching the sun gradually illuminate the mountains from the window of her studio apartment early in the morning, and how her soul used to rise with that leisurely infusion of light.

'Two for two,' he said.

## Chapter Five

# The Hand You're Dealt

Fate could deal some freaky hands, Daniel mused, as the Thunderbird cruised out of the city and hit the highway. One minute you were sitting next to the cuddly, curvaceous blonde you'd married only a few days before; the next minute you were leaving town with her smart-arse, skinny brunette sister. Daniel still wasn't quite sure how this had all gone down, but here he was at the table, staring at a hand of cards, with no choices left but to fold or play.

His spirit felt amazingly light, considering that he'd watched his new bride walk out of his life less than an hour ago. He palpated his heart, the way you'd probe a cracked tooth with your tongue, searching for those piercing arrows that warned of serious agony to come. But the only twinge he felt when he thought of Heather arose from south of his belt buckle.

*I'm going to miss making love to her.*

Daniel toyed with that thought for a while. Fair enough. What else? He rummaged through his memories, trying to recall something Heather might have said that would reveal a profound connection between them, some gesture of overwhelming love she might have made, any expression of shared passions (outside of the bedroom, the shower, the men's room at the Casbah, and everywhere else they'd had sex since the night they met).

There had to be something more. Daniel was too deep

to fall into that age-old trap of mistaking lust for love. True, he was a romantic, but he'd never been so moved by a woman that he went straight out to buy her a ring. Heather's beauty held something extraordinary, a promise of unrevealed mysteries, glorious secrets lying under the surface. It would just be a matter of time, he believed, before Heather's true self would unfold for him, and those mysteries would grace him in a sparkling rain...

'...beef jerky?'

Daniel was distracted from his thoughts by a swatch of brown leather poking into his peripheral vision.

'Huh?'

'I said, do you want some beef jerky?' Amity repeated, her voice raised so that she could be heard over the roaring wind she was creating by driving twenty miles over the speed limit. She was guiding the blue boat with one hand on the wheel while she waved a stick of dried meat with the other.

He'd have to give Heather more consideration later. For the moment, he had to focus on the road. They weren't even out of the city yet, and Amity's driving was already making him nervous. She drove too fast, cut off other drivers and forgot to use her signals whenever one of her favourite songs came on the radio.

'No! I want you to slow down!' Daniel shouted.

Amity's long hair, a defiant flag, whipped around her face. 'I always drive like this!'

'Not with me in the car, you don't. We're going to get pulled over. Or killed. I'm not a big fan of cops or death. Besides, if we get in a collision at this speed, your guitar is going to be a pile of matchsticks.'

'Whatever.'

Amity sighed and released her foot from the gas pedal. The speedometer slowly returned to double digits.

'That's better,' Daniel said. 'Now put this baby on cruise control and we'll be fine.'

'I don't do cruise control,' Amity said. 'You'll just have to live on the edge when you're riding with me.'

So much for Daniel's visions of cruising sedately down the highway. He'd be grateful if Amity would keep the car at a steady 75. This was the price he had to pay for flirting with Heather's stepsister. Amity was just too damn fun to flirt with; Daniel hadn't been able to help himself at the restaurant. Talking to her, looking at her, touching her skin even the slightest bit – every kind of contact created responses that she probably wasn't even aware of. When he stroked her callused fingertips, Daniel had felt a fluttering vibration running through her wrist. He'd felt the moist heat of her arm, the quick pulse inside the crook of her elbow, when he grasped her elbow to prove some point he was making. And when he had asked her to confess her biggest fear, Daniel had seen all the colour leave Amity's freckle-spattered cheeks, only to return in an intense wash of red.

Clearly, no one was loving on this girl, and sex with hound dogs like Zak didn't count. Watching Amity bite her lip in concentration as she pondered the things she feared the most, Daniel had felt a twitch of big-brother protectiveness. He shouldn't have left her alone with Zak; players like Zak weren't good for women like Amity. Under her heavy-metal exoskeleton, her wise-arse sarcasm, she took the things that mattered to her very seriously. All you had to do was watch how carefully she handled that battered guitar case of hers, or how her whole body seemed to harden into armour when anyone tried to take the instrument from her.

'What exit do I take for the trailer park?' Amity was asking.

It had been Amity's idea to start the quest at the same trailer park where Daniel had searched for Sadie O?

Grady years ago. His search hadn't been successful back then, but as Amity pointed out, they shouldn't overlook the obvious. One of the residents of the park would probably remember Sadie, her band, possibly even the black Gibson Epiphone she picked up one day from a pawnshop in Vegas.

Daniel pretended to consult the map. He had no patience with maps – he preferred to let destiny guide him to the right place, or the wrong one – but Amity seemed to be relying on him to navigate them on this journey.

'Um, when you see a bald piece of dirt that looks like a scene out of *Road Warrior*, and then a truck stop with a MacDonald's, you'll know the park is coming up. Take the nearest exit after that. You'll see a big sign that says Starlite Trailer Homes on the right.'

'Starlite Trailer Homes,' Amity said with a melodramatic sigh. 'How painfully romantic. So nineteen-fifties. Hey, speaking of the fifties, aren't we getting close to one of the old atomic testing sites? The map should show those, too.'

'Hmmm. I think so.'

Amity glanced over at Daniel. The map was flapping uselessly across his knees. 'You're not really reading that map, are you?'

'I'm reading it. I'm just not quite comprehending it.'

'What's to comprehend? It's lines with little numbers on them all spread out across a coloured grid.'

'My point exactly. Look, Amity, I'm no good with maps. You might as well hand me driving directions in ancient Greek; I'd have an easier time with the interpretation.'

'You don't use maps? Not at all?'

'Not for this trip. This trip isn't going to be like any journey you've ever taken, Amity. We're going to get where we need to go by intuition, not by following squiggles on a grid.'

Amity shrugged her shoulders. Daniel could swear that her sunburned arms were already sporting more freckles than the day before. The toasted skin on her shoulders was peeling away in patches, revealing clearings of tender pink surrounded by scraps of lacy white skin. He found himself falling into a daydream about rubbing baby oil on those shoulders, absorbing the second-hand sun from Amity's flesh through his fingertips. As he rubbed the oil into her skin, the brown and pink patches would begin to glisten. The hues would appear to melt together, like the strawberry and chocolate flavours in a carton of Neapolitan ice-cream.

'All right, no maps,' Amity relented. 'You're the boss. I'm just the driver.'

'Not "just" the driver. You're *my* driver.'

Daniel caught himself before he could reach out and touch Amity's shoulder. He'd almost done it – his hand had been itching to feel the smooth hot roundness of her skin. And if he wanted to, he could pull away the shoulder strap of her top to see the soft white line underneath.

He wasn't going to touch. His 'my driver' comment had already flustered her enough. She stepped on the gas again, and soon the speedometer's needle was soaring up to 110.

'Please, slow down,' Daniel said, speaking as calmly as a person could when shouting out in panic. 'The trailer park's coming up in a couple of miles. I see the golden arches in the distance.'

Daniel wanted to give Amity hell for driving too fast, but he couldn't blame her for speeding up. His comment had sent her into a flight response, like a wild animal running from an air-raid siren.

Daniel was feeling those danger signs, too. A quickening of his pulse when she looked him straight in the eye, a warmth deep down in his belly. And worst of all, a desire to peel her open, layer by layer, to find the gleaming secret that stirred his curiosity whenever she shot off one of her smart, quirky remarks.

Heather set off skyrockets of desire in his gut, but she didn't tweak his brain that way. Life with Heather was like falling into the waking dream of some potent, erotic opiate. Once the fog cleared, would there be anything left to uncover under all that dazzling gold beauty?

'Wow. This place is a hellhole.'

Amity brought the car to a stop beside the drainage ditch next to the Starlite Trailer Homes sign. The park lay ahead of them, a village of shells, trailers once painted in an array of ice-cream pastels, now battered by sun and desert wind into a uniform dusty grey. Some of the residents had planted hopeful arrangements of flowers in front of their trailers, but any greenery that hadn't been drowned by flash floods had browned and been withered by the heat. The place looked deserted. Amity's reference to the atomic testing site hadn't been far off-base.

'I guess everyone's hunkered down inside on a day like this,' Amity said. 'Let's start with the office. Lead on, captain.'

She put up the top of the convertible before locking up the car. Daniel agreed that this was a good idea. Though he and Amity probably didn't own more than two or three hundred dollars' worth of stuff between them, what little they owned would bring a princely sum for anyone who lived in a place like this.

The trailer marked 'Office' was set apart from the rest by the addition of a rock garden, a set of newer-looking lawn chairs and a blue plastic wading pool. Amity knocked on the door, with Daniel hanging back. Though he wasn't recognised on a regular basis anymore, he hadn't lost that paranoia that came from being the focus of unwanted attention. When he saw the woman who opened the door of the trailer, he had second thoughts about not wanting that attention.

The trailer park's manager was a stunner, a bit road-worn, but strikingly sexy nonetheless. Her see-through babydoll top revealed a pair of high, peaked breasts and a graceful curve of waistline that flowered into a pair of full hips skimmed by cut-off denim shorts. Discreetly looking down, Daniel saw a pair of legs that were as tight as any dancer's on the Strip. In the months he'd spent in Vegas, Daniel had got used to the fact that the population was full of dancers – past, present and future – but he never lost that growling thrill of delight when he met one of those beauties in surroundings that were anything but glamorous.

'You looking to rent a trailer?' the woman asked. Her pale green eyes squinted at Daniel through a cloud of smoke that trailed from her cigarette. She stepped out of the doorway into the sunlight to get a better view of her visitors, and Daniel's heart leapt into his throat.

In his mind, he heard the phlegmatic sneer of the pawnshop dealer describing the woman who had bought Daniel's guitar. *Redhead. Hot little number.* The park manager's hair wasn't exactly red, but it was a faded chestnut that could easily have been dyed at one time into a fiery mane, à la Ann-Margret.

It couldn't be this easy to find her. Not after all this time.

'Are you Sadie O? Grady?' Daniel asked.

His voice came out in a rough, interrogatory bark, nothing like what he'd intended. He sounded like an undercover cop, or maybe something even more sinister. The park manager shrank back into the gloom of her trailer. Daniel saw her hand dip into the shadows beside the door, and he knew that she was reaching for a firearm. Out of the corner of his eye, Daniel saw Amity stiffen. His own insides turned to ice.

'Who the hell wants to know?'

The manager's eyes turned to slits. She wouldn't have any problem using whatever weapon she had reached for. Daniel was struck by a vision of himself and Amity lying in a shallow pit somewhere out in that desolate grey wasteland, while residents of the trailer park shovelled heaps of rocky dust over their lifeless bodies.

At the same time, he saw the woman's curvy figure poured into black leather, bottle-red hair surrounding her like a burning bush as she stood on-stage, cradling his shining black Gibson Girl against her breasts.

'Did you ever play lead guitar for a rock band called the Dust Bunnies?' he asked.

He might as well have asked her if she'd ever been married to Elvis Presley. The woman gave him an incredulous stare, followed by a burst of raucous laughter that rang through the desert.

'You've got to be kidding!' she hooted, between snorts of hilarity. 'I wouldn't know the first thing to do with a guitar. Totally tone-deaf. I couldn't make it as a dancer – you think anyone would let me onstage to play music?'

'I thought you might be a woman who performed under the name Sadie O? Grady.'

'Sadie O? Grady? Lord, no. I went by the name Blaze, when I was dancing. My real name's Donna. Sadie O? Grady sounds like someone in a dirty joke.'

'Did you ever hear of a woman with that name?' Daniel pressed. 'Red hair, sexy. She lived on this park, say, four or five years ago.'

To Daniel's shuddering relief, the office manager brought both of her hands into the open to light another cigarette.

'Back then, I was still trying to make it in Vegas,' she said. 'I hadn't moved out to this dump yet. People here come and go. Sometimes they're only here a week or two. Me, I've only been here nine months. Feels like an eternity, though.'

I bet it does, Daniel thought. Time had stuttered to a halt at Starlite Trailer Homes several decades ago.

'Is there anybody who's been here that long?' Amity chipped in. 'Anyone who might remember a girl who played a black electric guitar?'

'Someone's got to remember,' Daniel said. 'If she ever played it here, she would have rocked every trailer in the park.'

Blaze/Donna considered this. 'You could go talk to Eugene. He's been living over there in lot 10 since the dawn of time. Been impotent for years, but he's still horny as a hoot-owl. The guy notices anything female that comes within a hundred feet of his place. He's probably standing at his kitchen window now, checking you out with his binoculars,' she added to Amity. 'Be careful if you go over there, honey. Watch out for your arse and titties; he's a pincher.'

It was hard to reconcile Blaze/Donna's thumbnail portrait of Eugene with the soft-spoken, tremulous old man who opened the door of the trailer in lot 10. The lot was as neat as a pin, its front yard still lined with the marks of a rake, and the interior, though shabby, was equally spotless. To all outward appearances, Eugene was more interested in observing desert birds and recording encyclopaedic notes about them than in leering at women, but he did remember Sadie.

More importantly, he remembered the black Gibson.

'Ah, yes. Yes,' he said, his eyes growing misty behind his bifocals. 'Sadie had the loveliest scarlet hair. The kids call that style a mohawk, but I always thought of it as a crest, because she wore it with such pride. She managed to keep her skin snow white somehow. Smooth creamy breasts. She often wore black, and she was almost entirely nocturnal. I remember seeing her with a black guitar. It was approximately nineteen-hundred hours, on a Friday evening. She was out on the porch, showing the instrument to a few of the n'er-do-wells who always seemed to flock to her. If she ever played the instrument, I didn't hear it. She didn't have electricity in her trailer.'

Daniel's fingertips tingled, the way they always did when he experienced a sudden connection with his lost guitar.

'Do you know what happened to her? Where she might have gone?'

Eugene lowered his voice to a gallant murmur. 'Can't say I know for sure, but rumour has it that she moved to Crescent Canyon to, well, work.'

'Work as what?'

'You know.' The old man's eyes widened, and he tilted his head in Amity's direction as if to indicate that she shouldn't hear the deep dark secret he was revealing. '*Work*.'

Daniel was drawing a blank.

'He's trying to say that Sadie ran off to be a hooker,' Amity drawled.

The elderly birdwatcher's mouth tightened into a prudish sphincter. Daniel had to choke back a laugh. The old man was probably saving up every spare penny to make a pilgrimage to the shrine of Sadie O? Grady's milk-white boobs.

'Would you happen to know if she's working independently, or is she employed by an ... er ... establishment?' Daniel asked.

'Last I heard, she was working at the Pussykat Ranch outside of Crescent Canyon,' Eugene said, lifting his chin. 'They say it's a very classy place. Completely reputable. Nothing shady about it.'

'Sounds like a slice of heaven,' Amity said.

Daniel grabbed her arm. 'Thanks for your time, Eugene. We'd better get going. Come on, Amity.'

He dragged Amity out of the trailer, and they stumbled down the steps into the glaring sunlight.

'"A very classy place. Completely reputable,"' Amity said, imitating the birdwatcher's prim tone. 'Why, I might just want to apply for a position there myself.'

'Which position would you prefer, madame?' Daniel laughed.

'Well, I like the view from on top.'

'Of course you do.'

Now that he'd rescued poor Eugene from Amity's sarcasm, Daniel could have let go of her arm, but he hung on to her, all the way to the car. He told himself that he was holding on because of the charge that was running between them, the shared buzz of finding their first clue.

'Wait out here for a second,' Amity said, unlocking the door of the convertible. 'I need to get out of these jeans. I'm burning up in the sun.'

Though he tried to hide his reaction to the image of Amity driving down the highway wearing nothing but a tank top and panties, she must have read something in his face.

'Don't worry. I'm swapping the jeans for shorts,' she explained. 'It'll only take a second. Then we can head off to the Pussy Farm, or whatever it's called. Keep your back turned till I pop the top of the car.'

Figuring that his back was always turned to something, no matter which way he was standing, Daniel stood at a forty-five-degree angle to the car while Amity changed. He glanced over his shoulder – purely by accident – in time to see her lean, bare thighs shuttling back and forth as she sprawled across the length of the front seat, wriggling her way out of her tight Levi's. Just a flash of tanned flesh, far less than what you'd see at your neighbourhood swimming pool, but his sense of victory at seeing something she didn't want him to see left him rock-hard.

This is beyond absurd, Daniel scolded himself. Grown men didn't get randy at the sight of a pair of naked knees in the twenty-first century. But he couldn't deny the fact that he was aroused by Amity's shyness and the stolen glimpse of skin.

This trip was going to be perilous. Mighty perilous, indeed.

Amity wished that Daniel would lighten up. Before they pulled out of the trailer park, he announced that he wanted to have yet another Talk – one of those capital-T talks – about speed. Amity didn't usually entertain critiques of her driving, but since it was Daniel delivering the lecture, she kept her mind open.

'Let's get one thing straight,' he said. 'This trip we're on isn't about getting anywhere fast. I've been watching my whole life go by in fast-forward. Wherever we're going, we're going to take our time getting there.'

'What's your point?'

'You're not going to drive like a maniac. You push this baby over seventy-five, and I'm going to have to take over.'

So much for open-mindedness. Amity tightened her grip on the T-Bird's steering wheel. 'Hah! Not likely. This car has only one pilot, and that's me. I doubt she'd even start up for anyone else.'

'Listen, Amity, this journey's going to be epic. We need to stay focused on the goal. This isn't going to be some crazy college road-cruise; I need to know that you can stay on course.'

'If you don't like the way I drive, you can take your epic journey on a bus,' Amity snapped.

She stared through the windshield, at the line of highway that wound over the dun hills of the desert. She hoped her profile looked tough, because her head felt like cotton candy – pink and airy, a tuft of nothingness. Daniel didn't think she was cool enough, or committed enough, to accompany him on his quest. Somehow she sensed that the worst thing she could do was look like she cared.

'I'll let you drive,' Daniel said, 'but you have to prove you're dedicated to the mission. First you have to kiss my axe.' Daniel held out the curly-edged Polaroid of himself as a kid, cradling the Gibson Epiphone. 'Then you have to kiss me.'

'I don't kiss musicians on the first date,' Amity said. She was doing her best to sound cool, but her body felt as hot and shimmery as the asphalt on the highway ahead.

'Who's on a date?' he scoffed. 'A date with destiny, maybe. Kiss the picture.'

Amity lifted the Polaroid to her lips and held it there. When she looked up, Daniel had edged closer to her on the seat. Under his black sunglasses, his mouth curved into a smile that sent Amity's heart into a crazed staccato.

'Now it's my turn,' he said.

Daniel leant in and put Amity to the test. The kiss was a long, hard dare; his lips demanded to know what she was made of, how far she would go.

This was one test she couldn't fail.

She wrapped her arms around Daniel's neck and held on, putting everything she had into the kiss. So he wanted life to slow down? She gave him slow – a hot adagio of lips and tongue. When he tried to come up for air, she hunted him down with her mouth and held him down; the whole desert had been swallowed by an ocean of Amity, and he could drown in it for all she cared.

Daniel pressed his palms against Amity's chest and pushed her gently away.

'Stop, woman, I need to breathe,' he gasped.

But after gulping a few mouthfuls of oxygen, he resumed the kiss. This time he was taking control, leaning Amity back against the seat and bearing down on her with an intensity that would have stopped her heart, if it hadn't already been racing ahead of itself, towards a head-on collision with Daniel's. Her hands worked their way out from under his body and found the back of his T-shirt, pulling it out of his jeans so that they could slide underneath. She copped a brief, glorious feel of hard back muscles, undulating under smooth skin, before he grabbed her wrists and put a stop to the groping.

'We can't sit here mashing in the middle of a trailer park,' he said. 'People are staring at us.'

'Who cares?' Amity panted. 'At least we're giving them something to gawk at besides television.'

Daniel sat back in the passenger seat and threw his forearm over his face. He sat there for a few moments, his chest moving in and out as he tried to recover. 'I don't need to give the afternoon soaps any competition. Besides, we have to get back on the road.'

'I thought you said we weren't going anywhere fast,' Amity reminded him. 'We could put the top up again, so no one could see us.'

Daniel shook his head. 'I also said we needed to stay focused on the goal. That was just a kiss to launch the cruise ship.'

'Yeah, whatever,' Amity muttered, turning the key in the ignition. 'Felt more like a runaway train to me.'

'I'm still married.'

Amity glanced at Daniel. He was staring up through his sunglasses, addressing the cloudless blankness of the desert sky.

'But you kissed another woman, and now you're heading for a whorehouse.'

'I'm complicated,' Daniel said irritably.

'You're confused, is what you are.'

Amity yanked the wheel. The T-Bird's tyres sprayed gravel as the car hurtled back onto the road.

'Hey! What did we just talk about back there?' Daniel shouted as the car fishtailed onto the highway. A semi-truck roared by in the opposite lane, trailing the indignant echo of its horn like a scarf of sound. 'Why don't you just park in the middle of the highway and beg the gods of the desert for a full-on wreck?'

'That's what you get for being confused!' Amity shouted back. 'You want slow? Then *be* slow. Don't put your hands and your mouth all over me and then expect me to turn off like a damn light switch just because you don't know what you want.'

Amity stepped on the brake. The car slowed down, then stopped in the middle of the pavement. The headlights of another distant truck shone through the heat ripples ahead.

'Is this more like the speed you were looking for?' she asked.

A jackrabbit, long-eared and leggy, stopped in the middle of the road to watch them. The animal's twitching face looked almost human as it investigated the car.

Daniel shook his head. 'You can't have everything black and white, Amity. I don't want to be at a dead stop, but I don't want to be breaking the sound barrier, either. Now could you move this thing forward? And please don't hit that rabbit.'

'I would never hit that rabbit. He'll get out of the way. Unlike some males around here, he knows when to stay put and when to make his move.' Proving Amity's point, the jackrabbit bounded off the road and cantered across the barren landscape.

'Whatever you're trying to say, Amity, spit it out now. I don't want to play games in the middle of the freaking interstate.'

Amity stared straight ahead. 'I don't want to play games, either. In fact, I'm sick and tired of it. I've been played so much, I feel like a pinball machine. Don't kiss me again, unless you mean it. If you don't mean it, don't bother.'

*Did I just tell the hottest man I've ever almost known not to kiss me?* Amity wondered. *Damn.*

She waited for Daniel to open the car door, lift his backpack, suitcase and Fender out of the back seat, and heave his belongings angrily over his shoulder. She waited for him to shout at her, to tell her he didn't need her skinny, smart-mouthed self, before he stalked off towards the silvery mirage of water on the highway ahead.

He didn't shout, or disappear. He didn't even move.

'Fine,' he said simply. 'I can respect that. Any other requests, before we get run over by the semi that's bearing down on us while we sit here chatting?'

Out of the corner of her eye, Amity caught a glimpse of Blue Molly propped up against the back seat. Her mind flashed back to the hallway of the Casbah Hotel, standing in the hallway with Molly slung over her shoulder, watching that pathetic blonde rummage through the trash on Daniel's room-service tray.

*Note to self: I'm the girl with the guitar. Not some love-crazed groupie*, Amity thought.

'One more thing,' she said.

Daniel groaned. 'What?'

'This trip isn't all about you. It's also about me. I'm a musician, too. Not your ... consort.'

'My what? Did you say *consort*?' Daniel repeated, laughing.

'Yeah.' Amity lifted her chin. 'I mean no.'

'You've been doing too many crossword puzzles, darlin'.' Daniel shook his head. 'Now would you mind steering this boat in a forward direction?'

Amity started the car again. Half of her wished she could scoop up the words she'd just said, especially the words about kissing, and throw them back into the void. The other half – the sane half – knew that she couldn't have said anything else.

She'd have to store that kiss in her memory bank, as a starving woman might relive a long-ago Thanksgiving feast, fondling the details of the meal, embellishing the turkey and stuffing with all the passion of lost opportunities.

Some girls got drunk when they were depressed. Heather danced. She was shaking for a fix right now, if she wasn't going to collapse, weeping, into a mass of Jello. Music, make-up and male attention were the holy trinity of Heather's happiness, and she knew exactly where to find them. All she had to do was point the taxi driver in the direction of the giant twirling birds that adorned the rooftop of the Tucan Club.

Heather sneaked through the back door of the club, flattening herself against the doorway to avoid a couple of delivery men bearing crates of liquor. One of the boys, a muscular dancer wannabe whose T-shirt was dark with morning sweat, gave Heather a wink and a leer. Instantly her spirits rose a couple of notches.

'Hey, you aren't on the payroll anymore,' whined one of the dancers as Heather hurried towards the dressing room. 'You're supposed to be on the way out of town with your rock star husband. What happened? He already dumped you?'

'I forgot a couple of things,' Heather called over her shoulder.

*Chin up, baby doll. She's a cheap piece of work*, crooned the Daddy-voice in Heather's head. Heather's mental father figure was never far away; he followed her wherever she went, comforting her on the nights when tips were low and the men were rude; singing her cowboy songs when she couldn't fall asleep at night; and always, always reassuring her that she was the most beautiful girl in the world. He'd been beside her when she walked the ten feet of purple-carpeted aisle at the Casbah Hotel's wedding chapel, with Elvis's 'Love Me Tender' playing in the background. And she could have sworn that he shed a few imaginary tears when she and Daniel were pronounced man and wife.

Now Daniel was gone, on his television quest, or whatever he'd called it, but her father figure was still there, opening the door to the dressing room for her and ushering her back into that old familiar world.

Heather slipped out of her skirt and blouse, keeping her head lowered as she stepped into a G-string and a pair of sequined pumps, applied a pair of star-shaped pasties to her nipples, then rubbed her skin with sparkly lotion. She played an old childhood game with herself, pretending that if she didn't look at the other girls in the room, who were smoking and having a bitch session in the corner, they wouldn't see her. She didn't recognise the other three girls; dancers were disposable commodities at the Tucan Club, and on any given day the stage might be graced by a whole new staff. The turnover was partly due to the relentless gropings and propositions of its owner, Tucan Tony.

Tony was a nocturnal animal; he rarely showed up at the club while the sun still had anything to say about it. But as Heather slipped through the green tinsel curtain that separated the back hallway from the lounge, the club owner was suddenly looming in front of her, blocking her pathway to happiness.

'What's the matter, honey?' he drawled, all fake concern. His goopy, oyster-grey eyes travelled over Heather's breasts. He'd seen her tits a million times, but he never seemed to get his fill of ogling them up close. 'Had a fight with your new hubby?'

Tony, who had named his club after the bird who'd earned him his nickname, had a beak of a nose that he was always pushing into the girls' business. He pretended that his interest in their love lives, their sexual preferences, even their monthly bloating and cramping, was all paternal, but Heather knew it was nothing but a perv's naturally twisted curiosity.

'No, I most certainly did not,' Heather said. 'I just

needed – I mean I wanted to dance a few more numbers before I went home.'

Tony grinned. His long yellow teeth seemed to go on forever. 'Can't get enough of this place, eh?'

'Guess not,' Heather said with a forced giggle. She batted her eyes, wishing she'd remembered to apply her glitter-caked false eyelashes. Throbbing music made her muscles itch to move, and an audience of grey-haired conventioneers promised plentiful tips. She felt like a crack fiend standing inches away from her pipe, separated only by a wall of panting flesh that refused to get out of her way. 'Hey, you don't mind, do you?'

'Honey, you always have a home here at the Tucan. Always.' Tony planted his meaty hands on her shoulders. Fake sincerity oozed from his pores like the stench of metabolised booze after a three-day bender.

'Great,' she chirped. Heather tried to make a break for the stage, but Tony was still holding her in place with one hand, while tweaking a ringlet of her hair with the other. Heather tried not to cringe, but it was hard not to wince when she was breathing in wafts of onion and chili from Tony's lunch.

'I can tell you're hurting, baby,' he said. 'Why don't we go back to my office and talk about what's going on in your life?'

'There'll be plenty of time for talking later. Right now, I'd like to see the lady dance.'

The deep voice came straight out of Heather's dreams. So did the golden eagle on the money clip in the stranger's hand. Even Tucan Tony had to take a second look when he saw that wad of cash. Heather wished she could kiss the hand that was holding that money, especially when those tanned fingers peeled away a couple of bills and held them out – not to Heather, but to Tucan Tony. She couldn't see exactly how much the stranger gave him, but it bought her freedom.

*Lady.* The man with the money had called Heather a 'lady' – not a stripper, a slut, or a bitch, but a lady, because that's what she was, even when she was wearing nothing but a G-string, a pair of high heels, and a couple of pasties shaped like stars.

'Ab-so-loootly, Sir. You want her, you got her,' Tony fawned, neatly tucking the money into his shirt pocket. He gave Heather a not-so-fatherly slap on the bottom and pushed her in the direction of the stage.

She scampered away, so relieved to get away from Tony's chili-dog breath that she didn't get a chance to thank her rescuer, much less check him out. She saw the silhouette of a tall, square-shouldered figure sliding into a chair at a table out in the lounge before a new song started – one of her favourites, a Top Forty hit from the 1990s that always reminded her of her high school prom – and Heather claimed her spot at the pole.

There were three other girls dancing, none of them pleased to be sharing stage time with Heather. She was one-hundred per cent natural: blonde on top, blonde down below, with her very own set of silicone-free breasts in between. Too much competition for a bleached, surgically enhanced stable of dancers; Heather was an all-American beauty, the girl next door gone bad. She played up her look by wearing stars on her nipples and a G-string decorated with red, white and blue stripes, and the men couldn't get enough of her apple-pie beauty.

As soon as she started to move to the bouncy beat of the music, adrenaline rushed through Heather's bloodstream, washing away the residue of the morning. Daniel's departure was starting to feel like something that had happened a long time ago, as distant as one of her high-school breakups. Thinking about high school while she danced made her think about cheerleading. She executed a few high kicks, shaking imaginary pompons in front of her breasts, and the grey-haired gents in the lounge went nuts.

*Nothing bad can happen to you while you're smiling*, her mother used to say. Heather had invested so much faith in those words that they'd probably be engraved on her tombstone.

Keeping her smile wide and bright, Heather played up the cheerleader role. She shook her mane of curls, did the splits in midair, landing gracefully and going into a full backbend. She used one of the poles to stabilise herself while she extended her leg high, flashing her audience a glimpse of the paradise inside her patriotic G-string.

She bounced like a shiny, sexy ball on the waves of the pop song, feeling so damn good that she couldn't even remember why she'd quit the Tucan Club in the first place. Heather didn't care what people thought about her current career path – no matter where she danced, she was the star of every teen beauty pageant she'd won, every sports event where she'd cheered the team on to victory with her solid-gold star quality. Amity might have gotten the most acclaim for the folkie crap she played at the Senior Talent Show, but it was Heather who drew roars of adoration for her lip-synched, dancing rendition of Tiffany's 'I Think We're Alone Now'.

Why couldn't 3-Way Dream write music that made her want to sing and dance and smile? The songs Daniel wrote were either dark and sad, or dark and angry. The guys never made any effort at a stage presence; before they went on-stage, they pulled on whatever rumpled clothes they'd worn the day before and rinsed their hair in the sink. It was all so deliberately grungy, as if they were trying to gross Heather out. And as hard as she tried, she didn't get the point of all those ugly noises they made with their instruments. Daniel's guitar had blown out one of the amplifiers at the Sultan's Lounge at the Casbah, and half of the audience had walked out before the band was done because they thought the lounge was having electrical problems.

Heather had been kind of embarrassed.

'Well, what do you expect?' Daniel had said, glowering over a beer later that night. 'They came to Vegas wanting to hear Barry Manilow, but they're too cheap to buy tickets. So they got a down-and-out indie rock band – for free.'

As much as she hated to admit it, being around Daniel had been a downer the past few days. The brooding hunk with the sultry mouth whose dark eyes had flashed at her while she did her dirtiest moves for him at the Tucan had been turned surly and distant, except when they were in bed. When they were making love, Heather had Daniel's full attention. She was that beauty-queen-cheerleader-lip-synching-dancer all over again, star of the show going on between her naked body and her new husband's.

Daniel did have a marvellous body. He liked to work out when he was pissed off, and since he'd spent the past few years being pissed off, he was buffed and tightened and lean like a mountain lion. Heather had loved to touch him, loved to watch the way he responded when she was sitting on top of him, giving him multi-textured caresses with her fingertips, her painted nails, her nipples, her long hair.

Her training as a dancer gave her the strength and endurance to do things to him that no woman had ever done before, like squatting over him with her hands balanced lightly on his chest, his cock standing at attention at the doorway to her pussy. She loved to use her lower lips to ease over the head and give it short, silken caresses. She could drive him wild that way for a whole hour, easing down the length of his shaft a centimetre at a time, before gliding up again and teasing him by taking his little snatch of paradise away.

Then when she had him so worked up that he forgot the words to beg her to let him come, Heather would suddenly slide down the full length of him, one smooth liquid motion that sent him into another realm, where there was nothing but the pounding friction between his body and Heather's, and the tidal sounds her wetness made as he thrust into her, and the mingled moans and gasps of two people who wanted each other more than anything else in the world.

A pang of longing for her husband hit Heather like a sucker punch to the gut. For the first time since the happy music started, her smile wobbled, and she stumbled in her high heels, almost falling on her butt. None of the bedazzled males seemed to notice the skip in her footwork, except for one. The square-shouldered man with the overflowing money clip half-stood in the darkness, as if he were prepared to stride up to the stage to catch Heather when she fell.

Her smile came back full-force when she saw that gesture, and so did something else, a feeling she hadn't experienced in ages. A lot of men turned Heather on, but nothing gave her that icy-hot shiver all up and down her body like a knight in shining armour bounding to her rescue.

Girls like Heather's stepsister, who liked everything from their lifestyles to their music to be 'independent', didn't believe that modern women needed men to save them. But the truth, as Heather had experienced it at the Tucan Club, was radically different. She gave the cowboy an extra-special smile and, because this would have been the second time he'd saved her in less than twenty minutes, she performed one of the moves she considered a speciality.

Turning her back to the stage, Heather arched her

back, settled her palms on her thighs, and glided down the length of her legs, until she was bent over to the floor, grabbing her ankles. She held that pose for a few beats of music, letting her audience's gaze linger on the perfect peach with the sweet wedge of pink tucked inside, before she planted her hands on the floor and suddenly kicked her way into a backflip, finishing up with a side-split on the floor, her arms high in the air, breasts still a-jiggle from her landing.

She'd timed the move so that it coincided with the end of the song. The perky synth beat died away into a slow ballad by a grunge band, the last thing on earth that Heather wanted to dance to. She got up and walked off-stage. Instead of going back through the green tinsel curtain, she headed straight for the bar.

Dancing could only do so much to lift a girl's mood on a day like this. Sometimes you needed a banana daiquiri with a blue plastic monkey clinging to the side of the glass to make you smile again.

'I'll get that drink.'

The rich baritone voice interrupted Heather's attempts to beg a free cocktail from the bartender. For the third time, the man with the broad shoulders and the golden money clip had come to her rescue. She looked up into a square-jawed face edged with thick silver hair, the face of the man who'd haunted her since she was a little girl, not with his presence, but with his absence. Because she still didn't trust that he was real, she treated herself to a head-to-toe inspection of his body, just to make sure all the details were true to her fantasies.

Soft silver hair, thinning just a bit at the temples: *check*.

Twinkly eyes with sunbursts of fine lines radiating from the corners: *check*.

Elegantly weathered skin, browned by the sun, not a tanning booth: *check*.

Marlboro Man moustache, minus the yellow nicotine stains: *check*.

Tall, sturdy body clad in the subtly expensive tailored Western shirt and jeans that an oil tycoon might wear when he was revisiting his cowboy roots: *check*.

Big ol' carved silver buckle on his leather belt – NOT with his name on it: *check*.

Gorgeous silver-toed boots, made of Spanish leather, so glossy and well cared-for that a girl could get down on all fours and kiss them, if she were into that kind of thing: *check*.

None of the men Candi had married had been a true protector to Heather. None of them had stayed around long enough to learn the little blonde girl's middle name or her favourite flavour of ice cream, much less to step into the role of the strong male guardian she'd always dreamed of, the prince who would love her, comfort her, buy her presents, and yes, discipline her when she'd been a naughty brat.

But here he was, on the worst day of Heather's life, saving her from dragons with chili-breath, poised to catch her when she stumbled, and buying her a banana daiquiri when the music got too dark to dance to.

'Where have you been all this time?' Heather asked the stranger.

There was a quiver in her voice, and she could feel her lower lip fluttering. As soon as the question came out, Heather realised that it made no sense, but the man smiled as if he understood. His lips were full under his salt-and-pepper moustache. Heather plunged into a vision of those twin wings of facial hair caressing her lower lips as he kissed her in the place where she most loved to be kissed.

'Waiting for you, little lady,' he drawled, tipping the brim of an invisible cowboy hat.

## Chapter Six

# Post-Atomic Bordello Blues

*Miles driven since Vegas*: 76
*$$$ spent on gas*: I'm just flashing the plastic and trying not to think about it

Driving thru this desert is like one long hallucination. No wonder they used to test atomic weapons around here – who would care if this place was decimated by a mushroom cloud? I feel like we're driving on some red and grey alien planet ... Mars with McDonald's and Texaco and the occasional Reptile Museum or Giant Ant Farm. We're heading for a bordello somewhere in the middle of this huge expanse of nothingness. Do men really haul all the way out here to the armpit of Hell just to get laid? Speaking of which, I think my chances with Sir Galahad are improving. He hasn't made a move since the Meltdown Kiss, but I caught him checking out my legs. I'm feeling guilty about Gwinny. Wonder how she'd feel if she knew I played tonsil hockey with her husband this morning. She'd probably try to fumigate both of us with her hairspray; that aerosol stuff is worse than nerve gas.

> *Seventy-six miles of driving*
> *Cruising the face of Mars*
> *Hearts on parallel highways*
> *Following separate stars*
> *You told me I had to kiss you*
> *Then you told me I had to drive slow,*

> *But your mouth made my heart go faster*
> *Than your head could possibly know.*

'What are you writing?' Daniel yawned, waking from his nap.

The T-Bird was parked in the shelter of a dilapidated auto shed at a gas station off the freeway, where they'd stopped to fuel up and buy dinner, a six-pack of cold soda pop and a king size bag of pretzels. The old man who operated the station – he'd owned the place since the Vietnam War, he said – had offered to let Amity and Daniel rest there for a while, since that shed could be the last source of shade before Crescent Canyon. The open structure was dusty and airless, but it offered some relief from the relentless glare of the afternoon sun, and that shelter was so soothing that it made up for the stifling heat.

'You kids be good in there,' the old man had said indulgently. 'I know how you honeymooners get when you can steal a few minutes alone.'

'Don't worry, Sir. I swore I wouldn't touch her till we get to the motel,' Daniel had said. 'Hands off till the wedding night, she told me. I've hardly even gotten to kiss her yet. It's killing me, but I have kept my word.'

Amity had rewarded Daniel with a hard kick in the ankle as they walked back to the car. Now, sitting beside him in the front seat, she slammed her notebook shut. 'Nothing. Just trying to figure out how much we're going to spend on gas.'

'I don't want to think about gasoline. Too much of a buzz-kill.'

'I don't want to think about it, either. But I have to make sure we can afford to drive *and* eat. We have to make every mile count.'

'Sure,' Daniel yawned. 'But seriously what were you writing about?'

Amity clutched the book to her chest. 'I just told you.'

Daniel smiled and crossed his arms behind his head. 'You were writing about a lot more than the price of gas, darlin'. Let me see.'

His left arm shot out like a scorpion's tail, hand grabbing for the notebook. Amity gave a blood-curdling shriek and shoved the book down in the seat behind her back.

Daniel laughed. 'You're crazy. You know it? I bet that's your secret erotic diary.'

'Give me a break,' Amity snorted, but her derision hid raw panic. Daniel couldn't see her notebook. If he found out about the code names she was giving him and Heather – SG, or Sir Galahad, was Daniel; Gwinny, short for Guinevere, was Heather – he'd never stop laughing.

'Oh, come on. You seem like a secret diary girl to me. I bet you have all kinds of steamy material that you put down in that book. Sexual fantasies and dreams of luhuhhv,' he teased.

'Sorry to disappoint you, but you're dead wrong.'

'Really? You don't have any fantasies at all?'

'Nope. Not that I write down, anyway.'

'Then you *do* have some. Tell me.'

Amity's laughter burst out in an incredulous whoop. 'No way.'

'Aw, come on,' Daniel wheedled. 'Just one. A little bitty one.'

He was making slow, cruel figure-8s on the seat beside Amity's thigh with the palm of his hand. Without touching her, he managed to create a palette of sensations on her naked skin. Her image of the way his hand would feel – the cool hollow of his palm, the length of his firm fingers – was so vivid that she almost whimpered, wanting so much to feel him stroking her.

But she couldn't come out and beg Daniel to touch her. Especially after that lecture she'd delivered earlier, the one entitled Don't Touch Me Unless You Mean It.

'Why do you want to know about my fantasies?'

'Maybe I'm just curious. We're going to be spending a lot of time together. I want to get to know you.'

'Well, none of them are about you,' Amity lied.

'I don't have to be the star of a woman's fantasies to be curious about what she thinks about when she's alone in bed at night. I'm not that much of an egomaniac. Look, all I'm asking for is one measly second-hand erotic dream.'

Amity searched his face for signs of mockery, his words for notes of irony. His eyes, his mouth and his voice were completely serious, as far as she could tell.

'OK.' She looked down at her lap and twisted the hem of her shorts. 'There's a scene I wouldn't mind telling you about, I guess.'

Daniel took Amity's chin between his thumb and forefinger and turned her face so that she had to look at him. Her heart took a dive, head-first, into the pit of her stomach.

'What are you doing?'

'I want to see your eyes.'

'Why?' she attempted to ask, through the wad of cotton that suddenly filled her mouth.

'Because I want to know that what you're telling me is true. I want to be sure this fantasy is something you honestly feel, not just a story you're making up to hide what you really dream about.'

'I wouldn't lie about my fantasies,' Amity said, though in fact she had been considering borrowing one of Heather's erotic escapades. Her stepsister's adventures were so much more titillating than anything Amity could cook up.

'Great. Go ahead.'

Daniel lowered his hand. Amity's cheeks burned. She felt naked. She wanted to look away, but she forced herself to keep her eyes level with his.

She took a deep breath. 'I've had this fantasy since I was thirteen years old, but it's got more explicit over the years. If you laugh, I'll kill you. If you smile, I'll kill you.'

'I won't even blink. Cross my heart,' Daniel said solemnly.

'It happens at a club, or a bar somewhere. It's a small place, kinda private, not much of a crowd. I'm standing on-stage, playing my guitar. There's a little dance floor out in front, and two or three couples are slow-dancing while I sing. My songs are mostly slow,' she added.

'Nothing wrong with that. Go on.' Daniel rested his arm against the seat and leant his head into his hand.

'So I'm at a club, performing for this small, intimate crowd. They all know my music, and they like me. Not in a big, rock-star-fan way. They just like my songs. I don't know anyone out there, except for one guy. He's standing somewhere out there; I can't see him clearly. It's too dark. But I know he's watching me, because no matter which way I look, or turn, or move, I can feel his eyes on me. His eyes pull at me like magnets, and the longer I stand there, the more I start to focus on him.'

'Do you know who he is?'

'Not yet. I've just noticed he was out there, so I still feel like I'm in control of my surroundings. But as the song ends and I start another one, I realise that this whole night is for him. There's an electric ribbon of energy running between us; I feel what he wants to do to me. My knees get weak, my skin tingles all over and I'm starting to lose my voice. I can't stop singing, though, because I don't want to let my audience down. And I don't want to let *him* down either. He wants to do all kinds of dirty delicious things to my body, but he's going to make me finish my performance first.'

'The show must go on,' Daniel said with approval. 'So is this guy undressing you telepathically?'

'Oh, yes. He's making me feel totally naked. I feel like I have to do his will; suddenly that's what I'm all about.'

'He's mesmerising you.'

'That's it. I'm moving the way he wants me to move – slow and sensual, holding my guitar as if I were holding him in my arms. His eyes make me conscious of every inch of my skin. I think about his mouth moving across my body, and it gives me this warm, squishy feeling between my ... I mean, in my stomach. By now, I'm singing just for him. No one else exists. And I can see him; he's stepped out of the shadows, and he's standing in a pool of light.'

'What does he look like?' Daniel asked.

*Like you*, she thought. *He looks like you, because he is you – he's always been you, since before I even knew who you were.*

'No one in particular,' Amity said, keeping her tone light. 'He could be anybody.'

'I find that hard to believe. He has this compelling power over you, and he just looks like some guy who might come over to hook up your cable TV?'

'No,' Amity said. She had to pick her words with extreme care. 'He doesn't look like an ordinary guy, I guess. He looks like an angel. A dark angel.'

'Much better,' Daniel said softly. 'I like this fantasy. So what does this angel want from you? More importantly, what do you want from him?'

'I want him to help me down from the stage, when I'm finished with my set,' Amity went on, 'and take me over to the bar and buy me a drink. While I'm sipping my drink, he can't take his eyes off me, he wants me so much. And when I'm done, he leads me away to take me home, but he can't wait to get there. He pulls me over into a corner of the club, that scummy corner that every club has where junkies do their deals on the pay phones, and husbands call their wives to tell them they're someplace else. You know what I'm talking about?'

'I know that corner well,' Daniel said. 'Had some

amazing up-against-the-wall sex in corners like that. Go on.'

'The stranger leans me into the corner. He pushes up the skirt that I'm wearing and pulls down my panties. My thighs are slippery inside, and my panties slide down to the floor, no problem at all. He has his hands all over my hips, my rear end, and he's whispering things into my ear that make me go hot all over. He's telling me I'm beautiful. He's telling me I'm sexy. He's telling me my voice does things to him that no woman has been able to do to him with her whole body.'

'Wow.'

'Yeah. Wow. I feel like I'm drunk by now; I can barely stand up by myself. He starts to kiss me, and it's so vivid that I can taste the whiskey he's been drinking. I can feel the tiny cactus needles of his beard against my lips. He unbuttons his jeans, and before I know it, he's in me. He takes me right there against the wall, hard and fast.'

'Against the wall,' Daniel echoed. 'My kind of guy. He's a player, isn't he?'

'Oh, yeah. But I'm the only woman he wants to play,' Amity said.

Even in the gloomy atmosphere of the shed, Amity could tell that Daniel's eyes were dilated. All pupil, enormously dark. She knew what that darkness meant. She wanted to slip into it, swim naked in it, but if she fell, who would help her out of that water? Not Daniel. He'd be the one holding her under, keeping her down until she had to burst to the surface. His heavy lower lip fell open just a little, and that slight opening triggered a flood of remembered sensations from the kiss earlier that day: the pressure of his weight pinning her to the seat, the searching warmth of his lips, the interplay of teeth and tongue, the shattering pleasure when his fingers brushed her nipple as he reached for a grip on her shoulder.

She was scared to death that he was going to kiss her again.

He didn't.

'I had fantasies like that, when I got my Gibson Girl,' Daniel said. 'When I was fifteen I never got noticed at school, or at home for that matter. I was the kid who was never enough of anything. Smart, but not smart enough for honours. Did a decent job in gym class, but I wasn't fast or strong enough for team sports. I wasn't a monster, but I wasn't good-looking enough to get the girls I liked. The first time I held that black electric guitar, I knew she was going to give me what I'd been missing. I knew that I'd be able to seduce people in ways I didn't even understand yet. You know what I mean, don't you?'

Amity nodded. She wanted to tell him about the night she'd seen him playing that guitar, years ago, in the warehouse-turned-underground-club, how he'd strolled on stage looking like a guy who could have been anyone in the crowd, until the music turned him into an angel of electricity and anger. But it didn't feel like the right time for more confessions. It felt like the right time to be back on the highway, in the sunlight, driving as fast as she could . . . at least until Daniel yelled at her to slow down.

'We'd better go,' Amity said. 'I don't want to drive through the desert in the dark.'

'There's a shocker. I thought you'd get a thrill out of coasting through the darkness with the headlights off.'

'Not me,' Amity shuddered. 'I like to drive fast. Not blind.'

'Well, that's a relief. I feel much safer now.'

'You should. I'm a damn good driver,' Amity declared.

'And a damn good musician, I imagine. When do I get to hear you sing?'

Amity kept her eyes averted as she guided the T-Bird back onto the road. Why was Daniel asking to hear her sing, when the images from her oldest erotic fantasy were still heating up the air between them? Her confession had left her way too open and tender for a proposition like that.

Maybe that's why Daniel had picked that time to ask. The moment was ripe, and he probably figured that Amity was ready to plop into his hands like a warm, juicy piece of fruit ... which was exactly what she wanted to do, in fact.

'Soon. Maybe.' Keep it vague, girly-girl, Amity warned herself. Vague is cool, and cool is what you need to be right now.

'Soon maybe? Those words contradict each other. I want a date and a time.'

'That's the best I can do. Take it or leave it.'

Daniel sighed as he lowered his sunglasses and adjusted them on his nose. 'I guess I'll take it, since I don't have a choice. And now, I'm going to take another nap. I want to be fresh and purdy when we pull up to the Pussykat Ranch.'

He folded his arms over his chest, slumped down in the seat, and promptly began to snore. Amity stole glances at him out of the corner of her eye, her foot surreptitiously pressing the gas pedal, giving the engine just a tad more juice. Her father used to say that any man who could fall asleep in front of a woman who was awake and alert had to be plain stupid, very trusting, or in love. So which one was Daniel?

The sun was sinking in the sky, its mellowed light tipping the fawn mountains with pink. Night shuttered down fast in the desert. Amity looked at Daniel again, making sure he was really asleep.

'Pedal, meet metal,' she said, smiling to herself as her big blue land-boat powered towards the horizon.

Fitting in seamlessly with the post-atomic landscape, the Pussykat Ranch looked more like a fallout shelter than a bordello. A cluster of storage sheds, fuel tanks and automobiles in various stages of repair graced the dirt yard, mingling with the tumbleweeds and cacti. If not for the ornate, wrought-iron sign that advertised the ranch, complete with an illustration of a top-heavy kitty cat batting fake eyelashes and offering its posterior to passers-by, Amity might have missed the ranch altogether. The T-Bird had exited the highway onto an asphalt road; the pavement soon turned into gravel, and finally into dirt. Driving down a dirt road in a convertible wasn't Amity's idea of heaven on earth. She could write her name in the dust that was accumulating on the white vinyl of the T-Bird's seat covers.

Daniel woke, annoyed by the interruption in his beauty sleep, as the car was jolting along on the packed earth of the road.

'Where are we? Did we blow a tyre?' he asked, lifting his sunglasses to rub the grit out of his eyes. He leaned over the edge of the open seat to spit dust onto the road. 'What's this stuff blowing around?'

'That "stuff" is commonly known as dirt,' Amity explained. 'It usually doesn't make up such a big part of the atmosphere.'

'I didn't think so.'

'Look! There it is.' Almost missing the sign, Amity yanked the wheel to the left. The car fishtailed, tyres squealing, as it spun on a patch of packed dirt. She waited for Daniel to shout in protest, but he was silent. Staring slack-jawed at the bunker up ahead, he didn't seem to notice the dirt anymore. Apparently he was mute with awe at being in the presence of a real live cathouse, filled with real live working girls. Amity squelched a burst of jealousy.

All he wanted was to find Sadie O? Grady, she reminded herself. Even if he'd wanted to tomcat around here, he couldn't have afforded it. He couldn't even afford to buy a pack of cocktail peanuts, at this point.

All Daniel would do would be to walk up to the door, with Amity in tow, and ask if there was a red-headed guitarist working there.

'The girls can't be all that hot, if they work in a place like this, out in the middle of nowhere,' Amity reassured herself out loud.

''Fraid you're wrong about that,' Daniel said with a sly grin. 'Some of the hottest girls work in places like this, in the middle of nowhere.'

'How would you know?' Amity tried to keep the wounded note out of her voice, but she wasn't very successful.

'Word of mouth,' Daniel said mysteriously.

There was no sign of life outside the low-built cinder-block building. The place had been painted a pale, queasy green, the colour of hospital interiors back in the 1950s. Somebody had some surplus paint leftover, Amity figured. So much for pricey girls; these gals couldn't be raking in that much money if they had to use surplus paint on the exterior.

Amity pressed the door bell. A security camera was hidden inside a small bird house hanging from the eaves over the front door. When she saw no signs of bird life in the area, Amity figured they were being recorded by something tucked inside that little house, which was shaped, ironically, like a white country chapel. She nudged Daniel's ribs with her elbow.

'Don't look up,' she said.

'Huh?' he replied, staring straight up at the bird house.

'Never mind; it's too late now. You're on Candid Camera.'

'Oh, that,' Daniel said, glancing up and dismissing the camera with a wave of his hand. 'One more tape for the Dan Goldstein Files.'

'You mean you don't care if people spy on you?'

Daniel shook his head and laughed. 'Sweetheart, we're

being recorded every day of our lives. Privacy is an anachronism in the twenty-first century. At least we're doing something worth watching tonight.'

'Speak for yourself,' Amity said, stifling a yawn. 'I'm wiped out from all that driving. I'd rather go sleep in the car.'

'No way. You kissed the Polaroid of my guitar – you're in this with me every step of the way,' Daniel said. Casually he slung his arm around Amity's waist, his hand draped along the outcropping of her hip.

That woke her up.

'What are you doing?'

'This is just for effect,' he said. 'Don't jump out of your skin. Whoever's in there is taking some time to open up. They're checking us out. I'd rather have them think we're a pair of lovers looking for action than a couple of dusty drifters whose car broke down on the freeway.'

'Don't even say that. You might jinx us,' Amity warned.

The door opened. A beaming middle-aged woman with impeccably bobbed ash-blonde hair and a pear-shaped figure squeezed into fuchsia satin opened the door. She was holding a tray of tiny paper cups filled with a pink substance that matched her dress. Amity had a flashback to trick-or-treating on Halloween.

'I'm Miz Bunny,' the woman said. 'And this is my a new recipe. Watermelon Jello shots. Wanna try one?'

Slowly and tentatively, like Hansel and Gretel taking candy from a witch, Daniel and Amity extended their hands to take the cups. The shots went down smooth, with a wiggle of gelatin and a sweet afterburn of liquor.

'Come on in,' Miz Bunny said. 'Welcome to the Pussy-kat Ranch. Care to join us for a few drinks before you select a main course?'

How many times had she dragged out that tired old line? Amity wondered. She couldn't get past the cognitive dissonance of seeing a woman who looked like someone's favourite aunt opening the door of a brothel. She was even more shocked when the motherly blonde reached out and engulfed her in a musky hug.

Miz Bunny lowered her voice to a conspiratorial whisper, as if she were asking Amity about PMS symptoms. 'What's wrong, sweetie-pie? Are you nervous about playing with a woman? This must be your first time.'

'No!' Amity yelped. 'I mean yes! I mean ... I'm just kind of surprised, is all. You look like my den mother back in Girl Scouts.'

The madame laughed, a high-pitched, warbling giggle. Combined with her squishy rolls of flesh, the giggle made her look like the Pillsbury Dough Boy's twin sister. 'Honey, that's a pretty damn accurate description of what I do for a living,' she said. 'Now why don't y'all come and meet my girls?'

She ushered Daniel and Amity into a lounge area, where a line of women had magically materialised, arranged in order of height, like a line of Rockettes. 'Some of the girls are bombshells, others are just plain bombs, but each of them has some special trait or talent that makes her unique,' Miz Bunny declared loyally. There was Angelfood, a chubby strawberry blonde named for her oral fixation; Dorothy, an apple-cheeked girl wearing mud brown braids and overalls who looked barely old enough to vote; Rodeo Randi, bronco-buster extraordinaire; and a wide array of others.

'See anything special?' Miz Bunny asked, batting rhinestone-studded false eyelashes.

Daniel was staring at the line of women. His jaw was slack, his eyes glazed. Amity couldn't tell if he was bedazzled or just overwhelmed, but the end result was that he appeared to have been hit with a sledgehammer. An inarticulate sound came out of his mouth in response to Miz Bunny's question, something between a grunt and a death rattle.

'Does a girl named Sadie O? Grady work here?' Amity

asked. 'The "O" has a question mark.' Apparently Amity was going to have to be the brains of the operation, at least whenever scantily clad women with corny nicknames came onto the scene.

Miz Bunny's face went blank for a moment. It wasn't the blankness of confusion, more like a deliberate effort to make her face as bland and unrevealing as the Pillsbury Dough Boy's.

'We don't have anyone named Sadie,' she said, her perky tone edged with something hard. 'How about one of our other girls?' She motioned to the rest of her chorus line with a theatrical sweep of her arm.

Amity felt like a shopper at some kind of perverted buffet. If she'd been a man, she probably would have been drooling like Daniel; instead, she found herself scrutinising each of the girls with a combination of curiosity, horror and awe. So many different identities, offering so many different ways to have sex. For Amity, sex had always been a fairly straightforward deal. She brought no costumes, no toys, no pseudonyms to the table. She was just herself, naked, with a man, doing whatever felt best at the moment. Now, watching these exotic creatures who probably had more sexual positions at their disposal than most people had changes of underwear, Amity wondered if she'd been missing something.

'Her,' Daniel said, coming out of his stupor to point to a twenty-something punk chick wearing a nose ring, an asymmetrical suicide-blonde bob with spiky bangs, and a spaghetti string evening gown that showed off multiple tattoos. She wasn't the one Amity would have chosen. Faced with the opportunity for a lesbian experience, she would have gone with Dorothy; she looked the least threatening, and Amity had to admit that she had a perky pair of breasts under those overalls.

'Veruka. Excellent choice.'

Miz Bunny's smile wobbled a little, as if she privately thought that Daniel could have done better. Amity tended to agree. Veruka looked like she could swallow a bowl of rusty nails for breakfast without so much as a hiccup. The tall blonde detached herself from the line and slunk over to Daniel, shoulders sloping in elegant indifference. Veruka was sexy, in a dangerous sort of way, but Amity preferred Dorothy's cupid's bow pout and chunky farm girl figure. Veruka would probably charge more than Dorothy, and Amity was already wondering how she was going to get out of this without going broke.

Great. I'm starting to think like a john, Amity thought, with an inward groan. What have I got myself into?

Veruka took Daniel's hand and led him over to the bar. They made a striking couple. Daniel's dark, angular form was like the negative of Veruka's chalky skin and platinum hair. Together they delivered a double dose of edgy apathy, but from the tension simmering under Veruka's pallid hide, Amity could tell that she wasn't exactly indifferent to tonight's date.

For a weekday night, the lounge looked pretty full. Men of all kinds – and a few non-working women – sat on barstools and gathered in groups with the ladies. Some of the men were dressed in Italian suits and looked like they spent more on a haircut than Amity had ever spent on a month's rent. Others were clad in paint-spattered jeans, work boots and vests. Amity had to hand it to the Pussykat ladies. They were equal opportunity all the way, showing no discrimination between their customers. Booze and boobs flowed freely to the sounds of America's Top Forty playing on the jukebox. A bouncy Madonna number segued into an overproduced Celine Dion ballad, and some of the ladies were taking advantage of the unctuous sounds to lead their 'dates' towards the money-making end of the Ranch.

Amity hung back and watched as the blonde ordered a double vodka for herself and one for Daniel, and paid for Daniel's cocktail. She was hanging all over him now, gesturing wildly with her black-taloned hands as she talked, and forgetting to hide her overbite behind a sneer. Far from being turned off by those scary choppers, Daniel appeared to be basking in Veruka's attention. First he fingered his collar for all it was worth, then he shifted his attention to the noodle-thin strap of Veruka's burgundy gown.

Within three minutes, Daniel had forgotten that Amity existed.

Comprehension dawned slowly, but it came: Veruka knew who Daniel was. She recognised his name, probably knew all of 3-Way Dream's lyrics by heart, just as Amity did. Her spray-it-don't-say-it chatter was the enthusiasm of a die-hard fan who's just met her idol.

Amity's stomach tightened like a fist. She didn't belong here, in this swanky little cathouse lounge with its forest of bleached, plucked, sequined working girls. She was a working girl, too, but one of a different species, the kind that made photocopies, or poured lattés, or asked, 'Paper or plastic?'

'Hey. Can I getcha a Coke or something?'

The question, and the perky voice that asked it, fit so seamlessly into Amity's thoughts that she didn't realise it was coming from Dorothy. The girl was standing beside her, hands shoved in the pockets of her denim overalls. In the bar's revolving purple lights, Amity could see the pretty auburn highlights in Dorothy's shiny hair. Rocking back and forth on the soles of her Keds, this homespun hooker might as well have been waiting for her turn at bat in a softball game on a warm summer evening.

'Thanks, but I kinda just want to get out of here,' Amity said.

'Why? Aren't you having a good time?' Dorothy's freckled nose crinkled.

'Hardly.' Amity gave Dorothy a closer look. 'Is your name really Dorothy?'

'Gawd, no!' the girl hooted. 'That's just my alias. My game. If Miz Bunny had her way, I'd be wearing a red-and-white-checked dress and carrying a straw basket, just like in *The Wizard Of Oz*.'

'And don't forget the flying monkeys,' Amity added.

'Don't give her any ideas. So far, Miz Bunny lets me get away with looking like I fell off a turnip truck. But she won't go for that yokel look for long. I haven't been getting enough dates to pay for my room. That's when you know it's time for a new game. Too bad, 'cause I don't really look all that hot in Spandex and high heels. What's your name, anyway?'

'Amity.'

'Amity,' Crissy repeated. She let her lips shape the word slowly, as if she were tasting each syllable. 'Is that your real one?'

'Of course. You think I'd pick an oddball name like that if I had a choice?'

Amity was starting to wonder if anyone had their own identity – their own 'game', as Dorothy called it – around here. This wasted dreamscape seemed to fill people's heads with crazy mirages, impossible ambitions. Daniel was just another victim, with his impossible search for the Holy Gibson. And now, so was Amity.

'What's your real name?' Amity asked.

'Christina, with a C and an H. But you can call me Crissy.' She stuck her hand out, and Amity shook it. Crissy had a solid handshake, the kind you could trust. She finished it with a sweet, lingering squeeze.

'Wanna go for a swim?' Crissy asked. 'There's a pool outside. It's not very big, but we wouldn't be training for the Olympics or anything. And there's bubbles.'

She tugged Amity's hand in a playfully imploring

let's-run-up-the-hill gesture. Amity caught a message in the soft lilt of Crissy's voice, the tilt of her head. Images of sweet girl-sex filled her mind; though she'd never made love with another woman, she had her little repertoire of fantasy and experimentation to guide her imagination.

'I don't have a swimming suit,' Amity said, though she knew before she got the words out that suits wouldn't be required around here. In fact, bathing attire was probably forbidden at the Pussykat Ranch.

'Perfect. Let's go.'

Amity's heart was doing a quick two-step. A sultry promise illuminated Crissy's cinnamon brown eyes, and her round cheeks were pink with anticipation. The twin mounds captured in the bib of her overalls jostled each other gently as she breathed, and Amity noticed for the first time that there was a tiny lavender butterfly tattooed on the slope of her right breast. With each rise and fall of Crissy's chest, that butterfly stretched its wings, getting ready to take off into a heaven of silken curves and long, strawberry-scented hair...

'Amity. We're out of here. *Pronto*.'

A male voice, rough with urgency, exploded Amity's sapphic reverie. Daniel had his fingers wrapped around her triceps, and she caught a quick snapshot of Crissy's sweetly dismayed face before he was steering her out of the lounge and through the front door as if they were a couple of armed robbers escaping the scene of a heist.

'What's wrong? What's going on?'

Daniel had Amity by the hand now – the hand that still held Crissy's warm invitation – and was dragging her across the scrabbly yard to the car. With its floodlights and surrounding barbed wire, the ranch looked like a prison yard in the darkness. Now Amity really felt like a fugitive. She half expected Miz Bunny to come bursting out of the building in her fuchsia gown, wielding a rifle and hollering 'Freeze, you sons of bitches!'

'We got what we came here for,' Daniel said. 'Now let's get going before that Jello-shot mama brings us a bill.'

Daniel's dark eyes blazed. Amity still had no clue why he was so frantic to bail all of a sudden, but his urgency was contagious. The adrenaline rush made her hands shake as she jammed the key into the ignition and started the car.

'We didn't buy anything,' she said. 'I didn't even have a Coke. And I thought that blonde was sponsoring your drinks.'

'All I had was soda water with lime, but who knows what that costs in a joint like this? Listen, Amity, everything costs money in Nevada. If they could charge you for breathing, they would. In fact, someone's probably working on that even as we speak. Besides, I got what I needed.'

'What's that? Did that Veruka chick give you a hand-job under the bar?'

'God, no! You think I'd let her near my package with those black claws of hers?'

As if she'd been summoned when Amity spoke her name, the door of the Pussykat Ranch opened, and Veruka magically appeared in a burst of light and sound that streamed from the lounge into the desert night.

'Danny!' She waved a scythe-thin arm. 'Come baaack!' The blonde began running across the yard, doing a geisha-girl trot in her long dress and heels.

'Floor it,' Daniel said, through clenched teeth.

He didn't have to ask Amity twice. Veruka might be doing a turkey trot, but she was moving pretty fast for a woman in platform shoes. The madame with the shotgun couldn't be far behind.

'You owe me fifty bucks just for picking me out of the lineup!' Veruka shrieked. Amity could see her in the rear-view mirror, her fists planted on her hips, hair flying in a white electric halo around her gaunt face.

'See what I mean?' Daniel said, as Amity threw the T-Bird into reverse and gunned the engine. 'It's all a scam.'

'If everyone's on the game, and nobody's using their real identity, and it costs money just to breathe, then what are we doing here?' Amity wondered out loud.

'Aww, don't get cynical on me,' Daniel said, patting Amity's knee. 'It'll all be over soon. We're going to some place much, much better. Some place real, where everyone's totally authentic, and everything's dirt cheap.'

'Where?' she asked hopefully.

Daniel's teeth twinkled in the moonlight as he grinned. 'Point this boat to LA, baby.'

## Chapter Seven

# Convertible Sexuality

Amity got the low-down on Veruka as they headed down the highway, looking for a place to pull over and spend the night. Daniel had suggested that since they managed to avoid spending any money at the bordello, they deserved to splurge on a motel room. Amity agreed. She wasn't sure what kinds of animals roamed the desert at night, but she doubted she'd get any sleep with coyotes and scorpions circling the car.

'Did you bonk that blonde chick?' Amity asked. Point blank was always best when you needed to know the answer to a question.

'Are you nuts?' Daniel laughed. 'When would any bonking have happened? You and I were apart for fifteen minutes. I can hold out a little longer than that, darlin'. Besides, she wasn't remotely my type.'

'You picked her out of the lineup,' Amity pressed. 'She must have pushed at least one of your buttons.'

'She didn't push any of my buttons. Well, maybe the one marked "Exit". She was a scary, scary girl.'

'Then why did you choose her? Was it her vampire complexion? Her bleached-out hair? Or just her good old predictable boob-job?'

'Stop! You're merciless! It was nothing about her body, OK? I picked her out because she looked like the only lady there who would have been tight with a rocker girl. Nobody else had the vibe. All I wanted was the 411 on my guitar. And you know what?'

'What?'

'I got it.'

'So tell me.'

Daniel draped his arm along the seat and leant closer to Amity. The dry evening breeze was ruffling his hair, pushing it off his forehead, then back into his eyes. In the dark, with only the light of the moon and the twin beams of the headlights to guide her, Amity was afraid to look straight at Daniel. But whenever she stole a glance at him, his eyes were focused on her, and when she tried to look away, the intensity of his attention kept pulling her back like a tide.

'Sadie O? Grady worked at the Pussykat Ranch for about eleven months. She definitely had my Girl with her; everyone knew Sadie was a rocker, and she liked the rep. Miz Bunny let her use the garage to practise in, when one of her Cadillacs wasn't parked in it. Veruka sings, so those girls apparently hooked up and were even thinking about doing some gigs together. Then Sadie got a phone call from an ex-boyfriend. He'd moved to LA, got a job in a recording studio, and he offered to help Sadie cut an EP cheap. Three days later, she packed up everything – including my axe – and disappeared. Veruka's still bitter about getting left behind.'

'Tell me something,' Amity said. 'Have you thought about what you're going to say to Sadie O? Grady, or whoever has their hot little hands on that guitar these days, when you catch up to them? I mean, whoever it is, she or he isn't going to be too cool about it when you walk up to them and say, "Hi. My name's Daniel. Give me *my* axe."'

'As a matter of fact, I have thought about that. I've played out the scene in my head a hundred different ways. Each time, it's a different person, a different place. Sometimes it's a girl like Sadie, and I can sweet-talk her out of it. She sees why I need to have my baby back, and she doesn't try to get in the way. Other times, it's some big brute of a guy, with no artistic calling whatsoever. He doesn't give a crap about my Girl; he's the type who doesn't care about any of his possessions until someone else shows an interest. Then he's all over it like a pit bull on a lamb chop.'

'What are you going to do if it's someone like that?' Amity asked. 'It's not like we're packing firepower.'

'No,' Daniel admitted. 'Violence isn't an option with me. That's why I've got a secret weapon.'

'What weapon?'

'You. You're skinny enough to sneak through any door or window. You'll be my cat burglar.'

'I only promised to be your driver,' Amity objected. 'I never said I'd steal anything!'

She wasn't thrilled about being reminded how skinny she was, especially by Daniel. More than anything, she hated being yanked back and forth on a string; one minute she was being kissed passionately, the next she was being asked to commit robbery.

'Hey. Calm down. I was kidding.'

Daniel toyed with a strand of Amity's hair that had blown across his forearm. He gently pulled the hair taut, running his thumb and forefinger down its length as if he were testing the resilience of a guitar string. He kept scooting closer to her as she drove; he was practically straddling the gear shift by now. He must be charged up from the experience at the Pussykat Ranch, and to tell the truth, so was she. Resisting her stepsister's husband for ethical reasons was starting to get old. Sooner or later, Amity was going to break down.

Besides, Amity's sense of ethics was wearing thin. Heather wasn't here with Daniel, covering miles of desolate desert on a wild guitar chase. The marriage vows she'd spoken apparently hadn't covered the pursuit of impossible dreams.

'We're not going to have to steal the guitar back,' Daniel went on. 'I know I can convince whoever has her that she belongs to me. That axe isn't just my instrument; she was my first love. I wrote some of my best songs on that beauty. When this person sees me holding her, they'll know we belong together.'

'You're a hardcore idealist, aren't you?' Amity asked.

'I don't know about "hardcore". I can be as cynical as the next guy, when something doesn't seem real to me. But when something's real – like my connection with this guitar – I'm with it all the way. I don't see any reason to settle for anything less than a hundred per cent conviction.'

That's exactly why we belong together, Amity thought. But she sensed that this wasn't the right time to say it. She thought back to the times that she had played poker with her dad, how he had told her to trust her instincts when she had a strong card in her hand.

'Don't pull that ace out of the hole till you're damn good and ready,' she heard her father saying. 'Keep your cards low, keep your face blank, and above all, don't let the clock rattle your nerves. A good poker game can go on for a week.'

'Did we just hit an armadillo?' Daniel asked. 'The wheel did something weird, like we were running over a small animal.'

'I don't leave road kill when I drive,' Amity declared, sounding more confident than she really was. She'd felt the bump, too, and along with it, a lurch of dismay.

'Then what's wrong? The car's wobbling.'

'It's the axle. It's out of alignment. Shit. Shit, shit!' Amity cried, smacking the steering wheel with the flat of her hand. 'How am I going to get this fixed out in the middle of nowhere?'

'Shhh. Calm down.' Daniel patted her thigh. 'We'll find a way. We're two pilgrims on a holy mission, remember?'

'If that were true, this wouldn't have happened in the

first place. It was that damn dirt road back at the Pussykat Ranch. I knew those potholes were going to wrack my baby!'

'Hang on, Amity. If we can make it to that little circle of lights up ahead, we'll be home free. It looks like a little town.' Daniel pointed to a cluster of buildings in a valley that appeared to be at least a million miles away. 'There's probably a gas station down there. We'll pull over, spend the night in the car, and in the morning we'll find someone to fix her.'

'We'll never make it all the way down there,' Amity grumbled.

'Sweetheart, we don't have much of a choice. Let's just keep driving and hope we don't get flattened by a big rig.'

The car did make it, weaving and bobbing down the grade to the valley where the postage-stamp community sat. Amity felt like they were entering the last outpost of civilisation as she steered the T-Bird into the parking lot of the Desert Mirage Motel, but the place did indeed look sweet to her. In fact, it closely resembled a vision of paradise at this moment, with its half-circle of white bungalows arranged around a teacup-size swimming pool. The water glowed pink and orange and aquamarine in the flashing neon lights of the Sweet Mirage.

'OK. We've died and gone to heaven,' Daniel said, echoing her thoughts. 'See? I told you something would open up for us. You're just going to have to accept that this is a charmed journey.'

'Don't keep saying that, or you'll curse us,' Amity warned, knocking on the dashboard's wood veneer.

'Aw, you're just superstitious.'

'Damn right I am,' Amity said. But part of her secretly agreed with Daniel's optimism. Especially when the motel owner informed them that there was exactly one room left in the motel – and that it had double beds.

'Let's go for a moonlight swim,' Daniel suggested, after they'd coaxed the ailing T-Bird into a parking spot and had checked into their bungalow.

The room, with its ochre drapes and fake oak panelling, wasn't anything to write home about, and the price the owner was charging them had made the blood drain out of Amity's face. But Amity thought she'd never seen anything more inviting than the two queen-size mattresses with their flat pillows and cigarette-scarred bedspreads.

'No way. I'm going to bed,' Amity announced, kicking off her shoes and flopping down on one of the beds.

'Oh, come on,' Daniel wheedled. 'The pool's heated.'

'I don't have a swim suit,' Amity said, her voice muffled by the pillow.

'Don't need one. Your bra and underwear will do just fine.'

'I don't wear a bra.'

'Fine. You wear panties, don't you?' Daniel was relentless.

'How do you know I have more than one pair?'

'I don't. But you have to wash them sometime, right? Here's your chance. Come on.'

Then Daniel was dragging her off the bed by her forearm, leading her out into the dry desert night, and Amity found herself being manipulated out of her clothes beside the pool. Daniel took his time peeling off her shirt. His palms swept up the length of her waist and brushed the sides of her breasts as he pulled the shirt slowly over her head. Blindfolded by the fabric, Amity knew that Daniel was checking out her belly, with its ankh tattoo below the navel, and her small breasts. Between the caress of the night breeze and the heat of Daniel's attention, her nipples felt as big as silver dollars. She could feel the twin nubs standing at attention, and she wished there were some way to order them to lie flat again.

'Very, very nice,' he murmured, his voice catching on the second 'very'. 'Now let's get you out of those shorts.'

Amity's shorts offered even less resistance than her T-shirt, and within a matter of seconds, she was standing there wearing nothing but a pair of white panties and an embarrassed look on her face. Thankfully, she'd put on one of her few pairs of underwear that didn't have holes.

'I don't have much of a lingerie collection,' she said. 'Heather's the one who shops at Victoria's Secret. All my stuff comes from Wal-Mart.'

'To tell you the truth, I don't notice a woman's panties all that much. I'm more interested in what's inside them.' Daniel's grin was diabolical. Amity had never noticed that his eyebrows almost grew together in the middle. She'd never been this close to him, for this long. She wasn't handling the proximity very well; her stomach felt like it was full of moths, and she was trembling as if it were nine degrees out here, instead of ninety-nine.

'Well, you aren't going to see what's inside these Wal-Mart panties,' Amity said. Not tonight, anyway, she added inwardly.

'That's OK. I've got a good imagination. It'll hold me over till the time is right.'

To Amity's relief, Daniel stepped away to strip off his own T-shirt and black jeans. Before she had a chance to check him out, he slipped into the pool. Underwater, his body was ribboned with light, quavering in the rings that he made with his sculling arms.

'Well? Are you going to come in, or are you just going to stand there admiring my masculine beauty all night?'

Amity stepped gingerly into the water. Daniel had been right, the pool was heated. The water felt like a warm bath. She sank all the way under, down as far as she could go, letting the chlorinated depths wrap her in a deep embrace. She closed her eyes, mesmerised by the exquisite sensation of having her sunburned, dust-caked skin rinsed clean. She wasn't aware of Daniel swimming up beside her, until she was suddenly wrapped in his muscular arms and carried to the surface.

'What are you doing?' she sputtered. 'You made me swallow a gallon of water, sneaking up on me like that!'

'I thought you were drowning.'

'Not a chance. I worked as a lifeguard at the community pool all high school. I could save both of us with my hands tied behind my back,' Amity snapped.

'Really? Now there's a nice image. I love a woman with her hands tied behind her back. Especially when she's saving my lousy life.'

With his thick, dark hair slicked back, his features stood out in carved relief. He had a five o'clock shadow on his jawline that looked like it had been doing duty for at least twelve hours. Droplets of water beaded his full lower lip and his thicket of black eyelashes.

In short, he looked so good that Amity wished she could dive into him and let the pool go to hell.

'You're staring at me,' he said softly.

'Only because I can't believe what a dork you are.'

'Careful. If you hurt my feelings, I might cry. Chicks can't resist me when I cry.'

'Oh, really? Watch me.' Amity tried to do a back flip out of his arms, but he was holding on too tight for her to make her escape.

'No, you don't. You can't get away from me that easily.'

Daniel's slippery torso was pressed against hers, hip to hip, waist to waist, chest to chest. One of their hearts was hammering loudly, but she couldn't tell whether it was hers or his. Then there were his eyes, those dark, dark eyes, that always tripped her up when she was trying to turn away from him.

This time, Amity wasn't trying to turn away. She couldn't have, even if she wanted to. The air rushed out of her lungs when he hooked her lower body with his right leg, and she felt the ridge of flesh, caught in his boxers, below his waistline. Amity felt a rush of gratitude for the two layers of cotton – his underwear and hers – that separated the two of them. If not for that thin net of fibres, she and Daniel would be a lot closer than she was ready for them to be.

Her body, specifically the throbbing pleasure centre between her thighs, was plenty ready. That hot little place seemed to have a mind of its own – her lower lips opening to be filled, then clenching, fistlike, in frustration when nothing came in to fill them. She had thought that her hips were rocking with the motions of the water, but she realised that they were moving of their own accord, doing a synchronised dance with Daniel's. He smiled as he watched this revelation dawn on her.

'It's you doing the dirty rhumba down there. Not the water. You want me,' he gloated.

'I do not,' she said. The denial slipped away, completely unconvincing.

'Yeah, you do. Admit it.'

'Your nose is running,' she lied, searching for a way to slow this party down. Everything was happening at warp speed, and warp speed was making her dizzy.

'Hmm. Maybe I've got a terrible disease or something. If it's contagious, it'll be better if we both have it, don't you think?'

Before she could stop him, Daniel leant in and rubbed the tip of his nose against hers. Amity had had no idea that the end of her nose was an erogenous zone of unbelievable proportions. All it took was a bit of gentle nuzzling to turn her into a wild woman. She wrapped her legs around Daniel's waist and held on for her life as she kissed him. No Eskimo kisses, this time; Amity went straight for Daniel's lips. The water had left his mouth slick, cool and faintly flavoured with chlorine.

Amity closed her eyes as if she were diving to the bottom of the pool again, and drank him in. His fingers wove through her hair as he kissed her back, using the wet strands like reins to guide her mouth. She heard a groan take shape deep in his chest; the sound reverberated through her flesh, making her moan in reply.

'Woo-hoo! Free sex! That's what I like to see.'

The shout crashed through Amity's consciousness. She looked up just in time to see a stark naked, plump female figure doing a cannonball into the pool. Next thing she knew, water was exploding all around them.

'What the hell,' Daniel muttered, as dazed and bewildered as Amity.

A round, vaguely familiar face burst to the surface of the water, beaming in satisfaction.

'Sorry. I couldn't let you two have too much fun in my mom's pool,' the intruder explained.

Amity squinted, trying to recall where she'd seen the apple cheeks, the cinnamon eyes. 'Crissy? Is that you? What are you doing here?'

'I live here,' said the girl also known as Dorothy. 'My mother owns this motel. I help her out with housekeeping and repairs, when business is slow at the Ranch. What are *you* two doing here?'

'Well, we were about five seconds away from some mind-blowing sex,' Daniel said. 'Then all of a sudden, Esther Williams leaps into the pool. I'm just glad you didn't land on our heads.'

Crissy giggled. 'Why? You got a problem with having a girl jump on your face?' She gave Amity a practised, flirty glance out of the corners of her eyes. Her hair, liberated from the hokey braids, dipped in a thick auburn swoop across her cheek. 'I bet your girlfriend's happy to see me again.'

'I'm not his girlfriend,' Amity said.

Crissy's curious brown eyes skated back and forth, from Amity to Daniel, then back again.

'Really? What kind of relationship do you have, then? I mean, when I came over here you looked like you would have needed a hose to get you apart. But then, you were already wet, so the hose would have been pointless.'

Amity wasn't about to touch that with a ten-foot pole. A long time seemed to pass while she waited for Daniel to supply an answer. He was smiling at her as he treaded water, probably enjoying himself immensely as he watched her squirm.

Finally she couldn't take Crissy's expectant silence anymore.

'He's my brother-in-law,' she admitted. Did that mean that what she and Daniel had been doing could qualify as incest? She'd never even thought of that.

'She's my fellow traveller on a mythical quest,' Daniel said at exactly the same time, drowning out Amity's reply.

'Mythical quest? Whoa. And here I thought you two were just looking for a party in the desert,' Crissy said. 'What's so mythical about it?'

Her berry-tipped breasts shimmered as she floated in the pool. Beads of water dripped from her hair, twinkling like tiny crystals against the rich red. She was a strawberry ice-cream girl, her skin all pink and white against the aquamarine. Daniel looked decidedly less annoyed with her now.

'I'm looking for something magic,' Daniel said. 'Something I lost a long time ago.'

'Looking for what?'

Daniel smiled. 'Long story. I'd rather hear about you. What's a cutie like you doing in a wasteland like this?'

Amity rolled her eyes. Envy started to dig its claws into her insides, then she felt Crissy's fingers clutch hers underwater. That sweet squeeze again – friendly, with something more. Crissy's hip sidled against Amity's, bumping and nudging her like a playful dolphin. Then her foot hooked Amity's leg, the arch of her foot running up and down Amity's calf. When her toes began to tickle the back of Amity's knee, arrows of pleasure shot up the insides of Amity's thighs.

'I've lived here ever since I can remember,' Crissy was saying. 'I can't really imagine being anywhere else.'

'So what's with the job at the Pussykat?' Daniel asked.

'Best job around, by a long shot. Money's great, you get to wear cute clothes, and there's lots of guys to buy you drinks. Plus, I love the sex. What can I say? I'm always horny.' She gave that giggle again, sending a corresponding thrill up the length of Amity's spine. 'And on the nights when it's slow with the dates, there's lots of girls to play with.'

'You like girls, huh?' Daniel's voice was huskier than usual.

I'm pretty sure she does, Amity thought, feeling the fabric of her panties sucking gently at her skin as Crissy tugged the waistband down. The elastic rolled past the curve of her bottom, and Crissy worked the cloth past the nook of Amity's crotch. The panties put up one last fight between Amity's thighs, till Crissy yanked them free. Once past Amity's knees, her underwear floated down to her ankles, and she kicked them off.

Free. Amity had never felt so free, or so terrified. Was that Crissy's wriggling body sending waves through the pool, or Amity's thumping pulse?

'I love girls,' Crissy replied. 'Especially girls like Amity.'

'What do you like about her?' Daniel asked. 'Tell me.'

'Uh, this conversation is getting weird,' Amity said.

Crissy gave Amity a coy, assessing look. 'She knows who she is. She doesn't put up with any bullshit. She's tough, but she's got a soft centre. All that's sexy, don't you think?'

'Absolutely. Makes you want to kiss her, doesn't it?'

'Oh, yes,' Crissy whispered.

She turned Amity by the shoulders and slipped her

hands around Amity's waist, supporting her body in the water. Her legs and Amity's were tangled together now, four sleek vines, all warm softness at the roots. Crissy's mouth was so close to Amity's that her soft breath warmed Amity's face. Crissy's lush lips, glistening with water, hung slightly open, and before Amity could say *Help!*, her mouth was filled with a fleshy sweetness, with the taste and texture of canned peaches.

Something round and hard was pushing Amity's legs apart, gliding upwards between her thighs, rocking against her pussy. With her senses still engulfed by Crissy's kiss, Amity didn't recognise the intrusion for what it was: Crissy's knee. She only knew that the most sensitive part of her body was being pried apart and massaged in a rhythm that matched the motions of Crissy's tongue.

The kiss was long, coaxing; it pulled unfamiliar desires out of Amity's body the way a magician draws scarves out of his sleeve. She'd never fantasised about doing the things that she was doing, but suddenly Amity wanted to touch every inch of Crissy's voluptuous body, not just with her hands, but with her lips and tongue. New hungers gave her the courage to sink her fingers into the deep curves of Crissy's breasts, while her thumbs brushed back and forth against her nipples.

Crissy moaned and tightened her grasp on Amity's waist. Her whole thigh was lodged between Amity's legs now, and Amity started to ride back and forth against the sleek surface. She had a vague memory of Daniel being in the pool with them, but she couldn't see him anywhere. Her consciousness had narrowed to the sensations that Crissy's lips and hands and knee – oh, that talented knee – were generating.

And because Amity didn't want to be the only passenger riding the pleasure train, she reached through the water and past the curves of Crissy's thighs to find the plump toy in between. Crissy had a strip of fur running the length of her mound, but her lips themselves were shaved bare. Inside, the plump shell was warm and unbelievably wet; the juices that had pooled inside her pussy seeped out over Amity's fingers. Amity found the familiar knot – easy to locate in its stiffened state – and rubbed it the way she liked to be rubbed, back and forth, then up and down. She found a tiny pulse beating behind Crissy's clit, and when she touched the throbbing place, Crissy's hips began to buck back and forth.

Amity never expected Crissy to come so quickly. She'd only been playing with that plump, squeaky-wet pussy for a few minutes before she felt the other girl go tense in her arms. Then Crissy's round brown eyes widened, her swollen mouth turned into an O of surprise, and a sound came out of those lips that must have woken everyone sleeping at the Desert Mirage Motel...

... which left Amity overflowing with the most incredible, sparkling thrill, her hands full of Crissy and her juices and her undulating flesh, like shiny coins spilling from a slot machine.

Did I do that? Amity wondered. Did I really do *that*?

But Amity didn't wonder for very long, because the surprise of Crissy's orgasm was melting into the reality of her own. The taut vibration of Crissy's body had set off corresponding currents in Amity's. When Crissy came, her leg scissored frantically back and forth in the groove between Amity's thighs, and that climactic dance sent Amity into her own la-la land. A wave of heat washed through her body, in delicious contrast with the slightly cooler water, and for a few seconds she was suspended in a tingling contradiction of sensations inspired by Crissy and the pool and her own emotions – warmth against coolness, firm muscle under satiny skin, lust and fear and a needle-sharp pleasure that was so close to pain that Amity didn't know what to do with herself – until the climax released her, washing away all those contradictions in one river of joy.

Daniel was there the whole time, somewhere in the background, silent as a shadow.

According to the rules of sexual behaviour that Amity had learnt from the few porno videos she'd seen, he should have joined the two women somewhere around the first kiss. He definitely should have broken into the action by the time Crissy was flailing and shrieking in the water.

So what was the problem? Had he been waiting for an engraved invitation? Or had Amity done something in the pool that night that turned him off her permanently?

Even with a giggling Crissy hugging her in the water, keeping her afloat like the world's sexiest inflatable pool toy as she covered Amity's face with grateful butterfly kisses, Amity felt a tremor of disappointment when Daniel pulled himself out of the pool, wrapped himself in a towel, and walked silently back to the motel room.

He'd never seen anything like that scene in the pool that night, not even in his most outrageous teenage fantasies. Back in the fat days of 3-Way Dream, there'd been lots of orgiastic post-concert parties where he'd watched girls wriggling around naked together on beds or floors or hotel coffee tables, but Daniel had always felt like he was watching their antics from a distance, either through a haze of booze, or from a pinnacle of boredom.

Those groupies were just a bunch of drugged-up party girls, interchangeably gorgeous, performing for the band. Looking back at everything he'd seen and done in those days, Daniel found it hard to believe that he'd never watched two sober women making honest love – not to turn a guy on, or to make themselves look like hawt bi chicks, or to promote their fledgling modelling/ acting careers, but just because they wanted each other.

Tonight had blown Daniel away.

Daniel had seen Crissy talking to Amity in the lounge at the Pussykat Ranch, wearing those tacky pigtails and overalls like some kind of twisted Rebecca of Sunnybrook Farm. He figured that when she did her naked cannonball dive into the pool that night, she was looking for some fun to relieve the monotony of working, to remind herself why she liked to have sex in the first place. It never occurred to Daniel that she'd wanted Amity from the beginning.

Seeing how much Crissy wanted Amity, watching the way she stared at her, stroked her, kissed her, and made her come like a mountain lion, confirmed something that Daniel already knew, but couldn't bring himself to admit.

He wanted Amity, too. He didn't just want to mess around with her the way he'd been doing in the car that day. He wanted to play her body the way Crissy had, and kiss her till she made those same imploring whimpers and moans. He wanted to make her come so hard she arched her back and bucked ever-so-slightly back and forth, the way she'd done in the pool, her hair swirling in the water behind her.

If he'd wanted to slide between the two girls, Daniel was pretty sure they wouldn't have objected. In fact, Crissy had thrown him a few flirtatious glances that made it clear she welcomed him to join in. At first, he wanted to ... god, how he wanted to. What could be sweeter than being at the centre of that knot of girlflesh?

Then he saw the light in Amity's eyes, heard the plea in her open mouth, and he thought, no. It didn't feel right. He would have been an intruder, stomping through her paradise in muddy boots.

So Daniel had just sat back on the concrete steps of the pool, drinking it all in with his eyes. And when the girls had had their fun, he got out of the pool and left. No sense in killing anyone's afterglow; by that time, he truly felt like a third wheel. He'd gone back to the motel room and done what men always did when they were alone and unbearably horny. Then he took a warm shower and crawled into one of the two double beds. He took the bed farthest from the air conditioner. After that scorching encounter tonight, Amity was going to need some cooling down.

Daniel's dreams were weird that night, weird and filled with women. He was cruising down the highway in the blue Thunderbird, but this time he was driving, and he was going it alone. The desert sky was Day-Glo pink, streaked with green and red. Purple tumbleweeds the size of Volkswagens skidded across the highway, and strands of orange-and-blue clouds flew in accelerated motion across the sky. Cacti rose out of the dreamscape like gnarled hands, and nothing broke the flat stretch of road and sand but a series of female hitchhikers.

Each female Daniel passed was a woman he knew, and every one of them was trying to thumb a ride with him. There was his mom, his kid sister, then the pretty second cousin he'd made out with at a family reunion when he was sixteen. A whole chorus line of ex-girlfriends materialised, then he saw Amity and Crissy standing together with their arms around each others' waists, two duffel bags at their feet. Heather appeared a mile or two beyond them, posed with one sexy leg extended, her blonde hair haloing a pouting face. Miz Bunny and her stable of pussycats formed their line at the side of the road, under a sign advertising a reptile museum called Bob's Herp-O-Rama.

All these apparitions were odd but predictable. The one woman Daniel didn't expect to see was Sadie.

Sadie O? Grady. The one and only. Unlike the others, she wasn't looking for a ride; she was already coasting through the air, her arms spread like wings, crimson mohawk glowing above a wicked grin. She loomed over the open convertible like a bird of prey, hovering so close that Daniel could almost touch her. Clad in skin-tight black leather from head to toe and a pair of Frankenstein boots, she looked like she was decked out for a mosh pit, or a leather bar. Daniel didn't care about her plans for the evening. All he wanted was his guitar. He reached up and made a grab for her ankle, but she zoomed away, lifted by an air current.

*Keep tailing me, Danny*, the vision taunted. *You'll never, ever catch me. Besides, what difference would it make? You hocked your gift long before you hocked that guitar.*

Daniel sat up in bed, waking with a jolt. Light from the fluorescent bulb hanging outside the room seeped through the ugly drapes. Amity was sleeping in the bed beside him. She slept on her back, her right arm crooked over her head. Lying next to her on the bed was Blue Molly, freed from her case, her neck resting on the pillow nearest to the window. Amity must have been working something out on the guitar before she went to sleep, some song that had been stuck in her head, or maybe just a riff trying to take shape.

She had the spark. Whatever it was that struck a flame in a person's soul and made them want to write songs, or dance, or dig ditches, or whatever they did, Amity had it. Her face was turned towards him now, and though he couldn't make out her features clearly, he could see her lips curving in a smile.

Amity looked pleased with herself for the first time since Daniel had met her. He hadn't known she had that *Mona Lisa* smirk in her repertoire of expressions. Wary, worried, skeptical and every now and then amused, but just plain happy? Daniel hadn't seen it.

He felt a pang of guilt.

She sighed in her sleep, and her smile grew even wider.

*Enjoy yourself, little girl,* Daniel thought. *You look damn pretty when you're having those sweet dreams.*

Country music usually made Heather want to puke, unless it crossed over into familiar pop territory. She didn't recognise the singer whose throaty twang she was dancing to in the swanky hotel room, but she sure as hell recognised the glimmer in Roscoe's eyes.

It was the light of the loaded, the illumination that came from having tons of money and a pretty girl to spend it on. Roscoe had already spent at least half an inch of the bills in his golden eagle money clip on Heather. He'd bought her the pretty white ostrich-trimmed nightie and white satin mules she was wearing, and the twinkly rhinestone tiara that was nestled in her golden curls.

'How do I look?' Heather asked, pirouetting in front of her silver-haired cowboy. Roscoe was sitting back in one of the hotel's arm chairs, a Louis XIV replica upholstered in pale-blue velvet. He sipped champagne – not Cristal, but it wasn't cold duck, either – from the glass flute that room service had delivered with the bucket of ice and the chilled magnum.

'You look so good in love, baby,' Roscoe crooned, echoing the country singer's lyrics. 'Lord, I never thought I'd live to see a gorgeous blonde angel dancing to George Strait.'

Heather paused for a moment. She pressed her forefinger against her upper lip and gave Roscoe a look of wide-eyed confusion.

'Gorgeous? Lil' old me?'

He gave her a gallant smile and lifted his glass. 'Honey, you're *ex*-quisite,' he said, putting the emphasis on the 'ex' in a way that sounded a bit tacky to Heather's ears. 'Just like this champagne.'

Heather had sampled the champagne. The bubbly had

tasted sour to her, and she hadn't recognised the name on the bottle. But she knew Roscoe was right about her beauty. Heather was a star, and her husband had been an idiot to leave her in Vegas alone. Without ever meeting Daniel, Roscoe had been able to give Heather the rundown on what kind of man he was. A lot of rock musicians burned out young, Roscoe said. Ran out of money and talent at around the same time, if they were lucky, and ended up wiping tables at a hamburger stand before they were thirty. When Heather told him about Daniel's search for his lost guitar, Roscoe had howled.

'Honey, I don't know whether to laugh or cry,' Roscoe had said, wiping a tear from his weathered cheek. 'That's a damn fool notion if I ever heard one. Thinking he could find that guitar is silly enough, but does the poor boy honestly believe it's going to make him rich again?'

'Daniel doesn't care about getting rich,' Heather had said. She felt like she should defend her husband, even though he'd dumped her to go on that foolish mission. 'He just wants to be able to play music the way he used to.'

'Listen, baby doll, he cares. That's all musicians want, money and tail. Trust me. I know.'

Roscoe did know – he was a music promoter, he said. He travelled around the Southwestern United States, going from bars to rodeos to county fairs, sniffing out new talent. Roscoe would take these young, wet-behind-the-ears performers and mould them into professional country music singers, who might or might not become stars.

'I could make you a star, baby doll,' Roscoe was saying. He squinted through the smoke of his cigarette as he watched Heather lift one leg over her head, then slowly lower it and slide down onto the floor into a full split. He'd told her not to wear panties under the short white gown, just a garter belt, sheer white stockings, and the white mules with pompons. He would have bought her a pair of fairy wings, but the exotic dancewear boutique was out of stock. Wings were a popular item in Vegas these days, the sales clerk had said. Lots of men with angel fetishes, apparently, or maybe they were just searching for some cheap redemption.

'Me?' Heather perked up. 'You mean you represent dancers, too?'

'No dancers. Just singers.'

Heather wrinkled her nose. 'I can't sing, Roscoe. Not even in the shower. I can lip synch, but my real voice sucks.'

'Hell, honey, that don't matter. We'll teach you to sing. The important thing is, you've got the look. That sweet Sunday school innocence, with just a touch of the nasty girl. Why don't you come on over here and we'll discuss the details?'

Roscoe's voice was deeply soothing, as if his vocal chords had been steeped in aged whiskey. He leant back in the armchair and patted his left thigh.

Heather pranced over, adjusting her tiara, and perched on Roscoe's leg. His muscles were taut and hard, like the tent rising between his thighs. He circled Heather's waist with his left arm and pulled her closer. The spicy smell of his aftershave, mingled with cigarette smoke and leather, was making her feel all moist and tingly down below. His long, firm arm felt strong enough to protect her from anything, even a broken heart. Wearing her transparent white nightie and sparkling tiara, sitting next to this older man with the suntan and the money clip, Heather had never felt so safe ... or so sexy.

She made a small mewling sound and wiggled her bottom. Roscoe lifted the feather-trimmed hem of her gown and lovingly patted her right cheek.

'You're such a beautiful little girl,' he said. 'Were you good today?'

Heather nodded. 'I was very, very good.'

'Are you sure about that?' Roscoe's voice took on a darker note. 'That's not what I heard. Maybe you'd like to change your story.'

'No. I was a good girl. I swear!'

Heather's eyes widened as she shook her head back and forth. Her denial was a bit too enthusiastic, and her tiara slipped down her forehead.

'Then why is your halo falling off, angel?' Roscoe put the tiara back in its curly blonde nest. His big fingers looked like they could wrap themselves all the way around a bull calf's neck, but they were incredibly gentle as they replaced the ornament in Heather's hair. And they were even more gentle when they worked their way under Heather's nightie, sliding up her thigh, and eased her legs apart.

'Good girls don't get this wet,' Roscoe drawled. ''Fraid you've been lying to me all along, baby doll.'

He inserted his forefinger between Heather's lips. The digit slid in effortlessly, proving his point. Heather gasped. Blushed. This was all so horribly, deliciously humiliating! Using his other hand, he cupped one of her breasts through the filmy fabric and rubbed her nipple with his thumb. The little pink bud had begun to stiffen before Roscoe touched it, but as soon as the calloused ball of his thumb made contact, the nipple got unbearably hard. Meanwhile, Roscoe had begun rolling his fingertip around the pearl at the heart of her pussy, and Heather was getting so wet that she was afraid of soaking Roscoe's trousers.

What would he do to her then? she thought with a shiver of terrified delight.

As if he'd been reading her thoughts, Roscoe's face darkened. His silver moustache drooped with the downward curve of his frown.

'You'd better not be making a mess on my trousers,' Roscoe said sternly. 'I just had this suit dry-cleaned.'

'I didn't do anything! I promise.'

'Move that bottom of yours so I can see for myself. Stand up,' he ordered.

Heather obeyed.

Roscoe ran his palm up the length of his thigh. There wasn't any visible dampness on the cloth, but he made a tsk-tsk sound through his thick moustache and gave Heather a disapproving scowl.

'Just what I thought. You can't control yourself, can you?'

Heather stared at the ground and chewed her lower lip. Tears welled up at the corners of her eyes, and gravity sent them spilling onto the carpet. Damn, Roscoe was good. The game they were playing felt so real that Heather was going to bawl like a baby if he kept going. How far was he going to take this? His hands were so massive, with their broad, toughened palms ... if he intended to spank her, Heather was going to be in for some serious pain.

'I didn't do anything,' Heather muttered. She twisted her finger in her mouth.

'Are you contradicting me?'

Heather pouted. 'No, Sir. I'm just saying that I didn't mean –'

'Hush,' Roscoe interrupted. 'I'm sorry, sweetheart, but I'm going to have to punish you. Sometimes a headstrong little filly like yourself needs discipline.'

He patted his leg again, only this time, the clap of hand against muscle had an ominous ring. 'Go get my hairbrush from the dresser, doll. Then I want you to come back here and bend over.'

'What?' Heather giggled nervously.

'Get my brush, then get over my knee,' he repeated. 'I want your belly right over my leg and your sweet arse up in the air.'

Heather knew she didn't have a choice. What's more, she didn't want a choice at this point. Mingled with her fear and shame was an excitement so keen that her legs were barely holding her upright. She wobbled like a newborn filly as she walked the seven or eight steps to the fake French dresser and found Roscoe's hairbrush. Sure enough, it was one of those wide, square-backed man-brushes with the tortoiseshell handle and the black boar's bristles, the only kind of brush that a distinguished cowboy like Roscoe would use on his thick grey hair.

She picked up the brush and teetered back to Roscoe's chair. In all her years of doing beauty pageants, talent shows, modelling and dancing, Heather had never felt so self-conscious in front of an audience. Roscoe's stern gaze was focused on her every step, and knowing what was in store for her, those steps were pretty damn unsteady. As gracelessly as she was walking, Heather might as well have been drunk, and right about now she was wishing that she was.

A little buzz would soften the edges of the pain.

Heather had met a few girls at the Tucan Club who claimed to be kinky. They talked casually about being handcuffed, spanked, or even whipped by their dates, as if all that stuff were as normal to them as having their legs waxed or their hair cut. Heather couldn't relate to that at all. Tears sprang to her eyes at any unpleasant stimulus; even a paper cut could make her want to curl up into a ball and cry. But here she was with this cowboy, whose eagerness to spank her was written all over his tanned, handsome face.

'Is something wrong?' Roscoe asked. 'You look like you're about to cry, angel. Don't be scared. I'll be gentle. Just bend on over and you'll see how gentle I can be.'

He accompanied this order with another resounding slap of his thigh. The slap wasn't very reassuring. Heather jumped.

'I don't ... I haven't ... I've never been spanked,' she said.

'Never? A naughty thing like you?' he teased. 'Oh, come on. There must have been a few times when you needed some correction. Your parents weren't those spare-the-rod types, were they?'

'No.' Heather wasn't even sure what that meant, but she was pretty sure that it didn't apply to her mother Candi or her parade of boyfriends and husbands. 'I just never got a spanking. I was always good. And the few times I was bad, nobody noticed.'

'Oh, baby.' Roscoe's voice lowered to a sympathetic croon. 'That's just pitiful. Nobody cared enough to spank you?'

'I never thought about it that way, but I guess they didn't. My mom was always off on a date, or at the hairdresser's, or her aerobics class.'

'And what about your daddy? Spanking is usually a daddy's job. At least it was on the ranch where I grew up.'

Self-pity zigzagged through Heather's heart, threatening to crack her open. Roscoe was right. Her stepmother hadn't cared about her, and her father, well...

'I never knew my dad,' she said with a sniffle. 'Neither did my mom. She got pregnant at a party one night when she was in cosmetology school. She couldn't remember the guy's name. She got married a few times after that, but her husbands didn't stay around for very long. Some of them didn't even know she had a daughter until they were in the middle of the divorce and she was claiming alimony.'

'What about your husband?' Roscoe prompted gently.

'Daniel? Oh, my gosh, Daniel wouldn't slap a fly if it was crawling across his forehead,' Heather said. 'He's *so* not into causing pain.'

'That's not what I meant, baby doll.'

'What did you mean?'

Roscoe fixed her with that penetrating, no-nonsense stare that turned her on so much. 'Doesn't your husband give you enough lovin' to make up for all those stepdaddies who didn't know you were around?'

Heather couldn't answer that one. A whole host of ugly thoughts came seething out of the dark place where she'd stuffed them. Daniel really didn't love her all that much; if he did, he wouldn't have run away, with her ugly stepsister, no less. Even if he were totally devoted to Heather's needs, as a husband should be, Daniel was never going to be a big success. Looking for that dumb guitar was just buying him time until he had to face the truth.

Heather lifted her chin. 'No,' she replied. 'My husband doesn't love me enough.'

'Just what I thought.' A sly smile spread across the cowboy's face. 'That's why you need some Roscoe in your life. Now scoot your little behind over here and let me show you how love feels.'

Heather trotted over to Roscoe and knelt between his long lean legs. He took Heather's slim white hand in his big leathery paw and planted it directly on the taut tent that had risen between his thighs.

'Feel that?' he asked. 'That's love.'

Heather nodded, mute with awe. The rod of flesh under her hand felt as thick as Jack's beanstalk. Roscoe was possibly the most well-endowed man she'd ever felt. How did she get so lucky, finding a man with money, an enormous tool, and a heart overflowing with love for her?

Next thing she knew, Heather had surrendered the tortoiseshell hairbrush and was draping herself over Roscoe's thigh. Promising once again to be gentle, he lifted the skirt of her nightie. The air conditioner's artificial breeze drifted across her bottom, giving her a chill and a thrill at the same time. She wiggled her hips against Roscoe's thigh, generating bursts of pleasure in her loins.

Roscoe chuckled. 'You want that spanking now, don't you?'

'Oh, yes!'

'Beg me,' he taunted, rubbing the sleek tortoiseshell back and forth against her nude bottom. 'Beg pretty.'

Heather begged. She pleaded. She made small, mewling animal sounds and confessed that she was a bad, bad girl who needed to be punished. She prayed for that spanking until she was flooded with honey-sweet humiliation, and just when she'd exhausted her last resources for begging, Roscoe raised the brush and landed a firm smack across her backside.

The sting of the swats that followed took her by surprise. At first, all she felt was pain, then the ache turned into something sly and warm and promising, a prickle that left her craving more. Soon she was arching her back, bucking and squealing. Her flesh was on fire, but she couldn't get enough. Roscoe moved from her bottom to the tender backs of her thighs, so that her entire lower body became one big pleasure zone, with her pussy right at the centre. By the time Roscoe inserted the tortoiseshell handle into the place that would please her most, Heather was completely infatuated with that hairbrush. She would never, ever fail to appreciate those ugly man-brushes again, she thought, as the in-and-out motions of the handle carried her into bliss.

When she recovered, Roscoe turned Heather's attention back to the pup tent she'd been admiring earlier.

'That was a star performance, baby doll,' he said, unzipping his fly. 'Now I've got a present for you that's really going to make you smile.'

Heather sighed happily. Reaching into Roscoe's pale-blue boxers to pull out his erection really was like opening a long-awaited gift. The rod of flesh was as impressive as she'd expected: pink and stout and beautifully sculpted, like a penis from one of those *Playgirl* magazines that she and her girlfriends used to titter over in high school. Most men's cocks couldn't come close to those idealised, airbrushed organs, but Roscoe's was so close to perfect that it took Heather's breath away.

She found her breath again very quickly as she set to work with her lips and tongue, performing one of the acts that would never be featured in her portfolio. That was a shame, because Heather loved fellatio almost as much as her boyfriends loved to get it from her. With Roscoe's gorgeous penis filling her mouth, she felt soothed, content and excited all at once.

Just like Christmas morning ... only better.

## Chapter Eight

# Fight-or-Flight Syndrome

*Miles driven since Vegas*: 118
*$$ spent on gas*: Still in denial

The situation with the T-Bird isn't as bad as I thought. The wheel itself wasn't wracked; we just blew a tyre. But the mechanic pointed out that the other three tyres were practically bald; we're going to need a whole new set if we're going to have a prayer of making it to LA. I didn't ask him how much it was going to cost, just shut my eyes and handed over my Visa.

Good news is that Crissy says we can make a few bucks back playing a gig at the roadhouse a couple of miles down the interstate. She's the grand-niece of the guy who owns the place (everyone here is related to everyone else – their genes must be way screwed up), and he needs a band to play tomorrow night. Sir Galahad by himself isn't exactly a band, but there are a few local boys who can back him up.

Which is why I don't understand why they want me, too.

Maybe they're short on girls out here in the desert, and they figure having a chick get up and sing will attract a bigger audience. Even if it's just me, with my old acoustic banging against my flat chest.

(Sorry, Blue Molly. You didn't hear me call you 'old'.)

Here's a stab at a chorus for that song I'm working on. If it works itself out OK, I might play it at the roadhouse.

*Maybe if I staged a collision*
*That tore this T-Bird apart*
*You'd love me for being a victim*
*Of my reckless head-on heart.*

Won't be the most sophisticated audience of all time – if they're drunk enough by the time I get up to sing, they won't even notice if my song sucks.

After they got the news about the car, Daniel spent the afternoon on the phone, making calls to LA on Amity's Visa. Why were musicians always so expensive? she thought mournfully, as she watched him punch in one ten-digit number after another. He seemed to be calling everyone in the Greater Los Angeles area, from guitarists he'd jammed with to backup singers to models to waiters to promoters. In LA, all of those roles merged into one big horde struggling to break through, or to make money off of someone who was breaking through.

'Any luck finding Sadie?' Amity asked. She was lying on her stomach on one of the beds, flipping back and forth between the two fuzzy TV channels that were available at the Desert Mirage if you didn't pay for cable.

'Everyone says they know someone who partied with someone who might have run into her at a gig or something,' Daniel said. 'Then they give me the cellphone number of that first someone, and I call that number, and they tell me the same thing.'

His voice was steeped in cynicism, and his body slumped as if he'd aged twenty years since he got on the phone. Amity studied him over her shoulder, but he didn't return the look. He hadn't made eye contact with her since they kissed in the pool the previous night. He probably assumed she'd gone over to the other side when she made love with Crissy instead of with him.

'At least you got to talk to some old friends,' Amity said.

'Friends? Darlin' you've got a lot to learn about the biz.' Daniel stood up and stretched, his jaw cracking in a giant yawn. 'Your friends are only your friends as long as you've got money, connections, or some good drugs. I have none of the above. I'm surprised any of those people spent cell time on me.'

'I still think LA is worth a try. We have to keep the faith. Don't lose your confidence just because you got a few false leads.'

Daniel stopped in mid-stretch. 'Did I just hear what I think I heard? Was that my sceptical fellow traveller expressing some faith in me?'

'I'm all about faith,' Amity shrugged. 'Otherwise I wouldn't be here at all.'

Faith, love, hope and charity – all the classic Puritan virtues had come into play on this little trip. Then there was love, that big messy monster that Amity kept trying to shove under the bed. She couldn't tell Daniel any of this; this wasn't a good time for confessions.

'Listen, I need to get out and shake this evil mood,' Daniel said. 'Want to come with?'

Amity didn't have to be asked twice; between Daniel's mood and the sulphuric light that filtered in through the ochre curtains, the atmosphere in the room was getting her down.

A blast of mid-afternoon heat scorched their faces as soon as they stepped out the door. One thing you could say for the Desert Mirage, the air conditioning was effective. By the time Amity and Daniel had walked down the interstate to Charlene's, the general store-slash-gas station-slash-autobody shop where Amity had left the car, they were both ready to pass out.

'Let's spend the next six hours in here. What do you say?' Daniel asked, as he opened the door of the store for Amity. 'It's air-conditioned. That's about as high as my hopes can get today.'

'Sounds good to me.'

Charlene's had no clearcut identity; the front half of the building looked like any other convenience store, stocked with overpriced soda pop and candy, plastic-wrapped bakery products of unknown shelf-life, and a mysteriously broad array of canned meats. One corner was devoted to automotive products, another to an assortment of obscene T-shirts and tacky gambling souvenirs. And in the very back of the store, in a corner that would have been invisible to casual shoppers unless they passed it on their way to the grubby public restroom, Daniel discovered a pirate's cove of ancient treasures.

'Hey! Records!'

Amity, who was pondering whether canned ham or canned chicken were more likely to be tainted with salmonella, replaced both cans on the shelf and hurried over to the corner. She found Daniel digging through a box of albums. They were actual vinyl records, arranged by decade in cardboard boxes. Most were 78s, but there was a small stack of 45s. Daniel's face glowed.

'God, these old covers were cheesy,' he said, holding up an album with a misty portrait of a barefoot nude with curly golden hair, looking more than a little stoned as she gazed across a field of daisies. Her daisy crown was tipping off her head.

'She looks a lot like Heather,' Amity said.

As soon as the words came out, she wanted to kick herself. Why on earth had she mentioned her stepsister, at the one time when Daniel was actually looking happy? Daniel's fingers stopped moving through the albums for a moment. His shoulders tensed. Amity waited for the inevitable breakdown and wished she could rewind the last thirty seconds of her life.

'Wow. I can't believe it. Check this out! I used to worship this album.'

Daniel turned around, holding *Electric Ladyland*, the double album by Jimi Hendrix. Amity saw no trace of Heather in his eyes, only excitement over the album he was holding.

Did you hear what just came out of my big, dumb mouth? Amity wanted to ask. Did you hear me blurt out your wife's name?

Daniel, if he'd noticed, showed no sign of caring. He was too excited about his reunion with Jimi.

'I've got to hear this again.' He waved the album in the air in the direction of the sales clerk. 'Hey, do you guys have a machine we can play these on?'

'They keep some old piece of junk in the employee lounge,' yawned the teenage clerk, pointing towards the back of the store. 'Don't ask me how to use the thing.'

'Let's go. Grab as many of those albums as you can. We'll sort them out when we get back there.'

Daniel piled records into Amity's arms, and they set off in search of the record player. The employee lounge was a windowless room, equipped with a refrigerator, sink and microwave oven; a cigarette-scarred card table; a set of folding chairs; an orange-upholstered sofa; and a lamp table. Instead of a lamp, the battered wooden table held a record player, circa 1975. Amity's father had owned one just like it. Strange how these machines and instruments and albums kept circulating through the music world, she thought. It was almost as if there were just a handful of those magical objects in the universe, all being passed around from one music fanatic to another at garage sales, pawn shops, second-hand stores.

'Cool. Here's our afternoon's entertainment,' Daniel announced, dumping his pile of records on the orange couch. He pulled *Electric Ladyland* off the top of the stack. 'This album came out in 1968,' he said, his voice lowered to a reverent hush. 'It's a masterpiece of psychedelic rock. My dad owned this album. I stole it from him when I was twelve. I played it constantly till I was fifteen.'

'What happened when you were fifteen?' Amity asked. 'Let me guess. You got a stereo with a CD player, and you threw your record player out your bedroom window.'

Daniel grinned as he slid one of the vinyl discs out of the sleeve. He stopped for a moment to gaze at Jimi Hendrix's face, cast in gold on the cover.

'I wasn't quite that shallow, Amity. Think back to the legend of Daniel Goldstein. When I was fifteen, I got my Gibson Girl, remember?'

'Oh, yeah. Like I could forget that.'

'I had to ignore the record player for a while so I could practise. Hendrix would have approved. When he was that age, he used to run around playing an old acoustic guitar that he found somewhere. It only had one string. Your first guitar means everything. Doesn't matter what it's got, or what it's missing. Doesn't matter whether you got it all wrapped up as a birthday present, or whether you dragged it out of a dumpster. With that first guitar, you work out the rest of your life on those strings. You engrave your story in your own flesh and blood.'

Amity considered this. 'Listen, not to question our mission or anything, but if that story's engraved in your flesh, what do you need that old Gibson for? She's already left her mark on you. Right?'

Daniel paused, holding the record between his palms as he pondered the question. He didn't look at Amity as he gingerly dusted the album's vinyl surface with his shirt tail.

'Did you ever get a scar when you were a kid, and you thought it looked cool, and you thought you'd have it forever? But then it changed, or disappeared, and you missed it?' Daniel asked.

Amity nodded. She was thinking about the tiny white half-moon that intersected her right eyebrow. She'd got the scar from the whip-thin branch of a tree that had smacked her in the forehead when she was walking home from school one day. Actually, the tree hadn't hit Amity; it had been the other way around. She'd walked head-on into the branch while strumming her guitar. Now the scar was invisible to anyone but Amity. Daniel was right; she missed that scar. It reminded her that on one day of her life, she'd been so lost in her music that she'd forgotten all about the world around her.

'And sometimes those scars get so faded that you can't find them, or they move to a different place on your body when your body grows, and you can't read them as easily,' Daniel went on. 'That's why I need my Gibson Girl. It's not because I don't have that story in my skin anymore, it's because I need her to teach me how to read again. Does that make sense?'

'Yes,' Amity said. 'It probably shouldn't, but it does.'

'It makes sense to you, because you're just like me,' Daniel said.

He settled the album carefully on the turntable, turned on the machine, and placed the needle on the vinyl at random. Before Amity could ask him what he meant by his last remark, he was changing subjects, as if his words hadn't made the ground quake under Amity's feet.

Did he really think that they were exactly alike? People could be 'alike' in a million ways. 'Alike' as in identical twins. Drinking buddies. Tennis partners.

Soul mates.

'What did you mean...' Amity started to say, but Daniel was already skating ahead with maddening grace and speed.

'I never start from the beginning of an album with Hendrix,' he explained. 'I just close my eyes and let the needle fall wherever Jimi wants me to go that day.'

The jazz groove of 'Rainy Day, Dream Away' filled the shabby room, and the heat of a desert afternoon suddenly dissolved into the cool percussion of a summer urban rainshower.

Amity wanted to forget, for a moment, about how frustrated she was with Daniel. She closed her eyes and swayed back and forth, letting the electric organ lull her into dreamland as the conga drums sent her into a private bump-and-grind. She was so lost in the music that she didn't hear Daniel step up behind her; she didn't know he was standing so close until she felt his arms slide around her waist, his fingers interlocking just below her belly button, trapping her in the muscular cage of his arms. His chin was resting on her shoulder, and his breath in her ear was like the hiss of raindrops after they slap against a warm sidewalk.

'Jimi made the perfect choice, as always,' Daniel murmured.

With the fingers of one hand, he toyed with the hoop in her navel, sending delicious little shockwaves through her whole lower body. With the other hand, he made his way from the crest of her hipbone, down across to her crotch. He stopped just before he got to the risky point of the V, where Amity was already feeling loose and warm and a little wet.

'Hey, don't forget, this is an employees' lounge,' Amity reminded him. 'People come in here to eat sandwiches and stuff. Someone could walk in any minute.'

'You catch on fast,' Daniel teased. 'There's probably some store clerk or janitor out there, thinking about coming back to the lounge to heat up last night's leftover casserole. His stomach starts to rumble. He looks at the clock. He's got seven minutes till he gets to take his break. That gives me just enough time to do this...'

Quick as a gunman in an old Western, Daniel unsnapped the top button on Amity's shorts. Before she could do anything more than squeak, Daniel had slipped a hand under the waistband of her panties. He held his hand still for a few moments, letting his palm warm to the temperature of her skin as he nuzzled the shallow groove that ran from her ear lobe down the length of her neck. A tremor shook Amity all over as the pilot light in the depths of her body flared into life.

Delicately he took her earlobe between his teeth and tugged, grinding his incisors against the flesh just enough so that she got a zinger of pain on top of the thrilling sensations he was making with his hips and hands. When she looked down at the floor, she saw his Converse sneakers planted on either side of her feet. His forearms were locked around her waist, and his chest was pressed firmly into the space between her shoulder blades. His pelvis rocked against her arse to the beat of the music; she couldn't have escaped that magnetic connection if she tried.

Amity was so seductively, skilfully trapped that she couldn't move anything but her mouth.

'What are you doing, Daniel?'

His laughter was deep and low and very, very raunchy. 'Trying to make you come in seven minutes. Six minutes, now.'

His hand shifted to a more strategic location. He was parting her lower lips with two fingers, and probing the warm folds inside. Amity had a pretty good idea what he was looking for. By the time he reached his hard pink target, Amity was halfway gone.

'Does this mean you weren't turned off by the things I did with Crissy in the pool last night?' Amity asked.

Daniel froze, but only momentarily. 'You've got to be kidding. I've waited my whole life to see something like that. I was so turned on, I thought I was going to pass out and drown.'

'Is that why you left?'

'That, and...' he hesitated.

'And what? Why did you get out of the pool?'

'I felt like I was in the way. Like I was spoiling a beautiful private moment between two unbelievably hot women.'

Amity turned her head, incredulous. 'You think I'm hot?'

Daniel sighed. 'I'm standing here with my arms wrapped around you, my hand down your pants, and my lips all over your neck. What does it seem like I'm doing? Waiting for a bus?'

'I thought you might be playing with my head. Like you always do.'

Amity couldn't believe it, but she found herself breaking away from Daniel, dousing out the flames. She loved the way his hands and mouth sent ribbons of lust curling through her belly. She loved his faintly smoky scent; Daniel didn't smoke, but his hair and skin always had a faintly woodsy smell, like a campfire. She loved the way he looked at her just before he kissed her, as if he didn't know whether to laugh at her or eat her alive.

She did not love feeling like she was standing in quicksand whenever he touched her. Amity buttoned up her shorts and smoothed her tangled hair.

Daniel groaned and shoved his hands in his pockets. 'Tell me what's wrong. We're going to be clocking a lot more travel time together, so you might as well spill it now.'

'Whenever you kiss me, or put your arms around me, you're playing a game. I don't know what it is, but I have a feeling I'm going to lose.'

'Lose? To Heather, you mean?' Daniel scratched his head, as if any competition between Heather and Amity were a big mystery to him.

'Bingo.'

Amity turned off the record player in the middle of

'All Along The Watchtower'. Hendrix's cover of Dylan. Amity loved both versions. She loved the way one artist could pay tribute to an artist he admired by recording a song he'd written. That was the way the music world worked at its best: one person giving to another. But when it came to passing lovers around, or leaping from one to another, giving could go too far.

'Heather,' Daniel muttered. 'You are so different from Heather, it's not even funny.'

'I know. That's my point.'

'Well, you'd better explain that to me, because I still don't get what your point really is.'

Amity had her mouth opened and was about to enlighten Daniel, when the door of the lounge opened. In walked the teenage clerk who'd been slouching at the counter in front of the store. The kid gave them a cursory wave, then ambled over to the refrigerator. He removed a Tupperware dish from the refrigerator and popped it into the ancient crusted microwave.

'Leftovers?' Daniel asked the clerk. He looked at Amity out of the corners of his eyes.

'Yeah. My mom made a tuna casserole last night. Boring as dirt, but I'm too broke to hit McDonald's today.'

Stifling laughter, Amity and Daniel carried their armfuls of records out of the lounge.

'Did I call it, or did I call it?' Daniel gloated, as they replaced the records in meticulous chronological and alphabetical order. 'A kid with a casserole. He was timing us. Too bad we weren't doing anything worth watching when he came in.'

Amity shot him an evil glare.

'One more word, and I'll bring up your *wife* again,' she threatened.

'Ouch,' Daniel winced. 'Look, I'll make you a deal. Let's call a truce, at least until tonight's gig is over. At the end of the evening, if we still want to hash this out, we can hit that all-night diner and fight over black coffee. What do you say?'

Amity scowled. She was trying to replace a copy of Olivia Newton John's *Xanadu* into an overpacked box, but the record wouldn't fit. No matter how she jammed the cardboard square, it wouldn't fit.

'Here. Give me that. You can't abuse a goddess that way.' Daniel took the album from her and eased it into the box with one smooth motion. 'Relax, darlin'. You don't want to fight anymore, do you?'

'The fight can wait,' Amity said ominously. 'But it's coming.'

'Can't wait,' Daniel sighed.

Heather lay snuggled up against Roscoe on the king-size bed, her arm draped across his chest. She dozed in the blissful aftermath of a double orgasm – or maybe it had been a triple. She'd lost count. Roscoe had been as good with his tongue, his fingers and his cock as he was with that hairbrush, and all of those tools had been focused entirely on Heather. When was the last time she'd been spoiled that way? He'd given her the doting, utterly indulgent love that she'd always longed for. Daniel's puppydog adoration seemed adolescent by comparison.

Roscoe's free hand was ensnared in Heather's curls, playing with the masses of blonde coils.

'Pure gold,' he murmured. 'One hundred carats. Sweetheart, if only that gold were metal, I'd be a rich man again.'

The romantic soundtrack that had been playing in Heather's head screeched to a hideous halt. Every muscle in her body turned to stone, but her senses were suddenly on hyper-alert. She looked around the hotel room, as if seeing it for the first time, and realised that the room was second-rate, its furniture nicked and shabby. Under Roscoe's expensive aftershave, she detected an acrid scent, which she hadn't been able to place until now. The smell was sheer desperation.

All of the loose mismatched details that Heather had tried not to notice had just clicked into place, forming one big ugly truth.

'You're broke. Aren't you?'

She sat bolt upright, her back as stiff as a board, and glared down at her new sugar daddy – the one who had just admitted that he couldn't afford to be *anyone's* sugar daddy.

'Babydoll, what makes you think I'm broke?'

Roscoe had an abashed look on his face. The part in his wavy silver hair was slightly off-kilter. Roscoe was not only broke. He was wearing a cheap toupee.

'You said "again". You said you'd be a rich man *again*. That means you're not rich now, right? Guys like you are either stinking rich or flat broke – there's no in between.'

Roscoe gave a disbelieving snort. He tossed his arm across his face. 'I never said I was rich.'

'Maybe you didn't say it, but you acted like it.'

'Where's your soul?' Roscoe asked in a wounded tone. 'Can't you love a poor man just as easily as a rich one?'

'There's only one man I'd ever be broke with, and that's my husband Daniel.'

Roscoe gaped at Heather. A chuckle rumbled in his chest, then exploded into laughter, loud and lewd. He laughed until he was wiping tears off his wrinkled cheeks. How on earth had Heather ever thought Roscoe's wrinkles were sexy? He was a lying old fart, plain and simple.

'Oh baby. You're as much of a fraud as I am. Sitting there like butter wouldn't melt in your mouth, pretending to be the faithful little wifey. That's the best laugh I've had in ages.'

'So you aren't a music promoter, either? I bet you're not even employed,' Heather accused.

Roscoe's laughter had died down to a rattle. 'Aw, come on. We both had a good time playing make-believe. When's the last time a cheap little stripper like you got treated like a princess?'

'Who are you calling cheap? You're the one with the rug from Wal-Mart.'

Heather kicked her legs free from the sheets and leapt off the mattress. Naked, she began to pick up her clothes – her own clothes, not the cheap fairy costume that Roscoe had bought her – and put them on. There was nothing that ruined the sex appeal of an older man more than a hairpiece. Bald was hot. Bald was distinguished. Toupees were a tacky cover-up for the truth.

Just like Roscoe's story about being a country music promoter. He probably hadn't had a job in years. There wasn't a damn thing he could do for Heather or her career. That story was just the shtick he used to get girls into bed.

'Honey, it's not my fault I'm broke,' Roscoe said. His voice was hitting a whiney pitch, and his seductive cowboy accent had mysteriously gone AWOL. 'My ex-wives are killing me for alimony. I just sold my Mercedes this afternoon, thought I'd treat myself to a nice hotel room, some booze and a pretty hooker. I always intended to pay you. Help yourself to a C-note, baby doll. My money clip's on the dresser.'

Heather stood in the middle of the room. Her skin was on fire. Her hair sizzled. A red mist covered her eyes. She was a lightning rod of rage, capable of doing anything to this sleazy, naked con man lying in front of her. His flaccid cock lay across his thigh, and his wrinkled pink balls lolled in the pocket between his legs. Heather's eyes travelled to the slim sharp knife that they had used earlier to slice a wedge of the inexpensive brie that Roscoe had ordered with the champagne.

'A C-note?' she said. Heather couldn't believe how calm she sounded, as if she weren't contemplating a spontaneous castration at all. 'That's a hundred dollars. Do you honestly believe that if I were a hooker – which I am *not* – I'd be satisfied with a lousy hundred bucks?'

Roscoe shrugged. How had Heather missed the fact that his shoulders were so flabby? His smile, as he looked Heather up and down, was a smug leer.

'Tony Tucan said you were affordable,' he said.

Heather took a step towards the table, where the blade of the knife glittered in the creamy cheese. She looked at Roscoe, then back at the knife.

'Listen, Roscoe, if that's even your name, you came this close to getting relieved of your "manhood" this afternoon,' Heather said. She held up her thumb and forefinger, pinching a microscopic space between them. 'But you know what? You aren't even worth the trouble. And I don't want your blood on my favourite mini-skirt.'

The last thing she saw, as she hoisted her bag over her shoulder and flounced out of the room, was Roscoe's slack-jawed, disbelieving face, so ridiculous under that off-kilter hairpiece.

The sleazeball wouldn't notice that his wad of cash was missing until Heather was halfway to Los Angeles, with the money clip tucked safely in the front pocket of her denim miniskirt.

> *Current status*: Slow chill at the Desert Mirage
> *Sexual forecast*: Cloudy skies. Intermittent showers. Chance of precipitation later tonight

If I had a dollar bill for every time Sir Galahad and I have almost had sex on this trip, I wouldn't have to worry about buying gas. I don't know what his problem is. Attention deficit disorder, maybe. Poor impulse control. Or maybe he just has a morbid curiosity with finding the hot spots on a girl who doesn't get laid very often.

But I'd swear there's more than that going on. He likes me. I know he does; I'm not all that dense about reading signals. Yeah, we go back and forth, but half the time it's me backing away before we can seal the deal. Wouldn't it be funny – funny and cruel – if this whole deep freeze were my fault? Wouldn't it be sad if I came this close to getting what I always wanted, then bailed?

Heather. I can't stop thinking about her. Neither of us can; she's always hanging around between us, whether we admit that she's there or not. Part of me feels awful about trying to get Galahad for myself, because the two of them chose each other before I came on the scene. Marriage is marriage, even if you're stinking drunk when you say your vows.

But the other part of me couldn't care less about Heather. As corny as this sounds, there's something deeper than horndog lust between me and Galahad, something going on at soul level. As much as I want to just tear his clothes off and jump all over him, there's something more than that, an energy running between us. It's been pulling us towards each other since the first time we saw each other; it was working on our hearts since before we met.

Whatever that 'something' is, it doesn't care that he got married at a dive hotel in Vegas, or that his wife is my stepsister. All it cares about is bringing us together.

Later that afternoon, Amity sat on her bed in the motel room, sipping Gatorade and crunching cherry antacid tablets, scribbling in her notebook, and praying that her head wouldn't explode. She'd be performing in less than four hours, and she still hadn't figured out the bridge for the new song she was writing. Worst of all, she had nothing to wear. She hadn't packed any sexy stage clothes for this road trip; the best she could do was wash one of her smaller T-shirts in hot water and pray that the cloth would cling to her breasts in a semi-provocative way. As a last resort, she could try that old stripper trick of putting ice cubes on her nipples. That could arouse some curiosity, if nothing else.

'Hey, Am! Open up. I know you're hiding in there.'

Amity shoved her notebook under the bed. She opened the door to find Crissy standing in the threshold. She was wearing a sexed-up version of her *Wizard Of Oz* getup, with a clingy white blouse tied around her midriff and a pair of cinnamon-red hotpants instead of the overalls. Her Dorothy braids were tied with big red ribbons, and she'd dotted her cheeks with a smattering of extra freckles.

'Working tonight?' Amity asked.

Crissy nodded glumly. 'It sucks. I'm going to have to miss your show.'

'Well, at least you look hot.'

Amity surveyed Crissy's curves with more than a little envy. Her red shorts looked like they'd been painted onto her hips and arse. Her legs, sturdy but curvaceous, tapered down to a pair of sequined red pumps with bows on their toes.

'Ruby slippers?' Amity asked. 'I thought you wanted to downplay the Dorothy thing.'

Crissy winked and clicked her heels together. 'There's no place like home. Listen, speaking of looking like a whore, I came over to see if you needed any help getting ready for tonight.'

'Nah. I've got clothes.'

'Right. My fifteen-year-old brother has T-shirts and sneakers, but that doesn't make him a sex goddess. In fact, his clothes are sexier than yours. Come on. Let's go to my place.'

Crissy grabbed Amity by the elbow, yanked her out the door, and muscled her across the parking lot to the suite of rooms behind the office of the Desert Mirage, where Crissy, her mother and her kid brother lived. Crissy's bedroom was decorated in an eclectic combination of styles: 21st-century hooker meets jock meets dreamy bisexual Hollywood wannabe. A poster of Catherine Deneuve from *The Last Metro* hung on her wall beside a shelf of trophies from her victories on the local women's softball and bowling leagues. A department store mannequin wearing a red Rita Hayworth wig served as an impromptu lingerie rack for a wild assortment of bras, garter belts and thongs in a rainbow of colours. A leopard-skin bedspread adorned her bed, her pillows were littered with teddy bears, and a massive electric blue silicon dildo sat on her nightstand beside a lamp with a silkscreened Elvis shade.

'Welcome to my Hovel of Love,' Crissy said. 'What do you think?'

'Nice.' Amity wasn't sure which of the ten thousand lurid details of Crissy's bedroom were included in that feeble adjective, but it was the only word that came to mind.

'OK. Let's get to work. Tell me what you see.'

Crissy steered Amity into the middle of a shaggy lime green rug and turned her to face a floor-length mirror. Amity gave her reflection a suspicious once-over. Stringy hair. Ratty T-shirt. Faded jeans. Red Converse sneakers.

'Not much. I look like an underage skateboard rat. The best I can hope for is a push-up bra and fake ID that says I'm thirty-five.'

Crissy sighed. 'First of all, we need to change your attitude. You want to sell sex, you've got to take a hard look at what you've got to offer.'

'I'm not selling sex. I just want to sing.'

'Give me a break, Am. You're going to be playing in a bar in front of a bunch of drunken truckers. They might be listening to your music, but they're going to be looking for tits and arse.'

'Then they're going to be disappointed, aren't they?'

'Nope. Because we're going to make the most of what you've got. And you've got way more than you think you do.'

'Such as?'

'Great hair, for one thing. It looks like limp Top Ramen the way you're wearing it, but I see potential. We'll do a quick tint job to make it look shiny, trim your fringe, and do some heavy eyeliner. I'm thinking Cleopatra here. We'll throw on some jewellery and strap you into something that shoves your boobs up to your chin.'

'They won't reach that far.'

'Oh, yes, they will,' Crissy insisted. She left Amity for a moment, dug through her bureau drawer, and produced a roll of silver duct tape. 'Here's my secret weapon. With this stuff, I could give a lizard cleavage.'

'Ouch,' Amity said in a tiny voice.

'Pain is good,' Crissy said soothingly. 'Pain is our friend. We'll start with your hair, then we'll work our way down. By the time we're done, you'll look so good that I'll be able to pimp your arse on any streetcorner in the world.'

'Wow. I don't know what to say.'

'Say thank you, Mistress,' Crissy delivered an authoritative slap to Amity's right butt cheek. 'Come on. We've got a lot of work to do.'

Daniel didn't have much to do that night before the gig at the roadhouse; the local boys who played back-up had already set up the gear. No fuss, no frills, just a wooden stage the size of a ping-pong table, a few amps, mics and a drum kit. He'd be backed by a bass guitar and a drummer. Same configuration as 3-Way Dream, only the guys drove semi-trucks for a living, and had been married for a combined total of forty-seven years to women they'd known since high school. There hadn't been time for any rehearsals; this whole night was going to have to roll on sheer faith.

The T-Bird was decked out with a new set of shoes, courtesy of Goodyear and Amity's Visa, and was ready for the journey to LA. If Amity and Daniel survived tonight, they'd leave town in the morning with 75 extra bucks in their pockets. As Daniel put it, 'A handful of arseholes get rich off rock'n'roll, the rest get beer money, if they're lucky.'

'I like this place.' Daniel surveyed the tiny stage, the exposed rafters, the small working-class crowd that had started to gather in search of a refuge from the evening heat. 'It reminds me of my touring days. God, we played in so many joints like this. We might have played here, for all I know. Those days are a blur.'

Hank Williams, Jr was playing on the jukebox, and a freckled, middle-aged bartender was pouring shots of Jack Daniel's for a fleet of men who had apparently gathered to worship her bountiful bosom. The bartender glanced up and waved at Amity, her plump cheeks turning into apples when she smiled.

She had to be related to Crissy. Everyone in this little desert oasis was someone's son, daughter, brother, nephew, ex-spouse or former cell-mate at the state penitentiary.

'You know, I could spend some time in a place like this,' Daniel mused. 'Maybe that's what I need to do, just fall off the face of the earth for a while and write songs.'

Amity didn't want to remind him that from the standpoint of the entertainment industry, Daniel and 3-Way Dream had fallen off the face of the earth years ago.

'What about your Gibson?' Amity asked. 'She's the reason we're out here, remember? It wouldn't do you much good to disappear if you don't have her.'

'Yeah. You're right.' Daniel stirred his Coke and lime with a swizzle stick. 'I'm nothing without that guitar. She was my first muse.'

Daniel didn't have that fanatical fire in his eyes tonight, and when he talked about his Gibson, he almost sounded as if he were repeating the words of a prayer he didn't believe in anymore. Onstage, his Fender waited for him in its black case, like a new girlfriend who knows she's going to get the adoration she deserves as soon as her man forgets his ex. That Fender was a gorgeous instrument, sleek and slim and mean as a snake. Any guitarist would have loved to get his paws on that beauty.

Amity didn't have to say any of this. From the way Daniel was playing with his drink, using the swizzle stick to stab the lime wedge, she could tell that his focus was drifting.

He felt her watching him, looked up and smiled. A lock of shiny black hair fell over his face. He was wearing a black T-shirt, specially laundered for tonight's performance, and he looked just like the existential troubadour from the poster in her bedroom ... only older and maybe a bit wiser. When his lips went into that wry curve, as if he were thinking about a joke that only the two of them knew about, Amity always went into a brief private cardiac arrest.

'I can still remember a time when I would have been sitting in my hotel room right about now, getting a blowjob from some chick I didn't know, maybe slugging Jack straight out of the bottle or snorting a couple of lines,' Daniel said. 'Now I'm sipping a Diet Coke at a roadhouse in the middle of a wasteland, waiting to play covers for a bunch of truckers who've never heard of my original music. But you know what? I don't care. I'm content tonight – not ecstatic, but content. And I'm happy to be playing –'

He stopped, tilted his head, and narrowed his eyes at Amity. 'You look different,' he said. 'What did Crissy do to you?'

'Fixed my hair. Did my make-up. Loaned me some clothes and jewellery. Stuff like that,' Amity said.

No need to mention the three strips of duct tape that were wrapped around the top of her rib cage, helping her fill out the black satin corset that Crissy had loaned her. The corset, several sizes too small for Crissy, had belonged to one of her girlfriends, who had blown town to launch a career modelling for an internet porn site in San Francisco. Crissy kept it around for the sake of nostalgia; tonight she wanted Amity to wear it for the sake of her career. Along with the corset, Amity was wearing her own jeans and combat boots, the only elements of her wardrobe that had Crissy's seal of approval.

'I like it,' Daniel said. 'Very much.' His slow smile made Amity's heart do that temporary arrest thing again.

'Really?' Amity tugged at a strand of her hair.

'Really. You look hot. Way too hot for a schmuck like me,' Daniel teased. 'You're going to be hopping a ride out of here with some guy who drives a Mack truck. You'll forget all about me and my holy quest.'

'If it were that easy to forget, I would have done it days ago,' Amity said.

'Listen, Amity. I need to ask you something. Two things, actually.'

'What?'

Amity felt Daniel's knees under the table, edging in to gently clamp her thighs. He took both of her hands and stroked her palms with the balls of his thumbs as if he were trying to read the network of fine lines in her hands.

'Do you think I'm crazy?' Daniel asked.

'Nope. I *know* you're crazy. Next question.'

His inky eyes were so grave, so intent, that Amity's mouth went dry. His knees tightened their grip on Amity's legs, trapping her in the world's sweetest vice.

*Don't ask anything that blows me open*, she begged inwardly. *Not here, at this bar, with country music playing on the jukebox.*

'Will you still love me after you hear me cover ZZ Top?'

Amity stared. She opened her mouth to fling off another sarcastic reply, but there was a huge rock in her throat, which got stuck there when Daniel said the word 'love'.

'Well? What do you think?'

'I think I will,' she said softly. 'We'll have to see how well you play "La Grange".'

The good ol' boys on-stage were doing their version of a sound check, calling out the names of their buddies in the crowd, making dirty jokes, grabbing their crotches and pretending to be Elvis. Everyone who spent any time in Nevada was required to impersonate Elvis at least once before they were permitted to leave, Amity had decided. It must be a state law.

Daniel had apparently heard of the Elvis law. After his intro, in which he was introduced to the crowd as 'Danny Goldblum from Freeway Dream, performing tonight with the Desert Rats', Daniel launched into a throaty, oversexed rendition of 'Suspicious Minds'. His hips rotated in true Elvis style as he played his Fender; every female in the audience had her eyes glued to his lean thighs, which tapered down to a pair of snakeskin boots.

He looked damn hot, and the crowd responded accordingly. Within minutes, the dance floor was packed, and customers were piling through the door as if the vibrations of the electric guitar had lured them like snakes across the sand.

Amity stayed at her table, playing with her Coke. The ice in the soft drink had long since melted, and there was nothing but tea-coloured sugar water in the glass, but Amity didn't notice. Nothing around her had any colour, taste or sound, except for Daniel; everything else was just a blur of meaningless matter and light.

Eight years ago, Amity had watched Daniel from the heat of a mosh pit. Impossible to believe that she was sitting here at this desert tavern, listening to him play a

Fender instead of that old Gibson, singing Elvis instead of his own dark songs, with their harsh vocals and dirty distortion.

It was weird, the detours a life could take, Amity thought. If you didn't have time to adjust, those quick turns could leave you carsick.

From Elvis, the boys swung into Johnny Cash, the Stones, Dylan, Neil Young, and yes, at the bartender's request, ZZ Top. Daniel just didn't quit; the longer he played, the faster his hands moved on the Fender. He was so hot he was smoking, eyes burning with a diabolical intensity, teeth bared in a grin of maniacal irony at every pause in his vocals. Amity couldn't tell if he was having fun playing, or just having fun playing the audience, manipulating their bodies and their emotions with his rich, gravelly voice and sinuous moves.

Whatever he was feeling down inside, Daniel was putting on a damn good show of having the time of his life.

Daniel didn't break until after midnight – the women in the room wouldn't let him. Old, middle-aged, or barely legal, females were clustered at the foot of the stage, shaking their assets and ignoring their men. The younger, prettier girls were making shameless bids for Daniel's attention, with jaded moves like panty-tossing and titty-flashing. This tiny non-town had probably never seen anything like this. If it weren't for the general shortage of women around here, there'd be a whole host of men filing for quickie divorces in the morning.

Amity would have been enjoying herself as much as anyone else, if not for the terrifying thought that dangled over her head like a bucket of blood in a horror flick.

She was going to have to follow Daniel.

On an acoustic guitar.

And sing with her girly voice in front of fifty-odd females on heat.

She was going to be torn to shreds.

'OK, gang. It's been fun tonight, but all good things must come to an end,' Daniel announced into the mic. A mask of sweat covered his face, and his T-shirt was so wet that you could have wrung a bucket of perspiration from it.

The tavern seemed to explode in a roar of refusal – no way was this crowd going to release Daniel. Not until he was a panting white husk on the stage.

'You guys are merciless,' Daniel laughed. 'We'll do one more number, then it's time for me to shut my big mouth. There's a very gifted lady who's going to entertain you for the rest of the evening. When you get a look at her, you're going to wish I'd gotten off the stage a lot sooner.'

Amity doubted that anyone in the audience would feel that way, especially the women, but the tempo of her pulse accelerated when Daniel winked at her. That wink was heavy with irony, but it made every female in the room envy Amity. She wasn't used to being on the receiving end of the green-eyed monster; usually she was the one being held firmly in its claws, fiercely jealous of someone who had something that she really wanted.

Tonight, for once, Amity had everything she wanted. A chance to perform in front of a real live audience. A promise of cash in exchange for singing. And Daniel.

So why was she shaking in her combat boots, instead of floating six inches off the ground on a current of sheer joy?

Daniel returned to Elvis for his encore, crooning a decelerated version of 'Love Me Tender' in a smoky, seductive timbre, sounding like a bastardised combination of Roy Orbison and Trent Reznor from Nine Inch Nails. He deliberately warped a few of the chords, adding just enough distortion to let his audience know that as much as he revered The King, Daniel was still an indie rocker at heart.

The next fifteen minutes were a blur of lights, motion and warm bodies. Someone grabbed Amity by the wrist and pulled her onto the stage. She saw a circle of expectant faces surrounding her – the audience, the Desert Rats, Daniel – but she didn't know what they expected her to do. Someone was draping a blue guitar over her neck, adjusting its belly against her torso. The instrument looked vaguely familiar; did she know how to play this thing?

She didn't have a clue what to do with that guitar. Her hands hung at her sides, as heavy and useless as sandbags. A rivulet of sweat trickled down her forehead; she wanted to wipe it away, but those hands refused to move. The lights were blinding her, but her eyelids didn't seem to work, either.

Time stopped. Amity's head filled with a muffled roar, like the sound of the ocean heard through a pair of earmuffs. She stared into the crowd, which looked like an endless expanse of faces, though there couldn't have een more than a couple of hundred people in the tavern that night. For a girl who'd only played on street corners, at coffee houses, and in half-empty nightclubs, this venue might as well have been Radio City Music Hall.

The first sound that penetrated the fog was the screech of wood on wood. A pair of hands was steering her backwards, planting her butt down onto something firm and reassuringly solid, then lowering the microphone to the level of her face. She was sitting on a tall wooden stool, just like the one at the Java Dive down the street, where she sometimes strummed away an afternoon in exchange for tips.

Suddenly Amity remembered what she was supposed to do. Blood rushed back to her fingers. The weight of Blue Molly's hollow body against her thigh brought her back to reality. Her hands fell into place. She leant up to the microphone, and miraculously, her lips moved.

'My name's Amity,' she said. There was a flutter in her voice, but hopefully no one heard it. 'I'm not famous or anything. I just write songs.'

Then Amity sang some of those songs: 'Dream Dogs', 'Watching Your Lips Move', 'Could I Sleep through August?', 'I Don't Love You', 'Stars, Fall Down'. For the first few minutes of her set, she kept her eyes fixed on her guitar's blue surface, with its familiar scratches and fingerprint smudges. When she realised that no one in the tavern was hissing, booing, or throwing garbage – though a few customers took the ballads as a signal that it was time to refresh their drinks – Amity was bold enough to check out her audience.

People were listening to her. They were doing other things, too, like talking to each other, lighting cigarettes, drinking, and making passes at members of the opposite sex, but Amity's music was the background for all of that, shaping and colouring the motions of the crowd. She had a connection with the audience; she could feel it as strongly as if there was a rope coming out of her heart, connecting her to those strangers, who were kind enough to stay in that roadhouse that night and hear the songs she'd written.

Amity opened up her throat, so that she could sing stronger and louder. Halfway through 'I Don't Love You', she felt the energy in the room shift. The song was raw, plaintive, painful; singing those lyrics made Amity's throat ache as if she'd been up all night trying to convince an ex-lover that he didn't have a chance with her anymore.

The customers who hadn't been paying attention to Amity had their eyes riveted on her now. She knew that she looked as good as it was possible for her to look, in Crissy's black satin merry widow and her own faded skintight jeans. Her heavy boots made her dangling legs look long and delicate, like a deer's. She wore Crissy's silver-and-turquoise hoop earrings, three layers of lip gloss, and enough black kohl around her eyes to make any raccoon proud. Mix all that froufrou stuff with a voice that had suddenly soared to a new height of sensual power, and you had a recipe for some hard-hitting sex appeal.

Once she captured the crowd's attention, Amity didn't want to release them from her spell. She sang about love, sex and broken hearts; whiskey, cigarettes and coffee at four in the morning. She let her long dark hair fall in a sleek curtain over her face when she wanted to look intimate and mysterious, then tossed it back when she wanted to be sexy and bold. The crowd wasn't engulfing the stage the way they had with Daniel, but she had them mesmerised. Couples had started to pair off and drift up to the dance floor again, and they were clinging to each other through her slow numbers, their mouths and hips merging to the rhythms she'd created herself.

Amity felt like a snake charmer, faced with a whole roomful of dancing cobras. She'd never experienced such a sweet rush of power in her life, and she didn't want that honey flood to ever end. The whole time she was singing, she never forgot that Daniel was out there somewhere. Though she couldn't always see much more than a shadow of his slim form cutting across the crowd, or hovering by the bar, she could feel his presence as distinctly as if she'd kept a finger on his pulse all night.

It was just like the fantasy she'd described to him, only so much better. Instead of being watched by some anonymous stranger, she was being watched by a guy she was in love with. And from the magnetic pull that he exerted on her as she sang, she was beginning to suspect that Daniel loved her back.

Like all nights, this one eventually had to end. Closing

time was at 2 a.m. It was 1.30 when Amity launched into her final song.

'I've got to warn you all about this one,' she told the audience. 'It's brand new, just out of the oven. I've been on the road for a few days, and I've been working this out at night in motel rooms, or by the side of the interstate. So I'm sorry if it's not as polished as some of my other stuff, but this one's important to me.'

The tavern fell silent, or as silent as a roadhouse can get on a Saturday night, when the patrons have been drinking for seven or eight hours straight. As Amity strummed the intro of 'Head-On Heart', the only background noise she heard was the click of lacquered balls from the pool table, accompanied by the clink of glass against glass and the stage whispers of drunks who were sincerely trying to keep their voices down.

'I think she's a real talented little lady,' drawled one of those beery voices. 'Could use a little meat up top, but that's what plastic surgeons are for.'

Amity smiled. Not too long ago, a remark like that would have stung her. Tonight it just seemed funny. She glanced into the shadowed sea of faces to see if she could tell who'd made the comment, and her gaze locked with Daniel's.

He stood at the edge of the dance floor, where two or three couples were still twirling in their own tequila-soaked dreamland. He'd changed into a white T-shirt that made him stand out against the darkness, and his hair had been washed and combed back against his forehead. Sweeping back from a widow's peak, his black hair caught the reddish lights overhead, giving him a satanic halo that fitted perfectly with his wicked smile. As Amity began to sing, Daniel mouthed the lyrics along with her.

How the hell did he know this song? She'd never rehearsed 'Head-On Heart' in front of Daniel; she'd never even practised it when he was in the shower. So unless he'd been lurking outside the motel room while she was playing, or...

*You read my diary, you son of a bitch!*

The thought struck her like a bolt of lightning. She didn't know whether to burst out laughing or sink through the floorboards. Still singing, trying to pour her heart into the lyrics, Amity ruffled through her memory to try to assess the damage. No state secrets or anything. But she didn't necessarily want him to know that she was in love with him, or that she'd written parts of this song with the imprint of his lips still warm against her mouth.

Working her way to the bridge of the song now, she stared straight out into the audience. Amity caught the eye of a young man wearing a cowboy hat on top of a dishwater blond mullet, and she sang straight to him, instead.

> *You told me I had to kiss you*
> *Then you told me I had to drive slow,*
> *But your mouth made my heart go faster*
> *Than your head could possibly know.*

Amity had been worried about performing a half-baked song tonight, but this crowd was eating it with a spoon. The dance floor was full again. Tears glistened in more than a few eyes. When Amity rolled through the final chords, she expected to stand up and bid the crowd good night, but the applause kept her right where she was, carrying her through a double encore. Amity sang Dylan's 'It Ain't Me, Babe', then covered a ballad by Sheryl Crow, because her skin felt too raw to play any more of her own music that night.

After her set ended the music was still coursing through her veins, making her throb, making her shake. Someone helped Amity down from the stage. Someone handed her a beer. The audience swallowed her in a love wave, but she pushed them away. The only one she wanted to see was Daniel, and there he was by the jukebox, an angular silhouette against the brightly lit glass.

'You told me you weren't much of a singer,' he said accusingly.

'I lied.'

Daniel lifted the beer bottle out of Amity's hand and drew an invisible moustache across her lips with the frosty glass. With his other hand, he hooked the waistband of her jeans and pulled her against him. The rhythm of her last song lingered in her blood. It matched the rhythm of his pulse.

'Let's get out of here,' he said. 'Let's take a ride down the highway with the headlights off and park in a ditch and gaze at the moon.'

'Only if you drive.'

Daniel's grin was unholy in the red light of the bar. 'You'd better believe I'll drive.'

She hadn't had a sip of alcohol that night, but the sight and scent of Daniel, the rumble of his voice issuing those invitations straight into the sensitive shell of her ear, were giving her that loose, lovely feeling that comes with a couple of beers and a shot of whiskey. But in the back of her mind, a question was still burning, like a cigarette left glowing in an ashtray.

'Did you read my notebook?' she asked.

A flicker of guilt on Daniel's face told her all she needed to know. 'Yeah. I can't tell a lie.'

'When?'

'This afternoon, when we came back from Charlene's. You were out with Crissy. I was alone. I saw your book sticking out from under the bed ... and the rest is a fairly sordid history.'

'Why did you do it?'

Daniel had the decency to hang his head, but Amity

could see a trace of a smile on his lowered face. 'I couldn't help it. I'd been watching you write in that book for the past few days, and you always slammed it shut on me. I had to see who all those love songs were about.'

'So you know.'

Amity didn't have to elaborate. Her diary was a simple document. There wasn't much in it but a record of who she was and what she loved: Daniel and Blue Molly, her T-Bird and music.

Daniel bent one knee in a mock bow. 'Sir Galahad at your service, M'Lady.'

'Great. Now you think I'm a fool, don't you?'

'Fool for luhhhv, baby,' Daniel sang, his smirk flaring into a grin. He was moving against her again, rocking into her to the beat of the tavern's last-call jukebox song. 'I'm going to make love to you in your car,' he warned. 'I hope you're ready, because we're going to be doing it in the desert until dawn. Hey, how's that for a song title?'

Amity tilted her head. 'I could say no. I should say no, after the way you invaded my privacy.'

'Hey, now that I've invaded your privacy, I'm not taking "no" for an answer. It's time that we consummated our mystical soul connection with some red-hot fucking. You and me are going to be out in the desert, doing the bump-grind in your car. We're going to make the jack rabbits jealous. Or we could do it right here. I'll back you up into a dark, sticky corner, slip your jeans down, lift your arse up against the wall –'

'Last call!' bellowed the bartender. 'You don't have to go home, folks, but you can't stay here.'

Her ruddy cheeks were slack with fatigue, and her voice was hoarse from shouting back and forth with her customers all night, but like the rest of the crowd that remained at the bar, she looked satisfied, as if the music had left her heart and soul well fed.

'Guess we're doing it in the car,' Daniel said. 'Come on. We've got sunrise in about two hours. I want to be inside you while I watch it.' He took Amity by both hands and started leading her backwards out of the club, never taking his eyes off of hers.

'I thought you wanted to get an early start to LA in the morning,' Amity said weakly. 'We're searching for the holy grail, remember? We should go back to the motel and get some sleep.'

But Amity's will power was threadbare. At this point, she would have followed Daniel to hell if he'd promised to make love to her beside a brimstone lake.

Daniel led her outside, where Amity took the first breath of fresh air that she'd had in hours. The sky was vast. Far from the urban light pollution, countless stars were visible across a background of sheer black, as if they'd been swirled on black velvet with a giant paintbrush. The gravel lot was almost empty. The darkness seemed to sing. The night, left to itself, was carrying on with its own secret life.

'You know, I may have already found it,' Daniel said, squeezing Amity's hands. He bent down to give her a kiss, and it was simple and sweet and almost chaste, like a gesture from an ancient legend.

Both of them forgot that they'd made a date that night to fight about Heather.

At two in the morning, the gamblers at the Casbah Hotel's casino were still hanging tough. In Vegas, debauchery went on all week long, but by Saturday the 24/7 party was in full swing. For the tourists who huddled around the blackjack tables, or plugged coins into slot machines, or drank the Casbah's special 'Hare-martinis' as they played video poker at the bar, the thought of Monday morning was as distant as a childhood fairytale.

Heather couldn't remember how she'd ended up at

the Casbah. Somehow, she found herself plopped down on a stool in front of a slot machine at the end of a night of casino-hopping. Bright and blurry as the tail of a comet, her scattered memories of the long night streaked across her mind. Dancing like a one-woman whirlwind at the Ra at the Luxor hotel. Playing roulette at Mandalay Bay, with a faceless high-roller who kept trying to get his hand up her skirt. Being presented with a crown of flowers by a knight at the Excalibur Hotel and told that she was as lovely as a princess.

She was still wearing her crown of plastic white rose buds and blue forget-me-nots, with its streaming pink ribbons. Wearing flowers in her hair felt a lot better than wearing that jackass Roscoe's fake rhinestone tiara.

Roscoe. Thinking about his leering mouth under that furry moustache, and remembering that those rubbery lips had crept over every inch of her body, made Heather queasy. The four margaritas, three glasses of champagne, one Blue Hawaiian, two Hurricanes and three Haremartinis she'd consumed that evening didn't help, either.

But Roscoe's money spent as well as anyone else's. Heather hadn't stopped to count the bills in that clip. She knew that there was a thick wad of them, and that the denominations were all higher than twenty. Any further inspection would have made her feel greedy. With drinks and gambling and a little therapeutic shopping, Heather had spent a quarter-inch of Roscoe's money. She still had enough left to buy a Greyhound ticket back to Denver, and as of two o'clock on Sunday morning, she was sober enough to remember that she wanted to get back home.

Eventually. At her merry-go-round stage of intoxication, Denver didn't sound like much fun. Besides, Heather had a new job: feeding the slot machine. She was mesmerised by its spinning fruits and bars and stars. The occasional cascade of coins rewarded her for her persistence, convincing her that of all the places on earth she could be, this one stool in front of this one machine was the perfect place for her to achieve her dreams.

'Cocktail?' asked a waitress, passing by in her harem-girl costume.

Heather squinted. The girl was about Heather's height and weight. Not as pretty, but she was cute enough to wear the costume without looking like a fool.

'Do you make a pretty good living as a concubine?' Heather slurred.

'Huh?' The waitress's blue eyes widened behind her half-veil. 'What's a concubine?'

'It's like, a full-time slut,' Heather explained, speaking very slowly so that the waitress could comprehend. 'Only you're with one guy, who has a lot of other girlfriends, and wives, too. You should know, honey, you're wearing the uniform.'

'All I do is serve drinks,' the woman shrugged, backing away.

The concubine/waitress was balancing a tray loaded with cocktails on her forearms. One of those drinks was a tall, slender glass of something clear and pink and sparkly. Heather would look perfect sipping that pink potion, with her blonde curls and her wreath of white-and-blue flowers. She snatched at the glass, but the waitress blocked her.

'That's for someone else, sweetie,' the waitress said. 'How about I bring you a cup of strong black coffee?'

'Fuck that,' Heather growled. 'Princesses don't drink black coffee. We drink *pink champagne.*'

Heather sounded like she needed an exorcism even more than a dose of caffeine. Through a multicoloured fog she watched her own hand shooting out to seize the glass. She saw the waitress taking a slow-motion step in the opposite direction. She saw her fingers taking another swipe at the pink bubbly stuff, and this time her hand made contact – not only with the drink she wanted, but with all the other drinks, and with the tray, and with the waitress's face.

Chaos followed. Heather heard shattering glass, the coarse voice of a pit boss, the shrill accusations of the waitress. She couldn't see anything because she was curled up in a ball between a slot machine and a potted palm, her arms shielding her face. Her heart pounded. She squeezed her eyes shut and prayed that if she couldn't see her pursuers, they wouldn't be able to see her, either. Giant paws were grabbing at her, trying to dig her out of her hidey-hole, and suddenly she was clawing and screaming and fighting them with all her might.

Then one pair of hands, which seemed gentler than the others, reached for Heather, not to maul her, but to help her to her feet. The voice that was coaxing her out of her dark nook sounded familiar. The solid arms that embraced her, the male chest that offered a rock-hard pillow for her spinning head, belonged to someone she knew. Opening her eyes, she saw a nauseating sight: palm trees silhouetted against a sherbet sunset, all lurid lavender and orange, painted on a polyester sports shirt.

'Zak!' Heather cried out in joy, looking up into the bass player's surf-blue eyes.

'Heather,' he replied, scolding, teasing. 'You've been a bad girl, haven't you?'

'The baddest,' Heather agreed, just before she threw up.

## Chapter Eight

# Starry, Starry Sex

Daniel drove the T-Bird down the highway until they found a spot that was just far enough out of town to escape its halo of fluorescent light. He pulled off onto a wide weedy space off the road, near the hulking shell of an abandoned building that looked like it might have once been a gas station. Then he turned the headlights off, and they took turns watching the night sky from the back seat of the convertible, just as Daniel had said they would.

Amity got to be the first to lie back and enjoy the show, rhinestone constellations spiralling through the universe, their dance so slow that it seemed motionless from the earth. When Daniel got into the back seat with her, straddling her knees, she reached up to kiss him, but he gently pushed her down, pinning her wrists over her head.

'You're going to lie back,' he ordered, 'and watch the star show while I give you the best orgasm of your life.'

'Is there a money-back guarantee?' Amity asked.

Daniel nuzzled her neck, his lips grazing the sensitive valleys along her throat. He didn't have to do much to get Amity wildly turned on. The smooth surfaces of his lips were already wreaking havoc on her self-control; her body was melting back into the seat, already preparing to yield.

'Not unless you're planning to pay me. The only guarantee I can give you is that whatever I make you feel is going to be as incredible as what you see in the sky.'

'You've got some tough competition,' Amity laughed. Her laughter died away into a moan when Daniel began to unfasten the laces of her corset. Unlike most of the guys who'd undressed Amity in the past, Daniel was skilful, thoughtful. Either he'd had more practice than the average male at removing complicated female clothing, or he was just better – period.

When he eased his way down to tease her nipples with his tongue, Amity decided that he was just better. He knew how to approach a pair of breasts, courting the outer edges first, moving in towards the areolae, leaving butterfly kisses around the pink circumference.

Then he pulled the corset open to reveal a few more inches of Amity's skin, and he froze.

'What the hell . . . is that duct *tape*?'

'Oh my god. This is not happening.' Amity threw her hands over her face. Her cheeks were hot under her palms. Maybe if the burning flesh of her face seared itself to her hands, she'd never be able to look Daniel in the eye again.

'What did you do to yourself, sweetheart? Looks like you broke a few ribs and got patched up at an autobody shop.'

Daniel let out a sputtering choke, then gave up and collapsed into helpless laughter. He laughed until his howls turned into silent, spasmodic whoops. Tears streamed down his cheeks; Amity could see them twinkling on his cheeks in the moonlight.

'It's not *that* funny,' she said. 'Crissy was trying to give me boobs. You know, those two protruding objects that most women have on their chests? Those jiggly things that get everyone's attention if you don't happen to have any talent?'

Amity wrestled herself out from under Daniel's

weight and sat up, yanking the open flaps of her corset over her duct-taped chest.

'Some of us aren't born with pretty ornaments that we can dangle in front of people,' Amity went on. 'So we have to fall back on boring things like hard work and talent.'

'And tape?' Daniel gasped.

'A little tape doesn't hurt,' Amity said, with as much dignity as she could muster.

'A little? Baby, you're wearing a good six feet of that stuff. I'm amazed you could breathe, much less sing the way you did tonight. You blew me away, darlin'. You blew everyone away. You could have sat up there wearing a ski mask and a plastic raincoat; your songs alone were enough to give every guy in the place a hard-on and a broken heart.'

Daniel's laughter had finally subsided into heavy breathing, broken by the occasional chuckle. He readjusted his long, lean body so that he could sprawl across the seat with his head in Amity's lap. He reached up and grasped her face with his hands, tilting her head down so that she had to look at him. Gazing up at her, he was the most beautiful thing she'd ever seen, even though his face was still streaked with tears of laughter.

'There's not a damn thing wrong with the way you look, Amity. You're sexy as hell, whether you know it or not. And look! Hey!' Daniel sat halfway up and pointed to the sky. A silver streak arched across the velvety, spangled blackness of outer space.

'A shooting star,' Amity said. 'No, two of them. There's more. It's a whole shower!'

Like the blossoming plumes from a fireworks display, stars were falling, leaving trails that travelled across unimaginable lengths of space and time, only to appear as momentary spectacles of light to the human audience on the earth below.

'That's got to be a sign,' Amity said. 'I think it means that we need to keep moving. We're getting closer.'

'Closer to what?'

'To finding the Guitar. What did you think I meant?'

'Sex. That's why we're here. Isn't it?' Daniel asked.

He had somehow manoeuvred Amity down into the seat so that she lay beside him, her head nestled in the crook of his arm. His fingers played with the strands of hair at the nape of her neck, and his mouth was so close to her ear that his voice made her eardrum vibrate deliciously.

'We're here because we're hunting down your Gibson,' Amity insisted. 'You seem to need a lot of reminding these days. What's the problem, are you losing your focus?'

'Not losing. Maybe just . . . shifting.'

And with that, Daniel shifted his weight so that he was lying directly on top of her. He was blocking her magnificent view of the sky, but she couldn't care less. The light in his eyes was more spectacular than any show of stars.

'It's been a long time since I felt that rush I had tonight,' Daniel said. 'And I don't really know why, because I didn't play anything original. Didn't break down any creative barriers. You know, I used to feel sorry for my dad, playing in his lame cover band, doing the rounds of all the weddings and bar mitzvahs. But he loved to play. When I was a kid, I'd wait up for him to come home from a gig so I could hear him and my mom talking downstairs. She'd pour them each a drink, and he'd sit there and tell her about the night, and you could hear in his voice how much he loved it. And after they'd been talking for about an hour, they'd go upstairs together and make love till the sun came up.'

'Nice story,' Amity remarked. 'You said the word "love" about a hundred times.'

'Does that make you all squishy inside?'

'Nah,' she scoffed. 'I just thought it might mean something.'

'Like what?'

'Like ... maybe you haven't been searching for a guitar. You're looking for love.'

'In all the wrong places?' Daniel teased. 'This feels like a good place to me. An excellent place.'

He buried his face in Amity's hair and began to graze along the side of her neck, as his nimble fingers unbuttoned her jeans. He moved his hips off of Amity's so that he could ease his hand down under the waistband of her panties, into the soft, moist heat below.

'That's not the kind of love I'm talking about,' Amity said. 'I was talking about your love for your music. That's the only true love there is.'

Her protest wasn't very convincing. Her lower body was melting under Daniel's touch; he was manipulating her tenderest flesh with a skill she'd never experienced before. He stroked, squeezed and fondled her as if her pussy had always been his main instrument, with the guitar coming in at a distant second.

'You're too cynical,' Daniel whispered into her ear. 'But I've got the cure for that right here.'

Her first orgasm with Daniel was so swift and stealthy that she never saw it coming; one second she was humming under his hand, and the next she was arching in the seat, her muscles quivering as currents of sheer pleasure ran through her, leaving her tingling from toes to scalp. Jeans pushed down around her knees, Amity lay shuddering in the sweet aftershock, wondering if she might have been struck by nocturnal heat lightning.

'Still feeling cynical?' Daniel asked. He grinned like a Cheshire cat as he unlaced Amity's boots, pulled them off and tugged down her Levis.

'Till the day I die,' Amity panted.

Daniel shook his head in mock dismay. He was stripping off his T-shirt now, and pulling down his own jeans. 'Guess I need to work harder to make you a true believer.'

'Believer in what?'

'You'll see.'

Amity was prepping herself to make a smart remark, but she lost her breath when he nudged the tip of his cock between her lower lips. His hardness felt so different, so strange, but at the same time so blissfully familiar that she couldn't do anything but lie back and let him slide slowly, slowly all the way in. Throughout that long glide, he never took his eyes off her. Her eyes fluttered shut when she felt the full length of him inside her.

'Keep looking at me,' he said. 'You're going to feel what I'm talking about, but you have to keep your eyes open.'

Then he began to grind his hips, and Amity felt the world go dark around her. Everything beyond that cocoon they were weaving together was reduced to starry static. He filled her up, filled her all the way, not just the tight nook between her thighs, but the inner hollow that she'd had for as long as she could remember. She hadn't even realised that the empty space had been growing, eating up her whole heart, until she felt herself overflowing.

Daniel started out thrusting at a leisurely pace, then he picked up the tempo. Amity lifted up her legs as high as she could. Her jeans still dangling from one foot, she wrapped her thighs around his back. She could feel his muscles tightening, hear his breath coming quick and fast, but he never closed his eyes, or looked away.

Neither did Amity. Through the haze of her pleasure, she watched his face go soft with something that looked suspiciously like love. On and on he went, rocking in and out, until it felt like they'd been born like this, joined together. Amity didn't have a second crashing orgasm, but her body seemed to be suspended in a mild climax that ebbed and flowed like an ongoing wave. She'd never experienced anything like it – a peak that didn't seem to end. What if she could live in that state, just hover here with Daniel in the limbo they were making together?

The darkness in the sky was just beginning to lift, slanting gradually from black to blue, when he shuddered and cried out and finally finished breaking the gaze that had held them together since he entered her.

'You don't feel so cynical to me now,' he said, after the last of his spasms had finished, and he was coasting from climax to afterglow in Amity's arms.

'How does cynical feel?' Amity asked.

'Frozen over. Shut down. It feels ... dead somehow. Or no, maybe that's the wrong figure of speech. A woman who's cynical about love doesn't feel dead. She feels like she's locked. The only way to open her up is to use the right key.'

'You did a pretty good job of unlocking me last night,' Amity murmured. Her fingers traced his hairline, running up his temples and down the widow's peak.

'I could tell,' Daniel gloated.

They moved around into a sitting position, so that they could watch the sunrise. The sun was climbing rapidly, splashing the sky with streaks of pink and green. The skeletal fingers of tumbleweeds and cacti were etched against that neon light display. Rocks that were mouse-brown in the heat of the day turned into giant gems under that illumination. The colours graced the old Texaco station, turning its silhouette into the ghost of a bombed-out church.

'Can I ask you something?' Daniel turned to look at Amity.

'Sure.'

'Why am I Sir Galahad?'

'Huh?' A blush was beginning to creep up Amity's neck.

'You know. In your notebook, you called me Sir Galahad. Why not Percival? He's the knight who usually comes to mind when I think of the Holy Grail.'

'Yeah. But Galahad pulled the sword out of the stone at that banquet with King Arthur. And he was the only one who was pure enough to sit in the Siege of Peril without being killed by God. Out of the three knights that King Arthur chose to look for the Grail, he seemed the most like you. I guess...' Amity's explanation trailed off into helpless silence.

'For such a sceptical girl, you have a pretty decent knowledge of Arthurian legends,' Daniel said. 'Isn't that stuff too romantic for your taste?'

'Some girls had a life in high school. I did my homework,' Amity said with a shrug.

'Fair enough. But I see a couple of problems. One, I'm Jewish. So in all that Christian symbolism, a knight like me would stick out like a jar of kosher pickles at a Catholic wedding brunch. Two, I'm a good guy, most of the time, but I'm not pure. Not even close. I'm a nice middle-class Jewish boy from Orange County who's been knocked around a lot by the indie rock world. That doesn't quite fit your fantasy, does it?'

'The world doesn't have to fit my fantasies,' Amity said. 'It never has. I doubt it ever will. Besides, I never asked you to read my notebook; everything I put down was supposed to be private. So don't ask me to explain what I wrote.'

She had edged away from Daniel while she was talking; now he drew her back, coaxing her into his arms by planting butterfly kisses up and down her shoulder.

'You're prickly,' he said. 'I like that. And I liked what you wrote in your notebook. Especially the song you sang last night. You have a gift, girly-girl. I hope you never lose it.'

'I won't,' Amity said, 'because I never want to have to go on another quest again.'

'Me neither,' Daniel agreed with a yawn. 'My holy mission is wearing me down to the bone.'

He rested his head against Amity's shoulder, and in a few moments, she heard his breathing fall into the adagio of sleep. She stayed awake, watching the sun climb higher into the sky, until its light grew so fierce that she had to leave Daniel snoring in the back seat and drive them both back to the motel.

Cheetos didn't make a bad breakfast, Heather mused, as Zak placed another one of the crisp orange tendrils between her lips. Especially when you washed them down with juicy, lingering kisses. She caught Zak's thumb between her teeth and bore down with just enough force to remind him of some of the other things she'd been biting the night before.

Zak didn't need much reminding. His grin had 'I've got a raging hard-on' written all over it, and his hands were already gravitating to Heather's hips. He scooted her bottom around in the seat so that she was facing him, placed another Cheeto between his lips, and fed her the cheesy morsel straight from his mouth. Once she'd finished chewing, Zak's tongue took the Cheeto's place.

French kissing on a Greyhound bus was deliciously tacky. Heather had never felt so slutty, or so blissfully happy. Her orange-coated tongue danced across Zak's lips, tantalising him with flickering motions that promised more delectable activities in their immediate future. She lifted her bottom so that he could edge his hand underneath her cheeks and explore the space between them with his fingers. He located the tight bud at the heart of the cleft and began to probe it gently, his index finger swirling around the spoked centre before wiggling into the core.

'Zak, don't,' Heather hissed. 'That blonde with the Farrah Fawcett wings is staring at us.'

'She's just jealous,' Zak reassured her. 'Besides, I can't help myself. I'm infatuated with your arse. If you give me a hard time, I'm going to have to turn you over my knee right here and spank you.'

A thrill of fear rippled up Heather's spine. Her bottom was still tender from the swats Zak had delivered the night before with his hard palm. Being punished gave her such a sense of release. The spanking had liberated her from her guilt about cheating on Daniel, and her tears had cleansed her of any nagging memories of her husband's sad, espresso brown eyes. Free of remorse, Heather had enjoyed some of the best lovemaking of her life in Zak's hotel room on the previous night. After a few acrobatic rounds of sex, with frequent breaks to dash to the bathroom to embrace the porcelain goddess, Heather hadn't even felt drunk anymore.

She should have been on a bus heading in the opposite direction right now, towards Denver, and her new job. Instead, Heather was following Zak to Los Angeles, with the faint hope of finding Daniel and dragging her marriage out of the coals. If her horrid experience with Roscoe had done anything for her – besides giving her an enduring distrust for men who wore oversized silver belt buckles – it had taught her two valuable lessons. One, she didn't want to spend her life trying to fill in the blanks of her childhood. Two, she didn't want to turn into her mother Candi, marrying any man who whistled at her and tossed her a bone, only to leave him two years later for an even bigger loser.

'Maybe I should try calling Daniel again,' Heather suggested. Her cellphone was tucked under her right thigh, digging reproachfully into her flesh. 'I don't know what's going on with him. He must have his phone turned off.'

'He probably doesn't know how to turn it on in the first place,' Zak grumbled. 'Danny boy doesn't know anything about technology, unless it's something he can plug into a guitar.'

'Well, I need to find him.'

Heather lifted herself off of Zak's hand, shoved his arm away, and adjusted her skirt with a few ladylike tugs. Zak groaned and leant back against the seat.

'You're killing me, Heather. I'm offering you some consolation here, and all you want to do is chat with your hubby. Who left you, I might add, to run off and look for an old piece of junk that he hocked back in the Dark Ages.'

'You don't have to provide an instant replay,' Heather snapped. 'I know what Daniel did. I haven't forgiven him for leaving.' A tear welled up in the corner of her eye, stinging the sensitive tissue, but the droplet refused to grow big enough to plop onto her cheek. 'You know what? I haven't stopped loving him, either.'

'You cheated on Dan with two guys in two days, Heather. Wake up. If you loved him, you'd be on the road with him right now. Instead, he's running around with your sister Amy. Probably boffing her, too.'

'Her name is Am-i-ty. She's my stepsister, not my sister. And he's most definitely not boffing her. Amity isn't Daniel's type,' Heather said with a sniff. She fluffed her hair and dug through her handbag for her compact. A peek at the small round mirror informed her that she was still the fairest of them all, even if she didn't qualify as Newlywed of the Year.

'How do you know what Daniel's type is? You've barely known the guy for a week,' Zak huffed. 'Listen, if you don't think Dan's hot for your stepsister, think again. Guys are simple animals. When a chick wants us, we tend to want her back, even if it's only for a quick test drive in a public toilet. Take a look at your stepsister sometime when she's in Dan's divine presence. She goes all soft and limp, like an overcooked noodle. Amity's had a crush on the guy since she was barely out of the jailbait phase. You must have known about it; you grew up with her.'

'I didn't grow up with her. Her father and my mother were only married for a few years. I was way too busy to pay attention to Amity's crushes. She had a thing for musicians. Daniel was just another poster on her wall.'

'That's not what she told me. She wants him.'

Zak curled up on his side, facing the aisle, as if he were going to go to sleep. Heather gave him a long look out of the corner of her eye. She could swear he was leering at the woman with the Farrah Fawcett hairdo. She was old enough to be Zak's mother, but that didn't seem to bother him at all. He was probably thinking about giving her a test drive in the bus's closet-size bathroom.

'Well, she's not going to get him,' Heather muttered to her reflection. Damn, she was pretty when she got pissed off. Competitive anger had stained her cheeks with pink, and her blue eyes sparkled with an intensity that was almost scary. How could Daniel want anyone but his gorgeous fresh-from-the-oven bride?

Heather yanked her cellphone out from under her thigh, flipped it open, and jabbed at the keypad.

'The customer you are trying to reach is not available. Please try your call again later,' droned the recording for the five-hundredth time.

'Still can't get ahold of him?' Zak asked with a yawn. 'I'll bet he turned off his phone so he could have some privacy while he's screwing your stepsister.'

He glanced over his shoulder at Heather, who was too outraged to reply. The smug knowing gleam in Zak's eyes made her want to smack him. Why did men have to turn so nasty after you had slept with them? she wondered. Daniel was the only lover, in her recent memory, who hadn't morphed into a snake, a fraud, or a childish jerk the moment she'd peeled her sticky body away from his. Whatever his flaws, Daniel's heart had always been pure.

Zak had turned back to face the aisle again, and was striking up a conversation with the would-be Farrah. Through her rage, Heather caught fragments of Zak's familiar shtick: *Bass guitar ... blah, blah, blah ... rock star ... blah, blah, blah ... yeah, big name label ... yah know, you're pretty hot ... blah, blah, blah.*

Heather tapped Zak on the shoulder. He might be a loathsome worm, but she still needed him.

'Zak?' she said, in the most angelic coo she could manage, 'What makes you so sure we're going to find Daniel in LA? How do you know we're not wasting our time?'

Zak interrupted his siege on the blonde to answer Heather. 'Hey, I'm not wasting my time. I can't wait to get back to LaLa Land,' he said. 'If I'd had things my way, I never would have left to do that zombie gig in Vegas.'

'What about me?' Heather batted her eyelashes and pouted. 'I'm scheduled to be in Denver tomorrow, dancing at the opening of a brand new club. I was supposed to be their headliner. I'm giving that up to look for Daniel. How do I know he's going to be in Los Angeles?'

'Danny boy always goes back to his roots,' Zak said. 'Under all that grungy, mad-as-hell stuff he does on stage, Danny's a family guy, pure and simple.'

'Pure and simple,' Heather repeated, as Zak returned to his game. Saying the words out loud made her wish that she knew how to cry without listening to Whitney Houston's 'All At Once'.

The interstate snaked across the desert, an endless nightmare of sizzling asphalt under the brutal midday sun. With each step that Daniel took, the empty gas can in his hand seemed to grow heavier, and his swollen feet sweltered in his snakeskin boots. Why hadn't he put on a decent pair of walking shoes before he set out on this journey? He should have known that he wouldn't come across a gas station for at least five or ten miles; all you had to do was take a quick look across the miles of sand to see that there was nothing out there.

Nothing but rocks, lizards, cacti and those damned tumbleweeds. If Daniel never saw another tumbleweed in his life, it would be way too soon to suit him.

Two things kept him walking, in spite of the blistering heat and his overwhelming desire to lie down and die in a pool of his own sweat: the vision of his Gibson, waiting somewhere in the miles ahead, and the thought of a skinny brown-haired girl waiting in a blue convertible somewhere on the road behind him. He couldn't blame Amity for the fact that they'd run out of gas on the way to Los Angeles. She'd been distracted. Her spirits were still soaring from her performance the night before, and her body was still humming from *his* performance afterwards.

Through the mask of perspiration that coated his face, Daniel managed to smile to himself. Sex with Amity had been even better than he'd thought it would be. She was hot, hungry, intense – he could still feel the way she writhed underneath him when he fucked her, all sinew and slippery skin, like an eel. When she came, her face had been transformed, its usual wariness replaced by wonder and joy.

But the detail that had sealed his fate was that ridiculous silver tape wrapped around her chest. How could you help falling in love with a girl who was insecure enough to mummify herself with duct tape for a performance, and gifted enough to sing with such honesty and passion that no one would have noticed if she'd been missing both breasts and all four limbs? The moment Amity opened her mouth on that stage, Daniel had known he was lost. Married to one girl, in love with her stepsister... how had his life gotten so screwed up?

An image in the distance caught Daniel's eye. He stopped in his tracks. The glittering white object in the distance had to be a mirage. Maybe it was a massive quartz-studded boulder in the sand up ahead, doing a terrific impression of a moving automobile.

Quartz-studded boulders didn't emit exhaust fumes. Daniel's downtrodden soul perked up. A big white Cadillac was travelling towards him at a Sunday-drive speed, its wide, shiny bumper undulating with the slight dips in the highway. Daniel stood still and watched, afraid that a twitch of a muscle could turn the vehicle into an hallucination. But the Caddy kept coming, and the vision continued to take on form and substance. Daniel smelt exhaust; he felt the asphalt vibrating gently under the battered soles of his feet.

When the car came close enough that he could see its hood ornament, Daniel dropped his gas can, waved both arms in the air, and yelled for all he was worth, as if the driver could miss a tall, thin guy dressed in black from head to toe on the middle of a scorching summer day.

The Caddy slowed, then stopped. The window on the driver's side glided down, unveiling a vision even more breathtaking than the car itself. Daniel wasn't used to seeing women like this, not without a box of popcorn in his lap and a big silver screen in front of his face. Green eyes, as guileless as a Persian kitten's, studied Daniel from the front seat of the car. Cotton-white hair formed spiky petals around an oval face that would have been shatteringly angelic, if not for the saving grace of a chapped, overripe mouth.

Even as she peered out the window, the blonde was chewing her lower lip, which already had the consistency of raw hamburger. Someone needed to give the lady some Chapstick, and Daniel, being the knight that he was, happened to have a supply of the stuff in his pocket. He pulled out the black tube and handed it to the driver.

'I think you need this more than I do,' he said.

She blushed. The wash of pink illuminated her face like the light through a ruby-red stained glass window. A milk-white hand reached through the window to accept Daniel's gift. Around the slim, elegant wrist was a spiked black leather cuff.

Nice, Daniel thought. That's my kind of angel.

'Oh, you're an absolute sweetheart,' the vision said, in a purr that could only belong to a movie star. 'I quit smoking yesterday. I'm still a nervous wreck. I really feel like I need to break down and buy a pack.'

'Give it a couple more days. You'll be glad you did,' Daniel suggested. Was he really standing here in the middle of the highway, having a chat about smoking cessation with a gorgeous platinum blonde?

'I don't know. I think I'm a lost cause,' the blonde sighed. She narrowed her green eyes at Daniel. 'You look familiar. I'm getting this vision of you playing a black guitar. Did you ever perform at Fiero's?'

'You mean that club in West Hollywood, near the rock'n'roll Denny's? Yeah. I practically used to live there,' Daniel said. 'Everyone plays at Fiero's, sometime in their career.'

Fiero's was a sleazy dive, the kind of place where musicians could hang out during the day and nurse a beer or two while swapping sob stories and lies with other wannabes. At night, those same musicians would take the club by siege, rocking their guts out on the tiny stage. Daniel had met Zak for the first time at Fiero's, what seemed like a million years ago. Daniel was freshly hatched from his family's split-level home in Simi Valley; Zak had been bumming around Redondo Beach before he drifted to Hollywood. Over a pitcher of draft beer and countless tequila shots, the two wayward Cali boys had launched a conversation that led to the formation of 3-Way Dream. Two weeks later, they would run into Randy at the same hovel, searching for a band that was willing to tolerate his highbrow experimentation with native drums. Fiero's was a place where people went hoping to hook up with destiny, and Daniel, in one way or another, had succeeded.

'That must be where I've seen you,' the blonde said. 'You used to play lead guitar for that alternative band, Four-Way Stop. Right?'

'3-Way Dream,' Daniel corrected her. 'Yes. I did. Still do, as a matter of fact.'

'You ought to go back there sometime. I think you'll find what you're looking for,' the blonde said. Her smile was a sly secret, offering nothing but mystery. 'Hey, thanks for the Chapstick. My lips were starting to feel like the surface of this highway.'

To Daniel's disbelief, the Caddy's window began to roll up again. He felt like a child witnessing the premature conclusion of a magic show – Daniel was supposed to get in that car and be swept away with that stunning blonde, into a glorious future that would include a full tank of gas, air-conditioning, and an old Gibson Epiphone.

'Wait!' he shouted, pressing both hands flat against the sleek window. 'Can't you see I need a ride?'

The blonde's face had all but vanished. He saw amusement in her eyes as she blew him a farewell kiss. 'You don't need a ride, Danny. You know exactly where you're going. I'll catch you on the flip side, 'kay? *Ciao.*'

'What flip side? Stop!'

The car was pulling away. Daniel's sweaty palms squeaked against the glass. He trotted alongside the car for a few paces, then fell to the ground, watching the white barge carry its lovely passenger down the highway towards Las Vegas.

'Daniel?'

He peeled his face off the asphalt and squinted up

into the light. A freckled face, framed by long sheaves of brown hair, was hovering over him. His fingers clutched at the ground. The earth felt slick and smooth ... like car upholstery with drool on it.

'Were you having a bad dream or something?' asked the face. She looked familiar, this chick. He could swear he'd had fantastic sex with her not too long ago.

'Hell, yeah. I think it was a nightmare.'

Daniel sat up and squeezed his temples with his fingers as if he were trying to juice his own skull. He was in the back seat of Amity's convertible, with nothing in his head but the lurid remains of his dream and a few staggering memories of the night before. Amity was sitting in the driver's seat. She reached into a brown paper bag and handed him a dewy bottle of blue Gatorade. He chugged the salty liquid, letting it spill over his sticky mouth as if he were guzzling life itself.

'That's what you get spending the whole morning asleep in the sun,' Amity scolded. 'I tried to put the top up after I pulled over, but you started screaming *Stop*!'

'Where are we?'

'At a truck stop. We're on our way to LA. You've been sleeping since early this morning; I loaded up our stuff in the trunk and got us on the road. I had to pull over when you started groaning and kicking the side of the car. What were you dreaming about?'

'Fiero's,' Daniel mumbled.

'Excuse me?'

'A club in West Hollywood. That's where we need to go.'

'Why? What's at Fiero's?'

'Destiny.'

Amity laughed. 'Whatever you say, Galahad.'

Daniel rubbed his eyes. The sun was achingly, gloriously bright. All of the objects around him, large and small, snapped into focus with visionary clarity. He saw

Amity's cinnamon brown eyes, lids crinkled with laughter, rimmed by a hundred tiny freckles. He wanted to kiss every freckle on her cheeks, one at a time, before helping himself to the fruit of her pink softly peeling lips. She was nibbling the lower lip right now, in a way that brought him straight back to his dream.

'I love you,' he said.

Amity stared at him, lips parted in mute surprise. Light shifted in her eyes, turning her face serious, then soft. Finally her mouth curved into a smile, and she laughed again.

'Go back to sleep, Daniel.'

'Don't you want to talk?'

'We'll talk later, when you're fully conscious.'

'I've never been so conscious in my life. Not even that time in college when I dropped acid with that cute teaching assistant from my music comp class. I see everything so clearly, Am. I know exactly where we're going. I know how we're going to get there. And I think I even know what we're going to find...'

'We'll talk about this later,' Amity repeated, turning back to take the wheel. 'In just a few hours, we'll be in LA, and we can talk all we want. For now, let's drive.'

'Later,' Daniel echoed contentedly. He curled up into a foetal position on the upholstered seat, using his forearm as a pillow. 'Just make sure we've got a full tank of gas. I don't need to be hiking down the highway in snakeskin boots, waiting for some leather angel in a snow-white Caddy to tell me I don't need a ride.'

Amity didn't even ask.

## Chapter Ten

# Losing Her, Finding Her, Throwing Her Away

*Miles driven since Vegas*: 297
*$$$ spent on gas*: Who's counting? Just open a vein and let it bleed

I always knew I'd make it to LA, but I never thought it would be like this. My Molly, a new man, everything I ever wanted. Galahad says he won't break into this book again, but I'm keeping his code name. He's too good with his sword to let that go.

The only tarnish on my silver dream is Gwinny. She called Galahad on his cellphone today. He finally remembers that he forgot to turn the thing on, and five minutes later it's buzzing like crazy, and Heather's on the other end. Wants to meet him in Los Angeles; she's on her way there with Zak so she can 'reunite with *her* husband'. She actually said the word 'reunite'; I wouldn't use a lame soap opera word like that. I don't know how this is going to turn out, but my pessimistic nature has gone into overdrive. When's the last time I ever succeeded at stealing a guy from Heather? Um, let's see ... never. We're going to meet her and Zak at Fiero's tomorrow. She'll be wearing some slutty outfit that turns every man in the room into petrified wood. Galahad will take one look at her and wonder what he's been doing, gnawing on a bone when he could be eating a juicy blonde steak.

No, stop it. Think positive, for once in your life.

You're not losing this time, Amity. You're not losing this time. You're not losing this time. Say it till you believe it. Say it till your blood sings it.

Traffic entering LA was everything that Amity had expected: monstrous, flashy, laboriously slow, like a giant chrome-coated serpent. She had to put up the convertible's top when the gridlock fumes and smog turned into a gritty soup that burned the lungs. Daniel was sitting in the passenger seat again, no longer dreaming. He stared out the window, drummed his fingers on the armrest, chewed spearmint gum. Palm trees and scrubby oleander bushes lined the freeway, and billboards advertising everything from rock radio to beer to rape hotlines kept Amity's eyes occupied, so she wouldn't have to watch Daniel brooding. Feeling overwhelmed and far from home, she put her tape of Bob Dylan's *Blood On The Tracks* in the cassette player.

'Don't you think we should have that talk about Heather?' Amity asked. 'We should get a few things out in the open before we see her.'

'Like what?' Daniel asked. The question was surly, glum.

'Like what you're going to tell her about us.'

'I doubt I'll have to tell her anything. She knows we've been alone together for a few days. She'll figure it out.'

'She'll never think we had sex. Not in a million years,' Amity argued. 'Heather thinks I'm a walking, talking form of man-repellant. She never used to let me hang out with her in high school because she thought I'd drive all the cute guys away with my hippie jeans and acoustic guitar.'

'Oh, God,' Daniel groaned, letting his head sink into his hand. 'Heather doesn't know anything.'

'That's my point exactly. She doesn't know that you and I slept together, and she won't know unless you tell her. So what are you going to say?'

'I don't know, baby. I've never been any good at preparing speeches. I just have to play it by ear. When the time comes, I'll open my mouth and start talking. That's the only way I can do this.'

Amity kept quiet for a while. The traffic snake's glittering chrome scales seemed to stretch ahead of them forever. She didn't have to worry about the confrontation with Heather; this car was never going to make it to West Hollywood. She and Daniel would be stuck here forever, moving about an inch an hour, living out the rest of their lives bickering in a car that had no air conditioning.

'Tangled Up In Blue', one of Amity's favourite songs of all time, was playing on the cassette player. Amity didn't want to be like the woman in the song, a distant memory to the singer, a forgotten love, the one that didn't work out. When Dylan sang the lines about driving the car as far as they could and abandoning it out West, a chill snaked down Amity's backbone.

'What did Heather say, exactly?'

Daniel sighed. 'She gave me a choice. I can have her back, or I can keep chasing my guitar. She still thinks my dream about finding the Gibson is absurd. The worst part is, I think I'm starting to agree with her.'

'Great.' Amity clutched the steering wheel. 'You have a five-minute conversation with Heather, and everything we've done seems like a waste of time.'

'Think about it, Amity. What do we have to go on? A few Hollywood rumours about Sadie, and a message from an angel in a stupid dream.'

'What dream? You didn't tell me about any dream.'

Daniel gave a bitter laugh. 'Never mind. It's not important. The point is, we haven't made any real progress. We're following a trail of crumbs.'

'I still believe,' Amity said.

Daniel remained silent ... for too long. 'Maybe you believe by yourself. I hate to say this out loud, but I'm losing my faith.'

'Are you going to go back to Heather?'

'I married her. I owe her something.'

Amity's heart plunged to the pit of her stomach. She couldn't feel her hands on the wheel anymore; her circulation had stopped. 'Do you still love her?'

Daniel's fingers hammered out a nervous staccato. 'I don't know.'

'She wants you back.'

'I know.'

Amity took a deep breath and turned to face Daniel's profile. She couldn't see much of his face under his dark glasses, but he knew the gears in his mind were turning. Traffic had come to a standstill. Rush hour was under way. Why were so many people going *into* LA at this time of the afternoon? Shouldn't they all be heading home, back to suburbia? The cars huddled bumper-to-bumper like misguided pilgrims, crawling towards the mecca of concrete and smog up ahead. Amity and Daniel might be following the same path, but at least they were pursuing a vision that was entirely their own, not some mass-produced pot of gold.

Peering up at the sky, Amity saw a clear blue space above the layers of haze. Floating in that patch of blue was a shred of a cloud, and on that cloud Amity saw the black silhouette of an electric guitar. The image shifted, turning into a dark city bird that coasted away on an air current, but for a flash of a second, Amity had been reminded of what they were looking for. She thought about everything she had to lose, then took her big dive.

'I want you, too,' she said to Daniel. 'I don't want to lose you. The past few days have been the best days of my life. Everything's been a dream up to now. Even my songs, even Blue Molly – nothing's been absolutely real. When I sang the other night, I knew I was meant to do two things: write songs, and be with you. And what we did later, out in the desert, proved that I was right. It was incredible. I don't see how you'll ever find that with Heather.'

A muscle in Daniel's jaw was working back and forth, as if he were literally chewing on Amity's words, absorbing them into his bloodstream.

'Can you just let me handle her?' he asked.

'Sure. I can do that,' Amity finally replied.

*And if you don't handle Heather, I will,* said a grim little voice inside her head.

After the heat of the road and the endless grind of traffic, Fiero's felt like a slice of heaven. When the cool, cave-like air of the bar kissed his skin, Daniel felt like he'd come home. The smells of spilt beer, cigarette smoke and male bravado were as familiar as the aroma of the roast chicken that his mother used to serve every Friday night, and the ragged shadows of the customers looked like nothing less than family. The beefy biker pouring drinks behind the bar was the same guy who used to pour shots for Daniel and his buddies years ago. The bartender glanced up at Daniel and gave him a curt nod of recognition, as if it had been five days, not five years, since Daniel walked through the door.

If he peeled through the layers of flyers and posters that were plastered all over the club's walls, Daniel knew he would find a few artefacts of the early days of 3-Way Dream. Maybe he'd even find the flyer with the black-and-white shot of himself holding his Epiphone. The flyer would be curled and yellow at the edges, and the tape at the corners would crumble under his fingers. The picture of Daniel in Xeroxed ink would be the image of a struggling poseur. Not a musician, not an artist, but a kid wielding his first electric guitar like an automatic weapon, screaming about rage and pain that he hadn't even experienced yet.

Where would that Gibson take him, if he found her

again? She'd carry him straight back to that hungry limbo, where longing and envy felt so natural that he couldn't imagine ever being content.

'So this is where it all started,' Amity said, reminding him of her presence. Daniel's fellow pilgrim looked out of place, transplanted into this old shrine.

'Yep. This is home. Or it used to be,' Daniel replied. He hardly recognised his own voice; it sounded cracked, defeated. 'I need a drink.'

They slid onto a pair of barstools. Amity ordered a draft beer. Daniel ordered a double shot of Stoli on the rocks. Amity didn't say a word, just flashed her credit card at the bartender and asked him to leave the bottle. Good girl, Daniel thought. She knew when her man needed his medicine.

*Her man.* Since when did he officially belong to this weird, freckly chick? Daniel wondered. There was no doubt that he'd felt something for her when she sang at the roadhouse, and when he was making love to her out in the desert. But somewhere in this city, a gorgeous blonde was still wearing the Super Deals ring that he'd slipped on her finger. He'd never promised Amity anything, other than a long journey that could lead absolutely nowhere. At least that was one promise that he'd managed to keep.

'Hot band tonight. Gonna rock you off your arse.'

A skate rat in dreadlocks strolled by, handing out glossy squares of cardstock promoting a group called Runic Fuck. Daniel took one of the cards. Cryptic blood-red symbols floated against a bank of black clouds. In the foreground, a young male in skintight leather posed with his electric guitar, pelvis thrust out in provocative aggression. Some things never changed.

'Runic Fuck, huh?' Daniel was impressed with the promo piece. Kids these days had come a long way from the old photocopied flyers that he used to crank out at Kinko's.

'Yeah. These dudes are, like, oracles,' the skate rat said solemnly.

'Maybe they can help us,' Amity suggested, polishing off her beer. 'We could use a little prophecy tonight.'

'Want something stronger to drink?' Daniel asked.

'No. One of us needs to stay reasonably sober,' Amity said. Something over Daniel's shoulder caught her attention. She stiffened. 'Because the bomb's about to drop in five, four, three, two...'

'*Daaaaan-neeeeee!*'

The jubilant female squeal silenced the bar. Along with every other guy in the place, Daniel hearkened to the shrill mating cry. An angel graced the doorway. The evening sun streamed behind her, rimming her hourglass figure with light. In her white tassled gogo boots, cherry red hotpants and white leather bra, she was the ultimate Hollywood wet dream, and every man's inner thirteen-year-old was suddenly wide awake.

With his senses dulled by vodka, it took Daniel a few moments to register that the stunner in the doorway was his wife. It wasn't until she came hurtling at him like a blonde cannonball that he recognised her. One moment she was flying across the room, the next she was filling his arms.

God, she felt good. She was all watermelon-scented hair and silky skin and warm firm flesh, and her curves fit so perfectly against his torso that he wondered why he and Heather had ever gotten out of bed after their wedding in Vegas. Daniel buried his face in her curls, burrowing through her hair to taste her sweet neck underneath. She tasted like peaches and coconut suntan lotion. Visions of her nude body assaulted him – Heather perched on top of his cock; Heather on all fours offering him her arse; Heather on her back, parting her thighs and showing him the golden gates to paradise.

'I missed you, angel,' he murmured into her ear. 'Why did you ever leave me?'

Heather stepped back. Her eyebrows furrowed, and for the first time since he met her, Daniel noticed that those perfect brown arches were pencilled onto her face. 'You left *me*, Daniel. You're the one who wanted to go off to find that lame guitar, when you had a much nicer one to play with.'

Heather glared at Amity as she said this, implying that the Gibson wasn't the only inferior toy that Daniel had left her for.

'I never did understand that, myself,' Zak chimed in, materialising behind Heather. 'He's got that beautiful Stratocaster, but he has to go chasing the old axe he got in junior high. But then, Danny's a mysterious boy. That's what makes him such a babe magnet, especially when he's all bummed out like he is now. Look at us, Dan. We're sitting here with two of the hottest women in Hollywood, and I'm not even buzzed yet.' Zak slipped his arm around Heather's shoulder. 'Buy me a drink, would you, babe? Better yet, why don't you buy us all a drink? You can afford it.'

'Fine.' Heather pulled a roll of bills out of her white leather bra top and peeled a fifty off the top. 'Hey, Mister Bartender, could I get a round of tequila shooters and a pitcher of Bud?'

'Where'd you get that stack of cash?' Amity asked. Her brown eyes were huge. 'I thought you were broke!'

Daniel had been wondering the same thing. Last time he saw Heather, she'd been reduced to shoplifting a box of rubbers from a drugstore on the Strip because he'd spent their last fifty bucks paying for the wedding ceremony. And the money clip with the gold-plated eagle wasn't exactly Heather's style.

'Aw, dude. You gotta hear this story.' Zak climbed aboard a barstool, licked the back of his hand and sprinkled salt on the wet skin. He downed his tequila, then shoved a lime wedge in his mouth and sucked noisily.

'Danny doesn't want to hear that boring story,' Heather said, with a nervous giggle.

'Yes, he does,' Amity said.

'I do,' Daniel agreed. 'I think I need to hear this, Heather.'

Heather fluffed her mane and sighed. 'After you ran off with the Amityville Horror, I went back to the Tucan Club. I just wanted to pick up a few bucks to get back to Denver. I met this nice older gentleman, and he offered me some cash so I could buy a bus ticket back home.'

'Yeah, sucking the chrome off the tail pipe wouldn't have got her very far on the Greyhound,' Zak said, with a snicker. 'Sucking an older man, on the other hand, seems to have earned her a pretty nice wad.'

Heather kicked Zak's ankle with the pointy toe of her gogo boot. 'Roscoe didn't pay me for sex, you bastard. I stole that money from him after he pissed me off.'

'Who's Roscoe?' Daniel asked. This reunion with his bride and former best friend was turning into a one-way journey to hell. Part of him longed for Heather to come up with a decent lie to extricate herself from this tale. The other part just wished someone would shoot him and put him out of his misery. Might as well end it all at Fiero's, right where he'd started, face-down in a pool of Stoli.

Heather stood up straight. Her lips tightened into a haughty pout. 'Roscoe was a country music promoter who wanted to help me launch my career.'

Zak snorted with laughter, spraying beer out of his nostrils. 'Get real, Heather. The only thing Roscoe wanted to launch was his red rocket – right off your pad.' He turned to Daniel and slapped him on the shoulder with mock camaraderie. 'Listen, Danny, you might as well know the whole story. Your wife slept with some old fart in Vegas, got peeved because he wasn't as rich as he said he was, stole his hoard in retaliation, and got drunk off her arse to celebrate. I peeled her off the floor at the Casbah, took her back to the room where I was staying, and played hide-the-sausage with her all night long. She swore up and down it was the best sex of her life. Isn't that right, Heather?'

Daniel looked at the woman he'd married. Heather's face was twisted up like a lump of Silly Putty. Her dainty hands were clenched into fists. For the first time that evening, he noticed that she wasn't wearing the pink Super Deals ring anymore.

'Where's your wedding ring, angel?' Daniel asked.

'Huh?' Heather answered his question with a blank blue stare.

'Your ring. You know, that flashy bit of junk I put on your hand as a symbol of our commitment to each other.'

'She thinks she left it on the bathroom sink in Roscoe's hotel room,' Zak said, supplying yet another ugly detail to the worst story Daniel had ever heard in his life.

'It wasn't my fault!' Heather threw her arms around Daniel's neck. 'Don't hate me, Danny. You left me without any money. I didn't know who to turn to. I didn't know what to do.'

'You could have called your mom,' Amity suggested. 'Or your boss at the club where you were supposed to start working. Or one of your stripper friends in Denver. Or –'

'We get the point, Amity,' Daniel said wearily.

'Don't be mad, baby. Roscoe was a fraud. He was a horrible, horrible man. You have nothing to be jealous about,' Heather whimpered. She was making sobbing noises, and her shoulders were shaking as if she were weeping, but her blue eyes were bone dry.

'I'm not mad, Heather. I'm not jealous. I'm not even sad about this whole situation. I'm just disappointed that out of all the strippers in Vegas that I could have married when I was drunk off my arse, I had to pick one who would be so fucking predictable.'

Daniel slid off the bar stool and stumbled towards the door. After a few unsteady steps, he stopped, turned, and staggered back to the bar, where Heather, Zak and Amity were still trying to absorb what had just happened.

'Come on, you,' he said, grabbing Amity's arm and pulling her off her stool. 'This journey ain't over yet.'

While Amity shovelled down chocolate-chip pancakes at the rock'n'roll Denny's in West Hollywood, Daniel kept company with a pot of black coffee, trying to get sober. It was still too early for the after-hours crowd, and the only celebrity that Amity had spotted so far was a guy who looked like Vanilla Ice.

'You get more beautiful every time I look at you,' Daniel said to Amity. 'I am so sorry that I lost sight of how incredible you are. I was blinded by blonde hair and a big rack.'

'Which makes you no different from any other heterosexual male. Keep drinking that coffee. You're obviously still wasted,' Amity replied, reaching for another carafe of syrup. She hadn't tried the boysenberry yet. The fruity sugar-sauce actually went pretty well with chocolate chips.

'How could I have been so ... trite?' Daniel went on. 'I never would have thought of myself as the kind of guy who would marry a total stranger in Vegas after a rough night of drinking. Even when I woke up the next morning, and looked at Heather and wondered who the hell she was, I kept trying to turn the scenario around in my head, avoiding any side of the situation that wasn't bright and shiny.'

'You can't help it, you're a romantic. You dream bigger than you live,' Amity said.

'Do you think this mission of ours is a lost cause?'

'Maybe. But see, where you're romantic, I'm just stubborn. I want to keep going.'

'So do I, but I don't think we can. Reality's calling, Amity. We can't live on the road for the rest of our lives. You'll hit the limit on your Visa one of these days, and –'

'No,' Amity said, in a hushed tone.

'What? You mean you've got one of those platinum cards that lets you keep spending forever?'

Amity shook her head. Her fork slipped from her hand and clattered onto the table. 'Check her out.'

A waitress with bobbed red hair was walking towards their table, full hips swinging under her brown polyester uniform. Though she wore the pre-ordained smile of the service industry, she couldn't seem to keep her upper lip from curling into a Sid Vicious snarl. Unlike the other waitresses, who wore white orthopaedic sneakers and support hose, this one wore Doc Martens and fishnets.

'That's what I call "scary-sexy",' Daniel remarked, glancing over his shoulder. 'You know her or something?'

'We might.' Amity pointed at the redhead's nametag.

In curly gold letters, the tag read Sadie O.

'No way,' Daniel whispered.

'I think it is,' Amity whispered back.

'It couldn't be.'

'Yes, it could. She came to LA, didn't she? And she was a rocker, so it only makes sense she'd end up working on Sunset Boulevard.'

'Oh, screw this whispering – we're not detectives. Let's just ask her. Excuse me!' Daniel said, waving his napkin. 'Could you come over here, waitress?'

Sadie, who had passed their table, stopped in her tracks. She turned slowly on one of her thick heels, like the tough kid in high school who's just been insulted by some pipsqueak. Her smile was still plastered to her face, but her green eyes turned into evil slits when she looked at Daniel.

'My name's Sadie. Not "waitress",' the redhead said. She jabbed her index finger at the strip of plastic on her chest. 'That's why I'm wearing this nametag here. So customers can read and learn, and nobody gets hurt.'

'Your name wouldn't be Sadie O? Grady by any chance? With a question mark?' Amity asked, in a tone that would meet any Sunday school teacher's approval.

'Yeah. So what?' Sadie planted her palms flat on the table. Her face was so close to Amity's that Amity could smell the wintergreen gum she was chewing. Her crimson lipstick was applied so thickly that it looked black, and her nose was pierced twice.

'How long have you worked here?' Daniel asked.

'This is my second shift. Look, did my parole officer send you over here to check up on me? You can tell that bitch that if she wants me to keep a job, she'd better quit breathing down my neck. I can't concentrate when her narcs are spying on me. Got it?'

'We're not narcs,' Daniel floundered. 'We're more like...'

'Fans. We're big fans of your music.' Amity jumped in to save him.

Sadie gave an incredulous snort, but Amity thought she saw the redhead blush under her layer of death-white pancake makeup. Sadie crossed her muscular forearms over her chest. 'You've got to be kidding.'

'No. Not at all. We heard you play at that club on Hollywood and Vine a few months ago,' Daniel said. 'You were amazing.'

'A few months ago, I was incarcerated,' Sadie shot back. 'Try again.'

'Maybe it was that club in Vegas,' Amity improvised. 'The dive off the Strip? You played lead guitar in a girl band. You had this black Gibson Epiphone...'

'You're right. I did.' Sadie's voice went soft at the edges. 'Nice axe.'

Amity and Daniel stared at each other. Amity felt Daniel's fingers make contact with hers under the table. She squeezed his hands. He squeezed back. His eyes glowed so bright that the coffee black lightened to dark gold.

Daniel cleared his throat, but his voice still cracked when he asked the next question. 'What happened to her?'

'Aw, she's somewhere at the bottom of the San Francisco Bay,' Sadie said, with a flippant wave of her hand. 'Before I got arrested, I'd gone up to San Fran to try to get in on a documentary series about indie rocker chicks. "Wild Girlz of Rock'n'Roll", it was supposed to be called. HBO was going to produce it. Turned out to be one more deal that fell through. We all got fed a bunch of lies and promises, then sent home. Happens every day, yah know? But for me, that was the last time. I didn't want to play the game anymore. Didn't want to play the guitar, either. I took it up to the Golden Gate Bridge and tossed it in the water. It was more like a symbol than anything else. The Gibson was just some old thing I picked up at a pawn shop. Plenty more where that came from, yah know?'

Sadie had warmed up to them now, leaning on the table with one hand as she snapped her gum.

'I know,' Daniel said. His voice was flat, no inflection for anyone to hang on to. No one could interpret those two dead words as anything but a total lack of interest – except for Amity. Daniel's hands had gone limp and cold. She rubbed them, trying to bring the life back.

'Look, you guys want anything else?' Sadie asked. 'How about a couple pieces of pie? We've got fresh lemon meringue. I can get it for you on the house.'

'That would be awesome,' Amity said.

After a big helping of pancakes and an even bigger helping of bad news, she had no appetite at all. From the blasted-out expression on Daniel's face, she thought he'd probably never want to eat again. But she couldn't bring herself to turn down the redhead's offer. She felt a sisterly bond with Sadie O? Grady, the woman who'd travelled all over the West trying to make it as a rocker – working as a call-girl, working as a waitress, all the while lugging around a pawn shop guitar.

'Awesome,' Daniel echoed, still absolutely blank. 'That would be awesome.'

The chilly grey air was laced with mist. A strand of fog floated in front of Amity's face. She reached out and let the cool scrap of air glide over her hand before it drifted away to join a bank of clouds over the water. Amity hadn't brought anything warmer than a T-shirt on this trip. Daniel had thrown one of his long-sleeved shirts over her shoulders, and he held her shivering body tightly as they crossed the bridge.

'Nice day for a funeral,' Daniel remarked.

He'd come out of his trance about six hours ago, but his remarks were still succinct, dry and utterly lifeless. But Amity still felt life in his flesh. His heart thrummed against her ribs when he hugged her in the cold, and his fingers sent her secret messages every time they squeezed her hand.

'This is not a funeral,' Amity corrected him. 'We're having a memorial service. Remember?'

'How could I forget?'

They stopped in the middle of the bridge and leant over the railing. In the dense fog, the water below was a steely stew, visible only through the rare gaps in the murk. Amity tried to imagine the Gibson slipping into the choppy San Francisco Bay. She saw Sadie lifting the axe high over her head and hurling it over the railing. She saw the instrument cartwheeling through space, before doing a belly-flop in the water with an undignified splash. Then she saw Sadie O? Grady wiping her hands on her thighs and heaving a sigh of relief. Amity knew exactly how the redheaded rocker must have felt

– she must have found a grim satisfaction in trashing a career that had never got off the ground in the first place.

'Where's the Polaroid?' Amity demanded, holding out her hand.

'Um . . . I dunno. I might have left it in the car,' Daniel said sheepishly.

'No, you didn't. I saw you slip it in your pocket. Come on, hand it over.' Amity wiggled her fingers.

'You're killing me, babe,' Daniel said, but he obeyed. 'Why do we have to do this? This picture is my only memory of my Girl.'

'We're not going to throw the whole photo away. Only half. You'll keep one half as a memento of her; the other half will follow her into the Bay, so that you can have a sense of control over this incident. We've had a long ride, Daniel. You need closure.'

'Closure,' he mimicked. 'Glad you're up on your pop psychology. I have a feeling I'm going to regret this for the rest of my life.'

'No, you won't. You'll feel a new sense of freedom. We have to end this journey somehow. We can't just yank the needle off the record.'

Daniel smiled. His lips stopped short of forming his usual wicked grin, but Amity saw a flash of his old self. 'I'm so crazy about you, Amity. Most chicks don't remember vinyl at all.'

He pulled her close and kissed her. His lips felt cool and waxy at first, but they soon warmed up under Amity's mouth. He rubbed one of his palms against her breast, chafing the nipple just enough to draw a moan from her throat. She rocked her hips back and forth against his, in that rhythm that he liked to call the 'dirty rhumba', until she felt him get hard through their twin layers of jeans. He guided her up against the railing and pinned her there, making her squirm when his hard-on found the soft swelling between her thighs and began to prod that sensitive spot through the cloth.

'People are walking by,' Amity reminded him, her warning muffled by Daniel's tongue.

'You think they can see us through this soup?'

'The fog could clear at any second.'

'Right, and hell could freeze over. Stop talking and kiss me. I've got a much better idea for how we can remember my Gibson Girl. Now, don't worry. If anyone asks what I'm doing, we'll pretend I'm tying your shoe. Besides, we're both wearing black. They might not even notice me down here.'

Before Amity could object, Daniel was sinking to his knees and unzipping her fly. She looked down, and suddenly she saw Daniel's fifteen-year-old self in the face that gazed up at her – that same glow of awe and delight that had illuminated his eyes when he held the brand new Epiphone. This was the first time she'd seen life in Daniel's eyes since he learnt about the fate of his first electric guitar.

'Amity, will you let me give you a mind-blowing orgasm on a public bridge?' he asked, with ironic formality. 'Please? In memory of my Gibson Girl?'

Amity nodded. She squeezed her eyelids shut to cut off the tears that were welling up behind them. 'You can do anything you want. Anything.'

Daniel lowered her jeans and panties just enough to reach the downy crest of her pussy. With his hands cradling her arse, he parted her cleft with his mouth, his tongue flicking back and forth between her lips until he had spread the folds wide enough to reach the prize in between.

Amity knew she had no choice but to give in; when Daniel was on a mission, he was hell-bent to complete it. He had propped her up against one of the steel girders, and she leant against the metal column, hoping that it would shield her at least partially from the traffic and pedestrians. After Daniel had been lapping at her lips for a few minutes, the world around her grew fuzzy, and the fact that she was being eaten out in the middle of a metropolitan area didn't bother her quite as much.

Daniel's hair felt thick and soft and slightly oily, like a seal's pelt, when she clutched it with her fingers. She felt a promising buzz spreading from the hard pink button at the heart of her labia through the surrounding flesh, spreading warmth throughout her body. Her knees began to tremble, her hands tightened their grip on Daniel's hair, and her hips started to twitch of their own accord, moving in time with Daniel's tongue. Her inner muscles tightened, her spine dug into the steel girder, and she came with gut-wrenching intensity into Daniel's mouth, biting back a cry of pleasure.

'Now that's what I call a memorial service,' Daniel said, 'Making my girl come. You're the most important thing in my life right now.'

'That was amazing,' Amity gasped.

'I told you, didn't I?'

Still floating, Amity didn't see Daniel stealing the Polaroid from the pocket of her jeans. She came to her senses just in time to catch him tucking the photo in his shirt.

'Hey! What about the memorial ritual?' she protested. 'You have to throw at least half the picture off the bridge.'

Daniel hung his head. 'I can't do that, sweetheart. I'm not ready to let her go yet. Some day, maybe this picture won't matter, but for now, it's all I've got.'

'Fine,' Amity relented. 'But one of these days, you're going to wake up and realise that you'll never see the Epiphone again. The truth will hit you like a ton of bricks. Are you sure you'll be able to accept that?'

'Oh, I can already accept the fact that my guitar is gone. The one thing I haven't accepted is that I'll never get that divine charge from her again. That's why I'm going to need *you*.'

Amity's mouth opened, but no sound came out. She had no idea what to say. Holy quests never ended like this. They ended with big splashy epiphanies, or with bloodshed, or with a round of the bubonic plague. They didn't end with two tired disenchanted musicians losing the object of the quest, and finding each other.

'Are you sure I'm going to be enough?' Amity managed to ask.

'Don't worry.' Daniel wrapped his arms around Amity's thighs and held her fiercely, as if she were the lost guitar, and he were drawing that forgotten energy from her flesh. 'You'll be more than enough.'